MADE FOR *You*

NEW YORK TIMES & USA TODAY BESTSELLING AUTHOR

KELLY ELLIOTT

Copyright © 2016 by Kelly Elliott
Published by K. Elliott Enterprises

Cover photo and design by Shannon Cain Photography
Photos shot at Sugar Berry Inn Bed and Breakfast
Editing and Proofing by Erin Noelle
Proofing by Holly's Red Hot Reviews
Interior Design and formatting by JT Formatting

First Edition: November 2016
Library of Congress Cataloging-in-Publication Data
Made for You – 1st ed
ISBN-13: 978-1-943633-23-4

www.kellyelliottauthor.com

For exclusive releases and giveaways signup for Kelly's newsletter at
http://eepurl.com/JoKyL

Prologue

Emylie

SITTING ON THE dock, the cool breeze blew my dark brown hair around in a swirling motion over my shoulders. The clear night sky offered up an amazing show. We'd already seen two falling stars and my wish was the same for both. *Keep Holden safe.*

This was the last night Holden and I would spend together before he left for the University of Southern California and I left for Texas A&M. My heart slowly sank as the clock ticked on.

"Are you nervous?" I asked, my voice shaky and unsure. I could hear the nervousness in my voice.

With a grin that still caused my stomach to flutter, he responded, "Nah. Don't get me wrong, I'll miss you and my folks. Probably will miss Mason, too, but I'm not holding my breath on that one."

I lightly pushed him as I let out a chuckle. "Stop it. Mason's like a brother to you. You're going to miss him."

Shrugging, he nodded his head and glanced away. "I'm looking forward to playing football. I only wish my father understood."

Closing my eyes, I silently prayed I would understand as well. Holden and I had always planned on going to Texas A&M and getting a degree in agriculture and life science. Then we would move back to our hometown of Brady and start our life together. When USC offered him a full football scholarship, he said he couldn't pass it up and it would be a new adventure. One he would go on without me. It wasn't like he didn't ask me to go with him. I wanted to be with him, but I also wanted to follow my dreams and Holden realized that.

"I'll miss you the most, Em. I hope you know that."

Swallowing hard, I bit down on my cheek to keep my tears at bay. I had promised myself I wouldn't cry and make this harder on Holden, even though it tore me apart. He said he needed this. It would be good for both of us in the end. I had a terrible feeling it was going to change everything.

Turning back to me, Holden's face lit up. "I love you, Em. I'll always love you."

Holden Warner and I had been practically inseparable since we were five years old and he pushed Mason Frank to the ground for pulling my ponytail and saying I was cute. We had been best friends since then. When we hit high school, Holden finally started to see me differently. I was no longer his best friend who did everything with him. I was Emylie, the best friend who started growing breasts and who liked to put makeup on and wear dresses. Our friendship quickly turned into something so much more.

I tried to smile and failed big time as I pleaded, "Promise me you won't meet some hot California bleach blonde and forget about me."

Holden placed his hand on the side of my face, his gaze fell to my lips as his thumb left a trail of fire across my cheek. "I promise you, Em. You'll be my best friend forever and the only woman I will ever love."

Closing my eyes, I let the tears fall as I whispered back, "I'm scared you'll forget me."

"Look at me, Em."

I stared into his blue eyes. "This will be good for us. Some time apart isn't going to be a bad thing. It will make us stronger."

I shook my head. "How can you say that? It's tearing me apart. How is this not doing the same to you?"

"It is. But going out and exploring new things, new people ... it will be good for me *and* you. This town is all we've ever known. Ranching is all I've ever done. How do I really know I want to run my father's ranch?"

Hurt filled my chest. "Because you love it."

"I do love it," he answered with a soft voice.

"What about us?"

Moving his finger along my jaw line, he smiled. "I can't imagine meeting anyone who could ever make me feel like you do, Em."

Lifting my chin, I attempted to keep my voice steady. "I can't imagine it either. I love you and I'm going to miss you like crazy."

He leaned over and kissed my lips. "I love you too. More than you'll ever know. This is going to be good for us."

His words rattled around in my brain. We would be okay. Our love was strong enough to be tested. If this was what Holden wanted, then I'd go along with it. Really, what choice did I have.

CHAPTER 1

Emylie

Five years later

A LUKE BRYAN song played while everyone two-stepped on the dance floor of Twin Oaks Dance Hall. I quickly glanced around.

"Do you see him?" my best friend Becca asked.

Shaking my head, I answered, "Nope."

"Good, let's have some fun!"

I followed Becca to the bar where she ordered us each a Bud Light. Placing the bottle to my lips, I caught Mason staring at me. I flashed him a smile as he replied back with a wink then said something to the girl standing next to him.

Turning away, I checked out the dance floor. "You know," I said, leaning over to Becca, "he could still show up."

Shrugging her shoulders, she replied, "Let him. I'm done with him and his cheating ass. I wish I had listened to my parents. My life would be a hell of a lot better."

Gazing down at the floor, I shook my head before glancing back at my best friend. Her strawberry blonde hair was pulled up in a ponytail that swung to the beat of the song. Her blue eyes seemed to sparkle tonight. Her divorce from her high school sweetheart was finalized today, and she planned on celebrating while my parents watched her four-year-old daughter, Sage.

"You wouldn't have Sage if you had listened," I contended, giving her a wink.

She simply nodded. "Only good thing that came out of that mess."

"Evening ladies," Mason said as he stopped in front of me. He glanced over to Becca and I couldn't help but notice the way his eyes explored her.

"Evening, Mason," Becca purred. She'd always had a crush on him. I'm pretty sure since the day he and Holden walked up to us on the playground in kindergarten, she was in love with Mason. Holden and Mason were best friends from the first moment they said hello to each other. Even after Holden pushed Mason to the ground for pulling my hair, the four of us did everything together. Mason had liked Becca in high school, but never went for it. Then she met her asshole of an ex and Mason lost interest. I thought for sure when I told her what happened between Mason and me she would have been angry with me, but that wasn't Becca. She understood the reason behind why it happened.

Mason was there for me when I got the call. The moment my life changed forever. If it hadn't been for him, I would have packed up and left college to move back home and cry myself to sleep each night. Probably would have ended up working for my parents at their bed and breakfast in the heart of Brady.

But I didn't pack up and leave college. I cried in Mason's arms for weeks before finally pulling myself together. Of course, the fact that I found myself in his bed also helped. He numbed the pain and made me forget how Holden had torn my heart in two.

"Want to dance, Mason?" Becca asked as she placed her hand on his broad chest. Turning away, I smiled and attempted not to laugh at my friend's shameless flirting.

Before Mason could answer, Troy Walker came up and asked Becca to dance. Turning to me, she raised her brows and gave me a naughty smile. Her one and only goal tonight was to get laid. I was pretty sure any attention from any guy would do the trick.

As Becca wondered off with Troy, Mason watched them intently. Was that a bit of jealousy I saw? He finally motioned to sit next to me. Smiling, I nodded.

"How's it going, Em?"

The sound of Mason's voice caused my body to hum. I hadn't seen him in over a week, and I longed for some … attention of my own. "It's going. How about you?"

Lifting his beer bottle to his lips, I watched him take a drink while I bit down on my lip. Mason didn't light my body on fire like Holden had, but he certainly knew how to make it come to life. His blonde hair and blue eyes were my weakness…and my crutch. More so my crutch, truth be told.

"It's going. I haven't seen you around the ranch. Where you been?" Mason asked as he kept his gaze out on the dance floor. He couldn't stop watching Becca dance with Troy.

Taking a drink, I tilted my head and surveyed him. "Have you missed me?"

Mason peered back at me and licked his lips. The way his eyes filled with lust made my chest tighten. A moan unintentionally slipped from my lips. "I have. A lot," He replied.

I knew it was unhealthy for the two of us to use each other like we did. Becca took every chance she had to remind me that Mason and I were nothing more than fuck buddies. We were okay with that.

Quickly turning and glancing out over the dance floor, I said, "My days have been consumed with helping Sam stock the tank and making sure everything's ready for next weekend."

"Sounds like fun," Mason chuckled. Mason was the ranch manager for the T-Bar Hunting Ranch, one of the largest and most premier hunting ranches in all of Texas. I also worked on the ranch as a wildlife manager. He struggled with the position for a bit, knowing it truly belonged to Holden with it being his parent's ranch. But Holden made the decision to walk away.

I could feel the heat building between the two of us as I moved about in my seat. "Was loads of fun."

Mason stood and reached his hand out for me. "Dance with me, Em."

Setting my beer down on the table, I took his hand and let him lead me to the dance floor. It wouldn't seem out of place for the two of us to dance. After all, we'd been the best of friends since anyone could remember. Little did they all know, we'd been sleeping together since our last year of college. The only person who knew was Becca.

The song changed and "Fly" by Maddie and Tae began playing. Burying my face into his chest, I closed my eyes and let him take me away from everything. It was easy to get lost in Mason. He was my safe zone.

Holding me closer, he placed his lips against my ear, "Come home with me tonight, Em."

Pulling my head back, I looked at him. We had an arrangement. When he needed me, I would be there for him. When I needed him, he would be there for me. As much as I tried to make myself feel something more for Mason, I couldn't and I knew he felt the same way. We made great best friends, but we'd never be good at being together. We tried and failed big time. "Okay," I whispered as he smiled.

The song ended and a faster tune started playing. "Let's show these assholes how you dance, Tink." Throwing my head back, I laughed as Mason and I two-stepped around the dance floor. He'd given me the nickname Tink after I dressed up like Tinkerbell for

4

Halloween one year. Holden had hated when Mason called me that. He stopped calling me the nickname when Holden and I began dating, but picked it back up again after the first time we slept together. Holding me in his arms as I cried over the asshole who had broken up with me over the phone, he whispered, "I'll always take care of you, Tink. Always."

And he has held true to that promise.

Unlike Holden.

Mason turned on the lights of the three bedroom, two bath ranch house. Scanning the room, I frowned as I surveyed the mess. Once Mason became the foreman of the T-Bar Ranch, Sam gave him the house to stay in. He complained at first about the house being too big for just him, but having Mason here on the ranch was important, so Sam insisted he stay.

"Holy shit, Mason. It's a mess in here," I commented as I walked over and picked up a pizza box off the coffee table. Lord knows how long it had been there. Glancing back to Mason, he gave me a sexy grin and opened the refrigerator and pulled out two bottles of beer.

"I'll clean up tomorrow. Or the next day."

Letting out a sigh, I began cleaning off the coffee table. Walking into the kitchen, I threw it all in the garbage, not before I did a quick once over on the kitchen. It was actually pretty clean for being bachelor pad.

"You need a girlfriend, Mason." I said as I walked back into the living room and sat down next to him on the couch. Handing me my beer, Mason laughed.

"Yeah, like you need a boyfriend, Em."

Shaking my head, I whispered, "Hell no. I'm never going down that road again." Then I added with a smirk, "I do know someone who would love to play the part of your girlfriend though."

He lifted his brow. "Who?"

Chewing on my lip, I replied, "Becca."

"Yeah, fuck that," Mason whispered.

I wasn't sure why Mason thought the idea of Becca was wrong. I saw the way he looked at her, and he loved Sage so much. He had been crazy for her in high school. Not being in the mood to push it, I sighed and let it go.

I leaned my head back against his arm and asked, "How did we end up like this?"

Mason cleared his throat and started with his explanation. "Let's see. It all started when Holden called you up at A&M and told you he had met a girl and he was planning on staying in California to start a new life with her ... causing you to fall into a serious funk that I, as your best friend, had to pull you out of."

"That's right. How could I have forgotten?" I replied sarcastically.

"Then, I walked in on the woman I thought I was going to marry having sex with some computer nerd who swept her off her feet and moved her to Washington DC."

Snarling my lip, I said with a sharp voice, "Bitch."

"Yeah, she is. And Holden is an asshole."

Nodding, I agreed. "Yep. Better off without the two of them."

After Mason had walked in on his girlfriend, he came to my apartment, which was right off of campus. I'd never seen him so upset. One thing led to another and we quickly found ourselves tangled up naked as we spent the rest of the night together. With Holden breaking my heart weeks earlier, and now Mason's girlfriend destroying his, it was only natural when the hugs turned to more.

We made a promise to each other that night that nothing would come out of our arrangement. We were simply two friends who were finding comfort in each other by having sex. A lot of sex. Hot and heavy sex that left me breathless and longing for the next time Mason would fill me. God, that made me such a slut. But it also gave me an escape. When I was with Mason, I didn't think about Holden.

Letting out a deep breath, I stood up and headed into the kitchen. My stomach growled and I was wishing I hadn't skipped dinner. Before I even made it halfway into the kitchen, Mason grabbed me and had my skirt lifted and my panties pushed to the side. He sunk his fingers inside of me, giving me what he knew I needed. We were soon lost in each other. It was the only time we were both able to forget the hurt caused by the very people we thought loved us.

I couldn't figure out the expression in Mason's eyes, but I had a feeling it had to do with Becca. Guilt quickly hit me square in the chest. I was going to have to talk to him about her. About his feelings for Becca, especially now that she was divorced and single again.

Sitting on the floor attempting to catch our breath, Mason turned to me. "Tink, how long are we going to keep pretending?"

Feeling the tears build, I knew my answer was going to be a greedy one. I didn't want to give up my vice yet and that made me feel like such a bitch. I let a tear fall and whispered, "Until we completely forget."

Mason stood and carried me into his bedroom where we both drifted to sleep while wrapped in each other's arms. I never stayed the night with him before, but tonight I think we both needed to not be alone.

CHAPTER 2

Holden

"HOLDEN, WE'RE GOING to be late!" Daphne shouted from the living room.

Rolling my eyes, I sucked in a deep breath and prayed that I'd get through this night without fucking anything up. Daphne's dad given strict orders to be at the restaurant at seven sharp, and with me having to work later than normal, we were already running behind by ten minutes.

When I walked into the living room I saw Daphne staring out over downtown Los Angles. She'd grown up here, the daughter of a movie producer. We'd met at USC through mutual friends. She flirted with me all the time. Everything changed my junior year, though. The first year I hadn't gone back home over Thanksgiving break to see my high school girl friend, Emylie. Had I gone home, things would be completely different in my life. Most days, I wished like hell I had gone back home. I thought of Emylie every single day. Longed to have her in my arms. There were so many times I wanted to ask my parents or Mason about her. I knew she was working on my father's hunting range. Fulfilling her part of our dream. The dream I messed up because of one stupid-ass mistake that I will regret the rest of my damn life.

With a shake of my head, I pushed Emylie from my mind. "Why am I thinking of Em?" I silently asked myself as I got my act together and focused back on the woman I was fixin' to ask marry me tonight. Not that I wanted to ask her. I was forced into it. Yet again, because of one stupid fuck up. Seems like I made those often.

Turning, Daphne smiled when she saw me. "My, oh my, Mr. Warner, you look handsome."

My gaze roamed over her body and the form fitting black cocktail dress she had on. It did nothing for me. I wasn't the least bit attracted to her. But I forced the words from my mouth. "And you, my dear, look hot as hell."

Frowning, she replied, "Always the romantic one you are."

My chest tightened. I never knew the right thing to say to her anymore. If I thought I was paying her a compliment, she took the opposite way. The whole relationship was fucked up.

Countless nights I wanted to call Em and tell her everything. Beg her to forgive me. But I knew Emylie, and I knew she would doubt I had stayed true to her at all.

Fucked. Up. All of it.

Daphne reached for her clutch as we made our way to the elevator that whisked us down from the top floor of our condo to the lounge Daphne's dad had rented out for the evening.

Making our way into the room, Daphne put her game face on. There were a few top producers here, and I knew she was hoping to catch the eye of one or two of them.

The night dragged on as Daphne and her father worked the room while I sat at the table in the corner and drank one drink after another. Taking in a deep breath, I pulled out my phone to see I had a missed text from my mother.

Mom: Holden, I really hope you'll think about coming home for the family reunion. I'm sure your father would love to see you. I would, you know. It's been almost three years since you've been home. You can't hide forever.

"Shit," I whispered as I searched for Daphne. She was in the middle of a conversation with her father and an actress I recognized from some hospital TV show.

Standing, I made my way out into the hall. Hitting my mother's number, I attempted to calm my beating heart. Any time I thought about heading home, I thought of two things. My father looking at me with disappointment at my decision to stay in LA and not return to the ranch, and seeing Emylie. I had made her a promise that I had broken. I still had nightmares of hearing her cry over the phone when I told her about Daphne. I felt like a complete asshole. I didn't even remember cheating. A part of me knew Daphne slipped me something that night, but I could never get her to admit it.

Daphne was the complete opposite of Emylie. Her endless flirting caught my attention, but I would have never acted on it. Yet, I got so wasted that night, I did act. That night changed everything. I wasn't me. I chased some stupid ass thing I thought I needed to do to make sure I was on the right path. Prove to myself that I really did want the life we had planned together. As if my love for Emylie wasn't enough. I was too blind to see she was all I ever needed.

"Holden! Sweetheart, how are you?" my mother said as she covered the phone and yelled, "Sam! It's Holden!"

Knowing my father, he wouldn't care less that I was on the phone. I cleared my throat. "Hey, Mom. How have y'all been?"

I'd worked for the last year on keeping my Texas accent at a bare minimum, but any time I talked to Mom or Mason, it came back in full swing. Daphne thought I sounded like a hick and reminded me all the time how much she hated my southern accent.

"We're doing good. It's been raining here a lot, but we need it, so I won't complain."

Nodding my head, I inhaled a deep breath through my nose and slowly blew it out of my mouth. The hallway felt like it was closing in on me. Kind of like my whole life these last few years. I deserved it though. What I put Emylie through was nothing compared to the hell I lived in. "That's good. I know how much y'all needed to get out of that drought."

"Darling, you sound so sad. Is everything okay?"

Glancing back toward the door, I saw Daphne throw her head back and laugh. My chest ached and I knew I should be feeling the total opposite of what I was. "Yeah. I wanted to call and let you know I'm … uh … well I'm asking Daphne to marry me tonight."

Sucking in a sharp intake of air, my mother stammered, "W-what? You're doing what?"

"Um … I said I was asking Daphne to marry me tonight."

The silence that followed had me wishing I hadn't even called.

"Holden, we've never even met this girl. I've only seen a few pictures of her. Are you sure … what about Emylie?"

My heart dropped. I wanted more than anything to have my mother's blessing. I needed to have them. "What about Emylie?" Was Emylie still single? Was she dating someone? Mason never offered and I never asked.

"Nothing, never mind. If Daphne makes you happy and this is what you truly want, your father and I will of course give our blessing to you both."

My eyes closed. If only she knew it was the last thing I wanted. But I had no choice. I was raised to do the right thing and that's what I would do. Forcing myself to sound happy, I replied, "Mom, you don't know how much that means to me. Maybe I could bring Daphne home with me for the family reunion? That way she can meet everyone."

"Oh … um … why that sounds … ah … yes. That sounds wonderful, Holden."

I could hear it in her voice. She didn't want to meet Daphne. To my mother, she was the reason I never came back home. The reason I broke the heart of the only woman I had ever loved. She was the reason for the sadness in my voice when I called home.

Daphne walked to the door and motioned for me to come back inside. Lifting my finger to ask for one more minute, she raised her brow at me before she turned and walked away.

I couldn't ignore the sick feeling in my stomach. I had tried to make things work with Daphne. I'd given up Emylie for her and the baby, thinking it was the right thing to do at the time. I had never told my parent's about the baby and felt guilty when Daphne had miscarried. The only reason I stayed in California was because of the guilt I was riddled with. Daphne blamed me for her losing the baby, and a part of me believed her. She had fallen into such a state of depression; if I left, God knows what she would have done.

When I told Daphne a month ago I was thinking of heading back to Texas and that things weren't working out, she started crying. What happened after that felt like a déjà vu. A fucking nightmare that was starting all over again.

"Is the reunion still held during the July Jubilee?"

Clearing her throat, my mother answered, "Yes. Can you come that soon? That's next week, Holden."

"Daphne and I both had planned on taking a camping trip, but I'm going to surprise her by bringing her home to meet y'all."

What I really wanted to say was I was coming home to see Emylie. To chance seeing her one last time before I let go of that dream. A part of me wondered if I told her the truth and she forgave me, if I could walk away from Daphne and my responsibility.

"Oh, darling. Do you think that's such a good idea? What if she wants an advance warning or something? From the little I've come to know about her, I don't see her taking this with a grain of salt."

Daphne was now standing back at the door, this time with her hands on her hips. I didn't really give two shits what Daphne wanted. "Nah, she'll love it, Mom. I can't wait to see y'all. I'm sure you're going to love Daphne."

"Uh-huh, I'm really excited." I could hear the hesitation in her voice. I knew she knew something wasn't right. I could never really hide much from her. I also knew what the risks were by bringing Daphne home. I had to take them though.

Walking toward the door, I said, "Listen, Mom, I've got to run. I love you. Give everyone my love."

"Good luck tonight, Holden. I'll have everything ready for when you come home with um … Daphne."

"Great! Bye, Mom." Hitting End, I pushed my phone into my pocket and opened the door.

"Damn it, Holden, you kept Daddy waiting. We've already missed the first few minutes of his speech."

Feeling the excitement of heading home deflate, I kissed Daphne softly on the cheek. "I'm sorry. I was talking to my mother." The last thing I wanted to do was upset Daphne. God forbid her world get rocked.

Walking ahead of me, she simply said, "Oh … that's nice." As she took her place next to her own mother, she plastered on her perfectly rehearsed happy face. The waiter walked by and I grabbed a glass of champagne. Daphne quickly pushed my hand down and shook her head. "I think you've had enough, don't you?"

My mouth gaped open as I attempted to push my anger aside. Tonight was special for Daphne and her family, and tonight I was going to ask her to marry me. Surely I could overlook Daphne's need to constantly tell me what to do.

She took a glass and went to take a drink, but I leaned in and said, "Should you be drinking that, darling?"

The glass stopped at her lips. "I forgot."

My stomach dropped. How in the hell could she forget she was pregnant? Taking the drink from her hand, I downed it.

Plastering on a fake smile to match Daphne's, I stood and listened to her father announce the movie he had signed on to direct and that his daughter had the lead role. The entire room erupted in cheers as Daphne soaked it all up. She was in her element for sure. I was still trying to figure out how in the hell she was going to pull it off, acting in a major motion picture while pregnant. Her father didn't seem to care either. All he told me was they would figure it out and it wasn't for me to worry about.

Not for me to worry about. Being the father of the baby, I had a right to worry.

Cheers erupted again as Daphne took her place next to her father to talk about how excited she was for this role.

Closing my eyes, I tuned everyone out. The only thing I could hear was the sound of Emylie crying.

Everything was indeed fucked up.

As the party died down, I finally had a chance to dance with Daphne. Holding her close to me, I smiled and asked, "Are you happy?"

Grinning from ear-to-ear, Daphne gasped, "Oh my God, yes! I don't think this night could get any better."

The fact that this made her happier than when she found out she was pregnant worked my nerves.

Taking a quick glance around, I noticed a good number of people had finally left. Stopping, I reached into my pocket as I took a step away from Daphne.

"Holden? What's wrong?"

Getting down on one knee, I opened the box and held the one-and-a-half carat diamond up and asked, "Daphne Marie Weston, would you do me the honor of becoming my wife and spending the rest of our lives together?"

Daphne quickly glanced around the room before turning back to me and covering her mouth. Tears began to roll down her cheeks as she nodded her head and dropped her hands. "Yes! Yes, I'll marry you, Holden."

Again, the room erupted in cheers, expect this time there were cameras surrounding us as flashes began going off. Daphne quickly turned and began posing as she held up her hand for me to slip the ring on. I had wanted this to be a private moment between us so it didn't end up in the paper. I always worried about Emylie seeing me with Daphne. But Mr. Weston insisted it be done this evening, and in this way. He said it would be good PR for Daphne. Seeing him standing across the room smiling, I was beginning to think it was good PR for him and his new movie.

I was buzzing from all the alcohol I had drank tonight. I needed it to make my way through living in my own personal hell. I knew it was nothing more than Karma. Life getting me back for being unfaithful to Emylie.

What I needed to do was stop thinking about my ex and focus on the woman who carried my child. The woman I could barely stand to be around. Maybe if I tried to be more romantic, things would be better. We hadn't had sex in weeks, which wasn't anything new. But lately Daphne seemed to be trying to get me to fuck her at every turn. It never worked though. Either I couldn't get it up, probably because I was thinking of Emylie, or I was working late. Something I did on purpose to stay away. Tonight would be different. I asked her to marry me, and the least I could do was be with her.

Walking into the condo, I grabbed Daphne and pushed her up against the wall. "I'm ready to peel that dress of you and—"

Giving me a push, Daphne shook her head. "Damn it, Holden! Why didn't you ask me earlier! Right after Daddy's speech would have been perfect. *Everyone* was still there then. It would have been all over the evening news."

Standing there staring at her, I felt my chest tighten. "Are you fucking kidding me right now? You're bitching at me because I didn't ask you in front of total strangers? It's bad enough your father strong-armed me into asking you at this event. This is a mistake. All of this. It's never going to work. Clearly I don't make you happy and you don't make me happy. The only thing we have in common is this baby."

Daphne's expression softened as she walked up to me and wrapped her arms around my neck. "Oh, baby! Forgive me. It was perfect. It was amazing, and I love you!"

I pulled back and stared into her blue eyes. "Daphne, I don't want to start out this marriage with you already bitching at me. Let's be honest, the only reason we're getting married is because of the baby. I was ready to move out a few months ago and head back to Texas."

Anger moved across her face. "That's the only reason, huh? I thought maybe you actually cared about me, Holden. You cared enough to fuck me that night in the restaurant that led us to this pregnancy."

"That was a mistake on my part."

"A mistake!"

I could see she was getting upset and the last thing I wanted was to cause her stress. If she lost another baby, Lord knows how badly she would handle it.

"I'm sorry. Daphne, I didn't mean to say that. You have to admit our relationship is fucked up."

She forced a smile. "It's been so stressful for both of us. We haven't been able to give each other enough attention. I know how much you like it when I give you attention."

Guilt washed across my body. Her idea of attention was to drop to her knees and suck me off, and I wasn't going to lie, I liked it.

"I can't wait to go camping. Just you and me and lots and lots of sex." Wiggling her brows, she took a step back as she motioned for me to follow her.

Sex. Yeah right. We hardly ever slept in the same bed, let alone fucked in it, which was fine by me.

Running her tongue across her lips, Daphne spoke softly. "Speaking of sex, I do believe we have an engagement to celebrate."

Reaching up and loosening my tie, I followed Daphne into our bedroom where we celebrated Daphne-style. Me making sure she was taken care of first and her doing as little as possible to return the favor.

Reaching for the drawer, I grabbed a condom. "Why are you wearing a condom?" she demanded. The frustration was evident in her voice. "Damn it. I'm pregnant for fuck's sakes."

I got into this mess because I didn't wear a condom, twice. Each time I was wasted when I fucked her without one and each time she got pregnant. It was the only thing that kept a barrier between us, as fucked up as that sounded. Every time with Daphne felt like I was cheating on Emylie. In some weird way, the condoms kept a distance I needed. That made me nothing but an asshole. If I really didn't want to be with her, I wouldn't. But I was a guy and jacking off in the bathroom got tiresome.

Once I came, she crawled off and said, "I'm going to sleep in the guest room. You're snoring keeps me up. Maybe next time we can forgo the horrible rubber. It irritates me."

The bedroom door slammed and I pulled off the condom and tossed in the trash. Cleaning up, I fell back into bed.

Staring up at the ceiling, I let out a gruff laugh.

Yep.

Karma indeed.

CHAPTER 3

Emylie

L EANING MY HEAD back, I let the evening sun hit my face. Texas in July was sweltering, and I longed to be somewhere cooler as the heat beat down on my face.

"Hey, beautiful."

With a wide grin, I turned to see Mason walking up. Sitting next to me, we both gazed out over the eighteen-acre lake. The nearly cloudless sky reflected off the water, offering a beautiful view. "How was your day?"

Mason shook his head and let out a long frustrated breath. "Fucking long. Sam and Debbie had everyone running everywhere to get things set up for the family reunion."

I shook my head and giggled. "Why do they always do it during the jubilee that they are both a huge part of? How many pies is Debbie making this year?"

Mason chuckled as he laid all the way back onto the deck. "Isn't it like fifty something pies?"

Shuddering at the thought of having to help Debbie make fifty pies, I shook my head and pushed it all from my mind. "We should go somewhere."

Mason crossed his legs as he kept his eyes closed. "You and me?"

I glanced down at him and couldn't help but notice the sweat-soaked white T-shirt that showed off his perfect abs. "Yeah. 'We' usually means two or more people, and since you're the only other person here, when I say 'we' … I mean you and me."

Mason sucked in a deep breath then blew it out. "Damn, that would be nice. Where would we go?"

I shrugged my shoulders as I peered out over the lake before I dropped back next to him. "Dunno. Maybe the coast?"

"Hell no. It's hot and humid there too, Em."

Giggling, I replied, "Okay, how about Colorado? I bet it's not hot there."

Mason didn't say anything for a few minutes before he quickly sat up. "Let's do it. You and me. Let's run the fuck off and spend a week somewhere. We could go fly-fishing. Rent a place along a river and do nothing but fish and hike and … fuck."

I rolled my eyes, sat up and rested my chin on my knees. "Jesus, has any of your old girlfriends ever told you how romantic you are?"

Mason tapped my nose with his finger and lifted his brow. "We aren't dating, Tink. I don't have to be romantic with you."

Pursing my lips together, I thought about what he said. "This is true. Fly-fishing, huh?"

Mason smiled bigger. "Fly-fishing, baby. And sex with me any time you want. What more could a girl ask for?"

I laughed and gave him a push as he pulled me with him. Landing on him, I met his stare while I chewed on my lip. "Do you think Sam and Debbie would suspect something if we both took off at the same time?"

Mason grabbed me and helped me up as we both stood and re-

KELLY ELLIOTT

garded each other. "I don't give a shit if people find out we're sleep-ing together, Em."

Feeling my heart rate increase tenfold, I swallowed hard. "I do! Mason, everyone will think you're this badass guy who's been screwing me the last couple of years, while everyone will look at me as a pathetic whore who has been sleeping with her best friend, who by the way happens to be my ex-boyfriend's best friend too. Then it will open up Becca's old wounds again."

Mason lifted his brows. "Becca's old wounds?"

Shit. I needed to lead him away.

"Mason, people will gossip."

"Fuck them, Emylie. No one cares. I wouldn't be surprised if people don't expect us to end up together anyway. Best friends, al-ways together. Besides, Holden is living happily in California, and who the hell knows where Suzy is. It's time we moved on."

Taking a step back, my mouth fell open. "Mason, what are you saying? Are you wanting to take this further?"

Mason held up his hands and said, "No! That's not what I mean. I'm not saying you and I start dating, but who cares if people know we're together. If you think about it, it makes sense really."

I quickly turned away and noticed Debbie standing on the back porch talking on the phone. I was tired of everyone trying to fix me up on dates … Debbie included. "Fine. How about we test it out to-night at Shifty's?"

He made his way over to me and pulled me into his arms and planted a long wet kiss on my lips. "I like this plan. Now my mother will stop asking me if I'm gay."

Mason quickly stepped around me and headed off to the main house. I lost it laughing as I followed him.

Walking up to Debbie, she smiled at both of us. "I hope you two don't have any plans next week. We have lots of things going on."

"Um … actually, Debbie, Mason and I were talking about how we wanted to head up to Colorado to do some fly-fishing. There is a

20

fishery up there that I would love to stop at and talk to them for a bit."

When the expression of horror moved over her face I instantly stopped talking. "You want to leave? You can't leave!"

I shook my head as I held up my hands and said, "What? No, I thought since Mason and I both needed a vacation, we could take one and do some fly-fishing and maybe do a bit of research while I'm up there. Not for a new job."

Debbie looked between Mason and me while she attempted to find words to speak. "Mrs. Warner, are you okay?" Mason asked.

Letting out a quick breath, Debbie attempted a smile. "Yes. Yes, I'm fine, but I'm afraid I'm going to have to say no to you both requesting vacation. The ranch is going to be bustling with people, and I can't handle this reunion without you. It's imperative that you're here next week, Emylie. *Imperative*."

Mason cleared his throat as he looked at me and then back to Debbie. "That's fine, Mrs. Warner. How about if Emylie goes ahead and takes a vacation. I can cover any work she would be handling."

"No!" Debbie shouted, causing both Mason and I to jump. "Kids, come on. This is the worst time of year to ask off. I need *both* of you here." She glanced my way again. "Especially you, Emylie."

Smiling weakly, I gave in to defeat probably easier than I should have. Ever since Mason and I graduated from Texas A&M, we had been working for Sam and Debbie without a single vacation. Mason was hesitant on taking the job that rightfully belonged to Holden, but Sam had begged him. He hadn't talked to his son since he informed his parents, me, and Mason, that he had met some girl named Daphne and would be staying in LA indefinitely. No other reason but this woman.

Disappointment rushed over my body. "No worries, Debbie. You know you can count on us."

Mason stared at me then shook his head. I could see how pissed off he was. As much as I wanted to leave for a bit, I didn't want to leave without Mason.

There went that safety net feeling. I really needed to work on that. Mason was not my crutch. Okay he was, but I needed to change that and do it soon.

"Oh, thank you, darling. I promise once we get past these two weeks, if you both want to head on out, you're more than welcome to. I have a feeling you won't, though."

Mason gave a polite grin and tipped his cowboy hat. "Thank you, Mrs. Warner."

Her response caught me off guard. What did that mean? *I have a feeling you won't though.*

Flipping her hand at Mason, she sighed. "Mason, I'm like your mother. Stop calling me Mrs. Warner and call me Debbie. How many times do I have to tell you that?"

He let out a soft chuckle and replied, "Yes ma'am. I'm going to head on back to work now."

Debbie turned to me with a smile I couldn't really read. "I have lots to do to prepare and lots of planning."

"Pies?" I asked with a wink.

Giving me a devilish look, she shook her head and said, "Oh no, darling. Much, *much* bigger plans." She danced excitedly into the house while quickly clapping her hands together.

I got the feeling those plans were going to end up giving me a lot more than just a headache and a missed vacation.

Mason and I rode up to the main house on horseback as we talked about scouting the whitetail deer sometime this week. Whitetail hunting season wasn't until the beginning of fall, but it would be here before we knew it. There were some prize bucks we had both seen. I needed to make sure the food plots were laid out in the right areas. The sooner the better.

"Want to head to the barn?" I asked as Mason stared straight ahead. Turning to see what he was staring at, I said, "Oh shit. Are there people coming already for the reunion? This soon?"

"Looks like it. Damn it. I didn't get mesquite for the grill, and you know Sam will want to start grilling the moment people show up," he quipped.

Turning to following him, I said, "I'll help. We can knock it out faster if we both get it."

Mason nodded. "Sounds good."

Thirty minutes later, we were riding up with mesquite wood in bags thrown over our horses. Coming up almost to the back porch, I slid off my horse and grabbed the bag. Mason was already two steps ahead of me when he ran into a blonde Barbie doll who had rushed out of the back door.

"Jesus! Watch where you're going. I mean, really! You about knocked me over … oh my … well … because you're so handsome doesn't mean you can be rude." The blonde eye-fucked the hell out of Mason. Something most women did when they saw how handsome he was. Add a cowboy hat to the mix and forget it; you'd be dreaming about him for days. From what it looked like, the Barbie was already deep into a fantasy of her own.

Mason looked shocked as hell as I attempted to hold back my laughter. Clearly, this family member was from the city and one we'd never seen before.

Turning to me, the blonde probed me. "Oh. A Latino girl. Do. You. Speak. English?"

My expression widened in surprise. Okay, so she was half right. My father was Hispanic and the reason for my dark hair and sun-kissed skin. But to flat out say that to me and talk to me as if I was stupid … and deaf. I swear if I could, I'd tell her ass off in Spanish. Giving her a polite smile, I said, "Excuse us, and we'll be gone before you know it."

Lifting her pointed snobby nose in the air, she flicked her hand as if dismissing me.

My mouth dropped open while I spun on my heels and walked over to Mason. As we unloaded the wood and piled it up next to the pit, I leaned over and whispered, "Can we say bitch?"

Mason glanced back over to the blonde. "Royal bitch. Jesus, I feel sorry for the guy who sleeps with that thing every night."

"Daddy, it's me. Yes, I'm stuck in God-awful *Texas*."

Mason coughed as he said, "Bitch."

Laughing, I pulled out the last of my wood as the blonde kept talking. "Apparently he thought he would surprise me. I'm not the least bit happy about this. I was *not* prepared to meet the country folk."

I stood and turned to gape at her. Holy hell was this girl a serious bitch.

Mason slipped his arm around my waist and said, "Come on, let's go."

As we began walking back toward the horses, Debbie came out of the back door that led from the kitchen. "Oh no," she said as she stopped dead in her tracks. Her gaze immediately went down to Mason's arm around me. Any other time, Mason would have pulled it away, but he clearly embraced this whole attitude about people knowing we were together. Kind of together. What surprised me even more was the evil smile that spread over Debbie's face. Like she was happy to see his arm around me, even though it was more of a friendly gesture than anything.

I went to speak but was stopped dead in my tracks, as did Mason. Holden walked out and looked directly at us. My heart slammed against my chest as Mason whispered, "Fuck." Dragging out the f-sound out much longer than he needed to. Holden glanced down at Mason's arm and we both quickly stepped away from each other.

Mason and I both said at once, "Holden?"

Swallowing hard, Holden attempted to smile, but failed. As for me, I was frozen in place. A million emotions rushed through my body all at once. Anger, hurt, sadness, lust for the man I thought I was over, only to see him and realize I was far from being over him, and then right back to anger again.

The three of us all stood there staring at each other before Debbie finally said, "Mason, Emylie, isn't it wonderful to have Holden home for the family reunion?"

Mason took a step closer to me and took me by my elbow. He must have noticed I had begun to sway as I felt my knees grow weaker.

Holden is here.

Standing before me looking as handsome as the day he kissed me goodbye at the Austin airport and told me he loved me … forever. Only to crush my world by telling me he had fallen for another woman after he returned to California.

"Yeah, it's a … um … it's a surprise to say the least," Mason said with an awkward laugh.

Holden held my stare. I tried like hell to break away, but I was lost in the pool of sadness. All I could do was think back to all those moments he had made love to me and professed how much he had missed me. How there would never be anyone for him but me. How he loved no one but me.

Lies.

They were all lies.

"Holden, darling. Are you going to introduce me to your *workers*?"

Mason gripped me tighter while he brought my body up against his. Holden's eyes narrowed and turned dark as he watched his best friend hold on to me.

Oh God. This is not happening right now. He brought her home.

Pulling my gaze from Holden, I glanced over at the blonde. She made her way over to him and kissed him on the cheek as bile began to build at the bottom of my throat.

"Mason," I whispered. I needed to get out of here. *He brought her home. Oh God.*

"I've got you, Em," Mason replied back.

Holden glanced between Mason and me, then back at the blonde and gave her a forced smile before focusing back on me. "Um ... Daphne, these are two of my best friends. Mason Frank and ... um ... Emylie ... Emylie Sanchez."

Quickly looking at Daphne, I felt as if all the air had been ripped from my lungs.

It was her. Daphne.

Two of my best friends.

Did he really just say that?

"Oh, how nice. I do believe Holden might have mentioned an Emylie before." Turning back to Holden, she gave him a bitchy smile before peeking back at me. "So, I'm sure you both already know that Holden brought me to his little home town to announce our engagement. We're planning on staying the entire week. How lucky are we?"

Whoosh.

There it went. The last of the breath in my lungs as Debbie and Holden both attempted to get Daphne to stop talking. It felt as if someone had rocked the ground so hard I was sure it would knock me over.

"Come on, Em," Mason whispered as he ushered me toward the horses.

I dug deep inside my inner self and forced him to stop in front of Holden and Daphne. There was no way in hell Holden would know how I felt. Or worse yet, his little whore. Forcing a smile, I replied, "That's news to us ... *Daphne*. But congratulations. I'm sure you'll both be happy together—" Staring into Holden's eyes, I added "Forever."

Turning, I made my way down the steps and to my horse without Mason's help. Climbing up on the mare, I quickly turned her around and took off toward the barn as Holden called out my name. The whole time I forced air in and out of my lungs as I tried to keep myself from totally losing control of the tears I had somehow managed to keep at bay.

He's getting married.

Holden's getting married.

He found his forever, and it wasn't me.

CHAPTER 4

Holden

I STOOD ON the back porch and watched as Emylie and Mason rode off toward the barn. The moment I saw Mason's arm around Emylie, I had to fight the urge to punch him. Knowing I had no right to feel that way, I tried like hell to not let the idea of my best friend dating my ex-girlfriend bother me. Or the hurt on Emylie's face when Daphne mentioned we were getting married.

Fuck my life.

This is why I never came home.

I was a coward who didn't want to face the one person I promised to love forever.

The one person I knew I still loved as much as the day I kissed her goodbye at the airport.

My mother walked up to me and placed her hand on my shoulder. "Maybe you should go talk to her."

"Her? That girl? Who is she, Holden? What's going on?" Daphne spat out as she grabbed me by the arm.

I closed my eyes and prayed I could disappear for a few hours. Opening them, I smiled at Daphne. "Daphne, you look tired. Why don't you go lay down for a bit, while I go talk to Mason and Emylie?"

Daphne motioned to talk to me alone. My mother took the hint and said, "I'll be inside making potato salad."

"Thanks, Mom," I replied with a weak grin.

The moment the door shut, Daphne started. "First off, I'm totally pissed that you brought me here and I'll never forgive you! *Ever!"*

Pulling my head back, I stared at her. "Why?"

She widened her eyes and gave me a disbelieving stare. "Seriously? Holden, had I known we were coming to meet your family … a very large portion of your family … I would have prepared differently. I have no jeans, no boots, no backwoods country attire at all!"

"You're worried about your clothes, Daphne?"

She slowly shook her head and sighed. "Yes, Holden, I am. I would have also liked to prepare myself mentally for all of this. It may not seem big to you, but meeting your future husband's family is kind of a big deal."

"I'm sorry for not giving you a heads up. I wanted to surprise you."

Letting out a huff, she replied back with, "Well you certainly did." She glanced off toward the barn. "I take it *Emylie* is your ex."

Swallowing hard, I peered over my shoulder. Mason and Emylie had rode into the barn and were now out of sight. "Um … yeah."

Daphne tilted her head while she flashed a satisfied smile toward the barn. "Looks like I wasn't the only one who was surprised. Better that she finds out now and get it over with. She's lucky I didn't mention the baby."

I couldn't believe my ears. What a cold-hearted thing to say.

Daphne examined me with an expression of pure evil. "I'm going to go lay down and pray like hell this headache goes away. Take care of the things you need to take care of, Holden, and please do it quickly. I'll be waiting for you."

Spinning on her heels, Daphne headed back into the house, screaming as she jumped and yelled out, "Spider!" Running quickly into the house, the door slammed behind her as I let out a frustrated moan.

I ran my hand through my hair as I made my way to the barn and tried to figure out what I wanted to say to Emylie.

As I approached the barn doors, I heard Mason talking. "Don't let it get to you, Tink. Please, please don't cry. Baby, don't cry."

My heart instantly hurt as the idea of making Emylie cry hit me full force. Mason had called me the day after I broke up with Emylie and bitched me out for over an hour. It was easy to push it away with the hundreds of miles between us. I had asked for it, after all. Away from the pressures of my father, enjoying life in another state. Exactly what I wanted. I'd met Daphne a few times before the party. She was a part of that other world I so desperately thought I wanted. After I woke up that morning in her bed, I knew what I truly wanted, and it wasn't Daphne or a life away from Texas. It took my huge fuck-up to open my eyes and make me realize I didn't want to be anywhere other than with Emylie and here.

When Daphne told me about the pregnancy, there was never a doubt in my mind what the right thing to do was. I never did tell anyone one though, especially Emylie. I knew it would have devastated her to know I had been careless and gotten another girl pregnant.

I sucked in a breath as I stepped around the corner and saw Emylie crying into Mason's chest. He held her tightly and spoke softly to her. She lifted her face and the way they regarded one another told me they were more than friends. Then Mason's words he whispered to her hit me like a brick wall.

"Don't let it get to you, Tink. Baby, don't cry."

With two steps back out of the barn, I placed my hands on my knees and began to drag in one deep breath after another.

Air. I needed air in my lungs.

"I've got to go," Emylie said as Mason called out after her.

Taking in a deep breath, I stepped back through the door of the barn. Emylie slammed into me, causing me to grab a hold of her. Electricity ripped through my body and we both inhaled sharply.

This was what real love felt like. Not lust or desire, but love.

"Em," I whispered.

Her eyes widened in horror, she pushed me away. "Don't touch me."

My heart felt like someone had reached into my chest and squeezed it as hard as they could. In that moment, I knew I had to tell her the truth. I needed her to know why I had done what I did. "Let me explain," I said.

Letting out a laugh, Emily took a few steps away as Mason quickly came to her side. "Explain? Oh, there's no explaining, Holden. You went off to California and found something better." Emylie's voice cracked as I shook my head.

"You didn't even have the decency to come back to Texas and tell me in person. You did it over the phone like a coward! Led me on to believe we had a future together!" Emylie shouted. Tears began to fall and I wanted nothing more than to reach out for her. "I hate you, Holden. I hate you with every ounce of my being."

My whole body trembled as I watched her fall apart. "No. Don't say that. Em ... please let's just talk ..."

Emylie held up one hand then covered her mouth with the other as she tried to calm down. Dropping her hand, she shook her head. "No ... I don't have anything to say to you, Holden. You left me feeling like a fool. You made promises you never intended on keeping."

"That's not true, Em. Baby, if you would let me talk I could—"

"Don't call me that!" Shaking my head frantically, I backed away from the heat of her body. "You said your goodbyes, Holden. Let's leave it at that. What we had is over ... the past belongs in the past. I hope you and your fiancée enjoy your time back home."

Emylie pushed past me and walked off quickly. Closing my eyes, I dropped my head and whispered, "Fuck."

With a quick look forward, I saw Mason staring at me. He gave me a once over and turned to tend to the horses. "Mason, you don't understand."

He dropped his hands and turned to me. "You're right, Holden, I don't understand. I've never understood, and you've never tried to help me or Emylie with that." Shaking his head, he pointed to me and said, "This … this guy standing in front of me is not the same guy who left here to go to California. That guy would have killed the person who made Emylie feel the way she's felt since you called and destroyed her entire world."

I glanced down and kicked at the dirt on the barn floor. "Things changed. I changed, Mason."

Mason mumbled something under his breath as he turned back to the horse. "What was that, Mason?"

Pulling the saddle off of the horse Emylie had been riding, he placed it over the rail. "I said, you're damn right you've changed. You know what's really sad, Holden. I hear it in your voice. Every time you call me, I hear how unhappy you really are. It's a damn shame you don't hear it too."

I made my way over to him with my fists clenched. "You have no fucking idea about my life."

Mason dropped the saddle, grabbed me by the shirt, and pushed me against the stall door. "Your life was with Emylie! Here on your family's ranch. Not living in LA and fucking some snobby ass bitch who clearly doesn't hold a candle to Emylie."

Pushing him away from me, I tried to stay calm. "Don't you talk about Daphne like that. You don't know a damn thing about her."

Mason took a few steps away from me and smirked. "You're right dude, I don't. But the little bit I saw today, I feel sorry for you. It's pretty obvious to me you picked the wrong girl."

He reached down for the saddle and headed to the tack room as my anger grew exponentially. "Well it looks like to me, Mason, you made out on that wrong pick. How long have you been fucking *Tink*?"

Mason dropped the saddle again and before I knew what was happening, he punched me in the face, causing me to stumble backward and fall into a hay bale.

He shook his head and pointed at me. "You left her alone and hurt. I was the only one there for her, and I'll always be there for her in any way she needs me. *Any.* I have nothing else to say to you, Holden. You're right ... you are a changed man."

Lifting my hand to my mouth, I quickly wiped away the blood as I watched Mason round the corner.

I dropped my head into my hands and let out a frustrated yell. "Motherfucker!"

The whole reason I had kept away from Brady, Texas was to keep from hurting Emylie. I wasn't back more than an hour and I had successfully caused her to cry, tell me she hated me, and walk away from me. I caused my best friend to punch me, and I was positive I had deserved a hell of a lot more than what he gave me.

Rubbing the back of my neck, I sighed. "Son-of-a-bitch. This is going to be a long week."

CHAPTER 5

Emylie

"**T**ELL ME YOU are kidding right?" Becca stated as she pushed Sage on the swing in the backyard of my parents' bed and breakfast.

Sitting on the steps that led to the yard, I replied, "Nope. He's back and he brought her home to meet his family."

Becca shook her head and uttered, "Wow. And they're engaged?"

Sage turned to Becca. "What's enraged mean, Momma?"

Becca smiled a sweet smile and answered, "See Aunt Emylie's face, baby girl?" Sage turned back to me and nodded. "That's the look of someone who is enraged. But Aunt Emylie said, 'engaged.' That means two people are gettin' married."

"Oh," Sage said as my mother chuckled from behind me and I frowned at Becca.

"I can't believe Debbie didn't give you a warning or something. I'm going to have to call her and give her a piece of my mind," my mother stated as she sat next to me.

I wrapped my arms around her. "Now, now, Momma. Don't be getting all upset. You might say something you'll regret and cause me to lose my job."

Brushing me off with her hand, momma shook her head. "Bullshit. Debbie and Sam would never let you go. They need you too much."

Becca and I both let out a gasp. "Momma! You swore," I exclaimed as I looked back at Becca who was attempting to cover her smile.

My mother never swore. I'd only ever heard her swear one other time, when I called to tell her Holden called and said he met someone else. She called him an asshole. I'll never forget it for as long as I live.

Momma stood up and placed her hands on her hip. "That's right, I did. And I'll do it again. I'm mad at that boy. How dare he bring her here? How dare he flaunt her right in front of you? I'm … I'm …"

"Pissed."

Turning around, my mouth dropped as I stared up at my father standing in the doorway.

"Oh hell, things just got really fun," Becca declared with a chuckle.

My mother pointed to my father. "Yes! That's right. I'm pissed. I'm pissed beyond belief. I'm so pissed that I'm going to go … go …"

I leaned forward and waited to hear what my mother was going to go do.

"What? What are you going to go do?" Becca asked with anticipation in her voice.

My mother dragged in a deep breath, slowly blew it out, and replied, "I'm going to bake my famous apple pie and bring it out to them. Welcome that jerk-off and his new girl back home. Then I'm going to tell Debbie I'm putting my apple pie and my lemon pie into the pie competition at the jubilee."

I covered my mouth with my hands and stood. "Momma! You know Debbie lives for that competition. If you put your pies in, she might lose."

My mother gave me a wink and shrugged. "Maybe it's time she did lose." Turning on her heels, my mother headed back into the house. "Come along, Mario. We have to go to the grocery store."

Glancing back over my shoulder at Becca, I shook my head and laughed. "What in the heck just happened?"

Becca reached down and scooped up Sage and started laughing. "Momma Sanchez got pissed, that's what happened."

Momma stuck her head out the back door and stated, "Girls, I think you both need to go dancing tonight. I'll watch Sage."

"Thanks Mrs. Sanchez! Sounds like a plan to me," Becca said as she began twirling Sage around. "Yay! Mommy gets to go dancing tonight."

I laughed as I walked up and took Sage from Becca while she kept dancing. Setting the little girl down, I began to dance with her as a familiar voice spoke.

"Y'all look like you're having a little bit too much fun."

Hearing Mason's voice made me smile. He walked up and took Sage in his arms and began dancing with her. Every now and then, he would dip her and make her start laughing. Stepping back, I watched how he interacted with Sage. My gaze drifted over to see Becca smiling at the two of them. Sage's father didn't have much to do with the poor little thing. He was more interested in his new girl-friend who lived in Austin.

Maybe it was time for me to move on? Clearly, dickhead Holden had moved on. Chewing on my bottom lip, I stared at Mason. I needed to let him go. It was becoming more and more clear to me how much Mason and Becca liked each other. Even though neither would admit it.

Laughing as he spun Sage, Mason stared at me and tilted his head. "What's wrong, Em?"

I lifted the left corner of my mouth into a smile, I shook my head. "Nothing. I was wondering if you wanted to go out tonight, dancing with me and Becca."

Mason gave me a sexier-than-hell grin then took in Becca. "Dancing with two beautiful women. Who would turn that down?"

Mason made his way over to Becca, slid his hand around her waist, and dipped her. I couldn't help but laugh at the exchange.

"Aunt Emylie! Uncle Mason and Momma are dancing!" Sage called out.

Seeing Becca laugh at the attention, I knew it was time to break things off between me and Mason. "Oh, believe me, Sage baby, I see."

Mason must have realized I was standing there. He quickly let go of Becca and headed back over to her daughter. With a kiss on the cheek, he said, "I've got to go, Sage. I'll see you later, okay?"

Sage blushed and whispered, "Okay, Uncle Mason."

He lifted his hand and waved to Becca as he called out, "Later, Becca."

Giving him a wave, Becca answered, "Yep. See ya later, Mason."

Taking my elbow with his hand, Mason began leading me out of the backyard and around to the front of the house. We walked to his truck in silence, stopped and I leaned against it. Mason placed both hands on his truck, pinning me against it. "I'm sorry he hurt you again, Em. I wish he hadn't even come back to town."

I swallowed hard and shook my head. "I'm not, Mason. I see now that it's time for me to put the past in the past." Pulling my lower lip in between my teeth, I searched his face. "It's time for us both to move on."

Mason's gaze peered into my own. I wasn't sure how to read him. "Time to move on?"

Slowly nodding, I smiled. "I see the way you look at her, Mason."

Glancing away, he replied, "You're wrong."

"Am I? Answer this for me then. If we didn't have this," I pointed between our bodies, "between us, you wouldn't be interested in dating another girl. In dating Becca?"

Mason swallowed hard. "I've dated girls, Em. You know that. I feel sorry for Becca, that's all. With the way that fucker treated her, she deserved better. I never did understand what she saw in him."

I placed my hand over his chest. "Mason, stop denying your feelings for her."

His eyes filled with terror. He was holding back something from me.

"Talk to me, Mason."

"It's different between you and me, Em. What we have is fun … an escape. What if things didn't turn out and I lost her friendship? I love spending time with her and Sage."

Mason brought donuts every Saturday morning to Becca's house. The three of them had a tea party on the front porch while they ate donuts and sipped orange juice from plastic teacups. I knew that time they spent together meant a lot to all of them.

"We can't hide behind each other any more, and we certainly can't keep using sex as a coping tool."

Sage sung as she skipped by us. Mason took a step away from me, realizing how close we were. He quickly glanced over to Becca.

Her smile was strained. I was probably the worse best friend on the planet to be sleeping with the man my best friend liked. In my defense, she had been married when it first started.

"See y'all later?" Becca asked.

Lifting my hand, I replied, "See ya later."

Without saying a word to me, Mason walked around his truck and got in. Stepping away, I watched as he drove off.

I wasn't sure how I was feeling right then. Scared. Angry. Maybe even lonely.

The one thing I knew for sure was that as much as it hurt to move on from the safety net of Mason, I knew it was the right thing to do. For him, me, and especially Becca and Sage. If Mason felt anything for Becca, I wasn't about to stand in their way.

Turning back to the house I had grown up in, I stared at it. The soft blue two-story house warmed my body. The historical marker on it was something my parents were both so proud of. It was now a bed and breakfast. I had long since moved out and into my grandmother's old house, giving up my room for some young couple in love.

My stomach turned thinking about Holden and Daphne. Now that he was bringing her home to Texas, that meant I'd be seeing them more. Could I handle that? Seeing him today only confirmed my feelings have not changed. I may hate him, but I loved him still. I'd always love him.

I pulled out my phone and sent a text message to a friend I had met in college.

Me: Hey! Long time no talk! How is Utah?

Jamie: OMG! Emmie! Utah is amazing. Come to me!

Chewing on my lip, I hit reply.

Me: I may be looking at relocating. I'm thinking a visit is in order.

Jamie: Do not kid with me, Em. Are you being for real?

Me: Yes.

A tear fell from my face and I closed my eyes. The only way I could truly move on was to leave the memories behind. Everywhere

I looked was a memory of Holden.

Jamie: Tell me when and I'm so there. I'll show you every-thing. Oh, Em, you would love Park City.

My chest tightened. Could I really leave the town I grew up in? Leave all of my friends? Mason, Becca, and Sage. What about my parents?

Me: I'm sure I would. I'll call you some time next week. We'll talk dates.

Jamie: Sounds good! I'm so excited!

The screen door opened and I glanced up to see my mother standing there. Forcing a smile, I pushed my phone into my back pocket and headed her way.

Walking up the steps, my mother held her arms open as I walked into them and silently cried into her chest.

CHAPTER 6

Holden

I PARKED NEXT to what I was pretty sure was Mason's truck. Would he be here with Emylie? I sure as hell hoped not.

"Holden, why must we be here?" Daphne whined in the seat next to me. "I wanted to go to Austin today to do some shopping and your mother had me in the kitchen almost all day. Ever since that Mrs. Sanchez woman dropped off a few pies your mother has gone insane."

I tried to hold my laughter back as I thought back to the look on my mother's face when Kim said she was entering her pies into the competition during this year's jubilee. I thought it would have been awkward with Emylie's mom being there, but it wasn't. She was pleasant like she always was. Welcoming Daphne to Brady with a damn apple pie. I quickly figured out what she was doing. Killing us both with kindness. I was half-tempted to ask her what she spiked the pie with.

"Daphne, I want you to see this side of me. This is a huge part

41

of who I am. If we're getting married and having a baby, I'd think you'd want to know a little more of who you're marrying."

Daphne shuddered as she glared at the entrance to Twin Oaks Dance Hall. "A run-down dance hall is a part of who you are, Holden? I think I liked being in the dark about this part of you. Besides, I know all I need to know."

Sighing in frustration, I turned to see my parents pulling up. My father had been polite to Daphne, but he had yet to speak to me. "It's the kick-off to the jubilee tonight. My parents are going to be here and I'm sure some friends I grew up with as well. It's an annual celebration and the start to our family reunion."

"Will Emylie be here?" Daphne asked.

It felt as if someone were sitting on my chest, I answered her honestly, "I'm not sure."

She rolled her eyes, pushed the door open, and got out of the BMW we had rented. Slamming the door shut, she immediately began bitching about having to walk on gravel in her high heel shoes. Why in the hell she had packed high heel shoes when she thought we were going camping was completely lost on me.

"Want me to carry you, Daphne?"

Daphne nodded her head and then laughed as I picked her up and carried her to the entrance. Stopping at the door, I slowly slid her down and gave her a kiss. Trying hard to make her happy. If she was miserable, I'd be miserable. "We wouldn't want you to ruin those heels now would we?" I said as I gave her a wink. It was rare that we were like this. Most of the time Daphne wanted to be left alone and I was more than happy to oblige.

"Gag me. Can we move along, Holden? Some of us would like to get in and get a beer."

Turning, I saw Becca standing there with Emylie and Mason behind her. My stare immediately zeroed in on Emylie. "Nice to see you too, Becca. I see you're still the same spunky girl."

She pushed past me while shooting me the finger as she mumbled, "Asshole."

Daphne's mouth fell open as she said, "Well, I've never. Holden, are you going to let her talk to you like that?"

Becca turned and observed Daphne. "Nice Louboutin's. Probably not the best place to wear them though."

Taking a step up, Emylie cleared her throat. "Becca, why don't we head on in?"

Becca gave Daphne a fake smile before turning and heading into the dance hall. Emylie peeked up at me through her lashes and I was almost positive she sucked in a breath. I knew she had seen my face where Mason had punched me. Looking away quickly, she and Mason made their way inside. His hand on her lower back, guiding her in.

Fucker.

I wrapped my arm around Daphne's waist, we headed inside. Smiling the minute I stepped inside, all the memories came flooding back to me.

"Damn, I had some fun times in this place," I said as I scanned the dance floor.

Daphne held onto me like we were walking down a shady alley in LA. She barely whispered, "This is what the country people do for fun, huh?"

I gave her a quick kiss on the cheek and chuckled. "Come on, Daphne, try and enjoy yourself. I can even teach you how to two-step if you want."

She lifted her hand and brushed me off while she checked her phone for messages. "I think I'll pass. I'll give you tonight to stroll down memory lane. But after this, I expect you to be back to your normal self, Holden."

I shook my head while my jaw clenched together. "Daphne, I'm not asking you to move here for fuck's sake. I'm asking you to at least try to enjoy this week. This is my family ... these are my roots, and if you can't accept me for where I came from, we have a serious problem."

Daphne stood before me with a stunned expression before she squared off her shoulders. "I'm sorry, Holden. You're right. This is all very ... new to me. I'm sure I'm just tired from the travel and thinking we were actually going—"

"Going where?"

Daphne glanced around and gave a weak smile to my parents as they walked in. "Fine, Holden, I'll tell you. I thought you were taking me to Mexico. Private beach, white sands, the whole romantic notion of you sweeping me away after you proposed to me is what I had in mind. Not being swept away to your family's ranch in the middle of nowhere. The stress of all of this is not good for me or the baby."

I pulled my head back in surprise as I asked, "Isn't that after the wedding day?"

She shot me a dirty look and replied, "I need a drink, Holden. The sooner, the better. And a table please. I'd like to get off my feet."

After finding a table and ordering Daphne a Coke, I excused myself and headed to my parents' table. My father was in a deep conversation with Mario, Emylie's father. Clearing my throat, I began to speak. "Mr. Sanchez, it's a pleasure to see you again."

Barely acknowledging me, Emylie's dad answered, "It's been a while, Holden."

I knew I didn't deserve much more than that. "Dad, are you enjoying the evening?"

My father glanced up at me. Disappointment filled his eyes as I felt my stomach drop. "It's fine. Your mother was looking for you and Daphne. She wanted y'all to sit with us."

I quickly scanned the area and saw my mother out on the dance floor with Mason. The way she was laughing caused a tinge of jealousy to race through my blood. "That was nice of her, but Daphne has a bit of jet lag and wanted to sit away from the music."

My father glanced over to Daphne who had her nose stuck in her phone. "That three-hour flight must have been hell on her."

I shook my head. "Dad, are we really going to do this right now?"

My father stood up quickly and got in my face. "I am, Holden, because you never had the balls to come home and do your dirty work in person. You come walking back into town with some fancy fiancée and you expect us all to fall at your feet with welcome arms. Well I'm sorry, son, my world doesn't work that way."

Feeling the anger build up, I slowly let out a breath as I replied, "So you're going to fault me for falling in love, Dad?"

He threw his head back and laughed. He glanced over to Mario and then back to me. "I call bullshit. If you love that girl, then God strike me down. Now, you had yourself a little fun, found a pretty girl who gave you some attention. Something new and different, isn't that what you said you wanted? But in the meantime know this, you hurt Emylie deeper than you'll ever know, and that is *not* the man I raised. You disappoint me in more ways than one."

"Lord knows we can't have you disappointed now, Dad, can we? And if you don't think I know how much I hurt her, then you are sorely mistaken. I'd give anything to go back and not che—." I instantly stopped talking.

My father glared at me. Slowly shaking his head, he said, "I thought so."

My mother stepped between the two of us and placed her hand on my shoulder. "Stop this right now. If you two want to work through your problems, that's fine, but do it in private."

Nodding, I gave my mother a knowing look. "Sorry, Mom. I'm going to head back over to Daphne."

"That's fine. Come on over and sit with us, okay?"

Not wanting to disappoint my mother, I nodded and said, "Okay, let me go get her."

My mother smiled and reached up to kiss me on the cheek.

45

As I headed back to where Daphne was, I saw Emylie and Mason dancing. Jealousy raced through my body for the second time tonight. Mason had my life. The life I openly walked away from.

Pulling my gaze from the past, I made my way to my future while I tried to shake the dreadfulness that swept over my body.

My father was right. He was absolutely right. I not only disappointed him, but my mother, Emylie, Mason, Kim, and Mario.

And most of all … me.

Ten Bud Lights and a few hours later, I was laughing and having a good time with Mason and a few guys I went to high school with. Daphne was sitting at my parents' table bored out of her damn mind. I'd tried over a dozen times to get her to dance with me, and each time she turned me down. I finally said fuck it and decided to enjoy myself. If she wanted to sulk, let her. I didn't really give two shits.

Mason and Tyler, a hunting guide who worked for my father, began talking about the upcoming season. I tried like hell to not pay attention to what they were talking about, but I was longing to add my input. Input I knew they neither needed nor wanted.

Mason glanced over my shoulder and smiled. Standing, he said, "If y'all will excuse me, a pretty girl is motioning for me to dance with her."

I glanced over my shoulder and saw Emylie. I had figured it was going to be Becca since Mason and Becca had pretty much been dancing together all night. Turning back to him, I acted as if I couldn't have cared less. I observed him as he walked up to Emylie and whispered something into her ear. She pulled back and smiled at him. Becca walked up and motioned for Mason to dance with Emylie.

The music changed and Emylie raised her brows as she led Mason to the dance floor.

Turning away, I asked Tyler. "How long have Mason and Emylie been together?"

Tyler frowned and shrugged his shoulders. "They've been keeping it on the down-low, but I think they've been together for at least a year. Heard a rumor they were together while at A&M. Something about Emylie had a bad breakup and then Mason walked in on his girl fucking some other guy. Since then, they've been rumored to be fuck buddies."

My blood began to boil at the idea of Mason with my Emylie. *That motherfucker.* Turning back to him, I fought the urge to bash his head into the floor.

"Fuck buddies, huh?" I asked as I turned back to Tyler.

Tyler took a drink of his beer. "That's the rumor. Shame, though. They both really deserve to be happy."

I gave Tyler a fake smile, I took another drink of my beer. "Sure they do."

Standing up, I pushed my chair back. "I feel like dancing," I mumbled as I made my way to the dance floor. Knowing how drunk I was, this was probably not one of my better ideas.

Luke Bryan's "Kick the Dust Up" played as I walked up to Mason and Emylie. Tapping on Mason's shoulder, I asked, "May I cut in?"

Mason took a step back and motioned to Emylie. "It's up to, Em."

I let out a gruff laugh and said, "You like calling her my nickname?"

Mason pulled his head back in shock. "What the hell are you talking about, Holden? We've always called her Em."

Pointing to myself, I said, "Nah, dude. That's what *I* called her. I guess it makes sense you would step into the role for me. I appreciate that, buddy. That's what best friends do. Take over fucking the girl, right?"

Mason's face turned red as Emylie stepped between us. "You're drunk, Holden. Why don't you go on back to your table? I'm sure Daphne is waiting for you."

"You don't want to dance with me, Emylie? Why?"

Examining me with a surprised expression, she slowly shook her head. "Holden, you have no right asking me to dance."

"Why not? I thought we were friends."

Mason reached for Emylie. "Come on, Em, I'll take you home."

I took a step toward Mason and poked him in the chest. "Oh hell. Whoa there, Mason. Dude, you really going to take her home right in front of me? Hell, why don't you just fuck her in front of me while you're at it?"

"Holden!" Emylie called out. Then she screamed. That was twice Mason had caught me off guard. This time he clocked me right in the eye.

Grabbing me by the shirt, Mason pulled me up to him. "You never were a good drunk, you asshole. Go home, Holden. You have a new life now. Remember? You can't come back and ruin Emylie's again."

My father walked up and pulled Mason's hands off of me. "All right, boys. That's enough. Let's go home, Holden."

As my father began to drag me away, my gaze caught Emylie's. She seemed so sad. "Em, I never wanted to hurt you. I swear to you! Baby, I still love you!"

Her eyes widened in shock. She turned away from me and walked right into Mason's arms as my father pulled me outside and over to his truck. Pushing me up against it, he glared at me.

"What in the hell is wrong with you, Holden?"

I let out a moan while I dragged my hands down my face. "Fuck, Dad. I don't know. I lost control when I saw Mason and Emylie together, and I know I have no right to be feeling the way I'm feeling."

"You think? You made a choice, Holden. For whatever reasons

you had to walk away from this life, you did. Now you live with that decision. You've got five days here, and I swear to God, son, you better make it up to your mother for being gone the last few years. As far as Emylie goes, you made your bed. Lie in it."

I peered up at my father, my eyes wet with the threat of tears. "I don't love her. Dad, it was one moment of weakness."

Tilting his head, my father stared into my eyes like he knew exactly how I was feeling. His gaze moved behind me as he leaned in closer and whispered, "That one moment of weakness better have been worth it, son."

He opened the door and pushed me inside. "He's pretty drunk, darling. Why don't you follow us back to the ranch in the car y'all rented?"

"Is he okay, Mr. Warner?" Daphne asked.

"Sam, call me Sam, Daphne. Yes, he never could hold his beer. Debbie, why don't you drive home with Daphne so she doesn't get lost."

I tried to push everything away. The way Mason and Emylie danced together. The sadness that filled her eyes when she gazed into mine.

My head dropped back against the seat while I let out a groan. *Where did it all go wrong?*

I already knew the answer.

The moment I met Daphne.

CHAPTER 7

Emylie

TWO DAYS HAD passed since the encounter with Holden at Twin Oaks. Mason had brought me home, walked me to my door, and wished me a goodnight. I hated that he and Becca didn't end up together that night. I knew it was because of me.

I mindlessly rode along the fence line. It wasn't a part of my job description to check the fences, but I needed to do something that took me away from the main house. My office was housed there and I couldn't bare the idea of running into Holden ... or Daphne. From the little I knew about her, she was vile and snobby. I didn't trust her. There was something about her that didn't feel right. I couldn't put my finger on it, and a part of me wanted to figure it out. The other part of me wanted them both to leave and get on with their happy lives in LA.

Closing my eyes, I thought back to this morning when I had overheard her on the phone.

"No, Jean, I'm not in Mexico on a white sandy beach. I'm stuck in the middle of Texas, where it's hot as hell and my hair will not hold a damn curl."

Daphne had wandered to the other end of the house where my, Mason's, and Sam's offices were located. My office door had been cracked open and I couldn't help but overhear her talking to a friend.

"Well, the plus side to all of this is I think Holden's mom is going to be throwing us an engagement party. I've already informed Daddy and he's sending someone to document it. Oh, yes, I've already cleared it with Holden. I think he needed to sow some wild oats. Once we get to back to LA, he'll be back to his normal self. Right now he's wearing Wranglers and a God-awful baseball cap backward. I will admit he looks hot as hell in it, but it's not the Holden I've worked so hard at grooming."

I rolled my eyes as I stood up and headed to my door. Before closing it, Daphne started laughing. "Oh, girl, sex with Holden has never been one of my complaints. No, unfortunately we haven't. I think he's worried about being in his parents' home. He won't be able to last too much longer without sex. He mentioned something about going to some cabin. He never could resist me."

My hand covered my mouth as I tried to keep the sick feeling down. The cabin is the first place Holden and I had made love. He was taking her there? How could he?

Pulling my office door open, I quickly walked down the hallway as Daphne let out a small scream. I needed to get out of this house.

I needed air.

I took in a deep breath and stared straight ahead as I tried to clear my mind of Daphne and Holden. Someone was on a horse up ahead in an open field. Pulling out my phone, I called Mason.

"Hey, Em. What's up?"

"Hey, are you out in the north pasture?" I asked as I kicked my horse into a trot.

"Nope, I'm living in hell right now listening to Sam and Tyler argue about something Holden mentioned."

With my curiosity piqued, I asked, "What did he mention?"

"A solar-powered system for the windmills." Mason covered the phone and shouted something about the men growing up.

Letting out a chuckle, I said, "You know, that's not a bad idea, Mason."

He responded with a sigh. "I know, but the idea came from Holden, so you know how that goes."

"Yeah. I know how that goes. His dad won't even entertain it. I'm going to see who in the hell is out here."

"It's probably one of the guides exercising some of the horses. Debbie mentioned wanting to take some of the kids on a guided horseback ride."

"Okay, that's probably it. Talk to you soon."

Hearing Sam raising his voice in the background, I smiled as Mason groaned. "Later, Em."

I slipped my phone back into my boot and gave Sunshine a squeeze and she took off in a full run. It didn't take me long to come up on the person. My heart began beating harder in my chest, the closer I got. Even out in the wide open, I knew it was him. I could feel it was him.

Turning his horse around, Holden stood before me looking like he did the last time we were in this field together. Bringing my horse to a stop, I fought to find my voice. Holden smiled and lifted his hand in a wave. "Hey, Emylie."

I finally spoke. "Hey. Sorry, I wasn't sure who was out here. I didn't mean to interrupt you and ..." Glancing around I searched for Daphne.

"Um ... where's Daphne?"

Holden shook his head and let out a loud laugh. "Daphne would rather roll around in pig shit before getting up on a horse."

With my lips pursed, I lifted my brow. "I don't see her as the type of girl to do either to be honest with you."

Turning his head away from me, he looked out over the pasture. "Yeah, she's not. She's more into shopping, photo shoots, and her acting career."

"Acting, huh?"

Holden turned back to me and smiled weakly. "Yeah. She's good at acting."

Not knowing what to say, I gave him a weak smile in return and lifted my hand to say goodbye. I couldn't stop hearing his voice replay in my head as Sam dragged him away. Shouting he still loved me. It had replayed over and over in my head the last two nights.

"I've got a lot of work to do so I'll see you around, Holden."

As I slowly moved away from him, I silently prayed he wouldn't call out to me.

"Hey, Em?"

Damn it.

I stopped my horse and glanced over my shoulder. "Yeah?"

His expression seemed so sad I almost felt sorry for him. *Almost.* "I'm sorry I hurt you. I didn't mean to."

I wondered if any other normal person would accept his apology. I knew my mother would. She'd smile and tell him what's in the past is in the past. Me? No ... I couldn't walk away from him now without saying what I've dreamed of saying to him. Sliding off my horse, I walked over to him. Holden quickly jumped off his horse.

Stopping short of him, I planted my feet wide, and if I hadn't known any better, I'd swear my nostrils flared. "How dare you come walking back into my life thinking all you had to do was say you're sorry? You know what, Holden? I don't give a flying fuck about your apology. You destroyed me. You destroyed us, and you don't get to get off that easy with a simple *I'm sorry*."

My heart was pounding in my chest and I was sure he could hear it. It was hot out already that morning, but a heat flashed through my body as I stood there staring at him.

"I cheated on you."

Those four words knocked me completely off my feet as I stumbled backward. "W-what?"

Holden shook his head. "I stayed back in LA over the holiday week our junior year because I had a huge test that following Monday. With our football schedule and all, I knew I needed to stay and study. If I failed that test, I was fucked. One of the other football players set up a study group early in the year. That's where I first met Daphne."

Placing my hands over my mouth, I shook my head. I didn't want to hear this. It was over … it didn't matter anymore.

"Please, Emylie, I need to tell you everything."

Tears began to fall freely now as Holden's eyes watered up. "A friend of mine had a party over the Thanksgiving break. They were all drinking and someone gave me something that had me flying high. I don't know if they slipped it in my drink or what, but I wasn't myself. Daphne started flirting with me, and that was the last thing I remembered. I woke up the next morning naked in bed with her."

I dropped my hands and took a few steps back before I turned and started back toward my horse. Holden ran up to me and grabbed my elbow. "Em, please wait."

Pulling my arm from him, I spun around. "You dirty bastard! You came home that Christmas break and didn't say anything to me. You never once mentioned you had met someone else. You kept me believing in us. We made love, Holden. I was with you after you … after you slept with her! I hate you so much."

A tear rolled down his face.

"Why? Why are you telling me all this now? So you can get married with a clear conscious? Fuck you! You obviously enjoyed her much more than me, you motherfucker!" I screamed as Holden grabbed onto both my arms.

"No! God, no Emylie. You have no idea how I felt that day. The aftermath of that one decision has haunted me since I woke up that morning and realized what I had done. I called you, but you didn't answer. I left you a voice mail … do you remember? I begged you to call me as soon as possible."

Trying to break his grip, I cried harder as the memories flooded my brain. "I called you back, Holden. I called you back, and you never once mentioned you slept with another woman!"

His eyes were filled with regret as he searched my face. "I tried to tell you. I tried so fucking hard to tell you. Then I heard your sweet voice and I couldn't do it. I couldn't hurt you like that. I thought if I forgot about that night, pretend I hadn't slept with Daphne, everything would be okay. I even started looking into transferring to A&M for our last year."

My mind was spinning. "What? Why didn't you tell me? What made you go from that, to calling me after Christmas break, the Christmas break we spent with each other. Making love and making plans about our future, to telling me you'd met someone and had to stay in California?"

Pulling my arms out, I stepped back and held up my hands when I saw the look in his eyes. "No. Never mind I don't want to know. Please leave me alone and go back to your Barbie doll. I'm sure she's wondering where you are."

"Damn it, Emylie, stop!"

Grabbing the reins of my horse, I quickly climbed up as Holden stood in front of Sunshine. "Get away from me, Holden. None of this matters anymore. You made a choice. You picked her over me. End of story."

Holden shook his head and said, "No, there's so much more to the story."

Wiping my tears away, Holden stepped aside and pushed his fingers through his hair. "Our story's over, Holden."

"No, Em. Please let me talk to you."

I gave a kick to Sunshine, she took off in a full run. Feeling the wind hit my face, I began to cry again before the cabin popped into my head. Turning her around, I headed back to Holden. He was walking back to his horse when he turned around and stopped. Coming to a fast stop, I jumped off of Sunshine and quickly made my way over to him. Pulling my arm back, I swung and punched him square on the chin.

Holden stumbled back and called out, "Motherfucker! What in the hell?"

Pain instantly shot through my fist and up my arm, but I held it in.

"That was for even thinking of taking her to our cabin. That was *our* place, Holden." My voice cracked as he stared at me. "She may be getting you for the rest of her life, but I had you first. That cabin was where you and I … where we …" Closing my eyes, my heart raced. I fought to find the words I wanted to say. Tears streamed down my face as I sobbed. "How could you take her there?"

Holden walked up to me and pulled me into his arms as I hit his chest repeatedly. "How could you?"

His hand laced through my hair as he pulled my head back and met my gaze. I'd never admit how amazing it felt to be in his arms again. Or how the way he was looking at me had my stomach in knots. "Em, I'd never take her to our cabin."

I felt like a fool and I was pissed I was letting Holden see me so upset. "She said on the phone you were taking her to a cabin."

Closing his eyes, he slowly shook his head. "I was going to take her to Russ's cabins for a night. I wasn't taking her to our cabin."

Oh fuck. Now I really feel like a fool.

I stepped away from Holden and whispered, "I'm sorry. I'm sorry I hit you."

"Emylie, you don't ever have to say you're sorry to me. I deserve everything you throw at me. You have no idea how much I hate myself for what I did to you. What I did to us."

My knees felt weak, and I needed more than anything to get away from him. "I … I have to go."

Slowly making my way back over to Sunshine, I started to mount her when my body came to life. Holden grabbed my hips and lifted me up as I threw my leg over.

Don't look at him. Do *not* look at him.

"She was pregnant, Em. I did what I thought was the right thing to do at the time."

Trying to control my trembling hands, I stared at him. I couldn't believe what I had just heard. I didn't want to believe it.

"Wh-what?"

Holden glanced away. "When I got back to LA, Daphne showed up at my apartment and told me she was pregnant. I didn't know what else to do. I knew if I told you the truth, you'd hate me even more. You'd be disappointed in me, and I couldn't stand that thought."

"You have a child?" I asked in a panicked voice.

I shook my head. "She lost the baby before we had a chance to tell anyone."

His words hurt me more than he would ever know. All I could do was turn the horse and slowly walk off.

Another dream of mine erased.

Carrying Holden's child.

There was a light knock on the door to my office as I heard Debbie call out my name. "Emylie?"

"Come on in, Debbie."

Opening the door, she smiled big. "Are you headed down to the jubilee, darling?"

I shrugged my shoulders and returned her smile. "Probably. Becca wants to take Sage to see the fireworks."

She grinned from ear-to-ear as she leaned against the door jam. Sitting back in my chair, I let out a giggle as I asked, "Why are you looking at me like that?"

Debbie glanced at her fingernails while making an indecisive face and said, "You do still remember you signed up for the volley-ball game, right?"

I glanced at my calendar where I had it written down. "Yeah, it's tomorrow though, right?"

Pursing her lips together, she said, "Yep. Wear your bathing suit. It's going to be hot."

"I am not wearing my bathing suit, Debbie," I stated with a roar of laughter.

"Okay … if you say so. Will you be joining us tomorrow evening for the reunion kick-off dinner?"

I slowly shook my head as my heart sank. "I don't think so. It would be awkward for me to be there with Holden and Daphne."

She nodded her head and gave me a slight smile. "Of course. Take the rest of the day off, sweetheart, and go enjoy yourself."

Wanting to leave early to pick up a few snacks for Sage tonight, I stood up. "I think I will. Tonight's going to be crazy."

Debbie gave me a look that said she knew something I didn't. She let out a quick breath and said, "You have no idea."

CHAPTER 8

Holden

"WHAT DO YOU mean there is going to be a camera crew with us?" I asked Daphne as she walked out of the bathroom and into the small room of the cabin we were renting.

"Daddy thought it might be a good idea to get some raw footage." Turning and giving me a smile that said she was up to no good, Daphne sat down on the bed. "Besides, I know about the dinner."

I stared at her like she had lost her damn mind. "What dinner?"

Laughing as she shook her head, she tilted her head and stared at me like I was the one who was losing it. "The dinner tomorrow? You know ... the one celebrating our engagement that your parents are throwing for us?"

I stared at her with a disbelieving look. Was she for real? She really thought this dinner was for her? "What?"

Daphne stood and spun on her heels as she talked. "Ugh, really, Holden, I hate when you play dumb. I know about the damn dinner, so stop trying to hide it. Daddy wants the cameras there to document it all."

Holy freaking hell. She honestly believes that tomorrow's dinner is for her. Unbelievable.

"Daphne, I don't know how to break this to you, but tomorrow's dinner is the kick-off to the family reunion. It's the same dinner my parents have hosted since I can remember. It has *nothing* to do with us. Nothing."

Dropping her mouth open, Daphne tried to speak. "W-what? Why ... seriously? Your parents have no intentions of throwing us a party? What in the hell did we come here for?"

My hands dropped to my side while my body slumped forward slightly. "For me. For my family to get to know the woman I planned on marrying. So you could see a little bit of where I came from. To break it to them you're pregnant."

She let out a frustrated moan. "For fuck's sake, Holden. We could have flown your parents out to LA and showed them a good time. We didn't have to come all the way here and deal with all this horse shit, and foul smells, and looks from your mother. And excuse me, but did you say *break it* to them. Like they won't be happy?"

Pulling my head back, I asked, "Looks from my mother?"

Daphne dropped her towel and quickly pulled on a pair of jeans she had overnighted from Austin. "Please don't play coy with me. It doesn't become you. We both know your mother is in love with that little country hick, Emylie. For Pete's sake, they have her working at the ranch. It's all over her face she wishes that woman was the one sharing your bed ... not me."

I walked up to her as I shook my head. "You're not giving my mother a chance to even get to know you. You're either on your phone or locked away in the room and now ... now you have us staying at these fucking cabins! And yes, I seriously doubt my parents are going to be happy about this pregnancy, if you want to know the truth."

Daphne glared at me while she stomped her foot. "There are people all over your house! And that house is bigger than my father's. That's saying something. Everywhere I turned, there were people. I wanted privacy, so excuse me for that. God, had I known what my life would have been like, I would have never said I was—"

My heart stopped beating and the room instantly became silent. "You'd have never said what?"

Pulling a T-shirt over her head, she closed her eyes and counted to ten. "Baby, emotions are really high right now, and I feel a panic attack coming on. That can't be good for *our* baby. Maybe we should stay here tonight. I'm really not in the mood to watch fireworks anyway."

I glanced down at her bra that she neglected to put on, I picked it up and tossed it at her. "Put it on, Daphne. You want my mother to like you, to get to know you better? Well, tonight that's going to happen. I plan on telling them about the baby before we leave, and I'd really like for my parents to at least feel like the woman carrying my child gives two shits about them."

The music from a local band was playing off in the distance as we walked around Main Street. Booths were set up and kids were running everywhere as Daphne walked next to me. We headed toward my parents when I saw them.

Catching a glimpse of us walking up, my mother turned to us. Holding out her arms, she wrapped Daphne up in a hug. "Daphne, darling, I hope you were able to get some sleep. Holden said you weren't use to all the hustle and bustle of our home."

Daphne plastered on a fake smile and shook her head. "Oh, no, that wasn't it at all. It was a bit awkward being in the same home as Holden's ex-girlfriend. I'm sure you understand how difficult that must be for me."

Choking on my own spit, I stared at Daphne as my mother's mouth dropped open. *I cannot even believe she said that.* "Oh, my dear … you have nothing to worry about. Emylie and Mason are an item and have been for some time."

I went from choking to not being able to breathe.

"Really?" Daphne asked with one raised brow.

Waving her hand as if to brush off the conversation, my mother said, "Yes. Old news. Now let's start introducing you to family."

Daphne gave me a look of horror as she whispered, "Oh, yay me."

Fifteen minutes later, I had downed three beers as I stood there and listened to Daphne go on and on about herself. I was almost positive Uncle Joe fell asleep twice.

I lifted my beer to my lips then froze when I saw Emylie walking down Main Street with Becca. Mason was behind them with a little girl on his shoulders. It had to have been Sage, Becca's little girl. It had been awhile since I'd seen her.

It pained me to see how happy they all looked. How I longed to get out of this town once upon a time, and now I wished like hell I was in Mason's shoes. He had the life I wanted. It took one fucking moment to change my entire world.

Turning to Daphne, I tapped her shoulder. She was deep in conversation with one of my cousins who is a dancer in New York City. "I'm going to go say hi to a few people."

She lifted her hand to dismiss me and said, "Sure, sure, darling." She never even looked at me.

I rolled my eyes and headed over toward Emylie. She was currently helping the little girl aim a pretend gun that shot out water.

"Hey," I said as I slapped Mason on the back.

He turned to me and frowned. "Hey, Holden." I hated that he looked at me the way he did. We used to be like brothers.

Emylie barely glanced up before going back to helping the little girl.

"Who's this?" I asked as I smiled.

"I'm Sage."

Her little face beamed as she looked up at me with big green eyes. "You're very beautiful, Sage."

"Sorry, Holden, she's a little too young for you." Becca flashed me a fake smile before peering over my shoulder. "Besides, it looks like your future bride isn't too happy with you right now."

I quickly glanced over my shoulder only to find Daphne shooting daggers either at me or Emylie. Probably both of us.

"She's fine," I mumbled before refocusing back on Sage and Emylie.

"I won! Mommy, I won!" Sage screamed while jumping.

Everyone cheered and I couldn't help but notice how Mason stood next to Emylie. As if acting like a shield against me. Sage ran up to him. "Uncle Mason, I won! I won!"

"I know and I'm proud of you, squirt. Told ya you had nothing to worry about."

Sage's little cheeks blushed. Apparently Mason had a way with the girls, young and old.

Becca took her daughter's hand and said, "Come on, I'll take you to get an ice cream cone, baby."

Mason and Emylie both glared at me. The awkward silence that filled the air grew tense.

With a concerned expression, Mason said, "Maybe you should get back to Daphne. She appears to be upset." Emylie looked into my eyes and I was completely lost in her gaze. What I wouldn't do to see them every morning I woke and every night I went to sleep.

"I wanted to make sure you were okay, Em. You left before we finished talking."

Pressing her lips together, she nodded. "I'm fine."

All I could do was nod. "I'll see y'all around," I said as I reached out and shook Mason's hand. The idea that the two of them would end up in bed together tonight did things to me.

With a quick nod, Mason said, "See ya."

Emylie remained silent as she stood next to Mason. "Bye, Em."

Her gaze quickly peeked over my shoulder to Daphne. I'd have given anything to know what was running through her mind. When she finally turned back to me, she simply turned and walked away.

I didn't think my heart could have broken anymore than it did right at that moment. Mason gave me a weak smile and followed her.

"For someone who is engaged to another woman, you sure look devastated at the sight of Emylie and Mason together."

My mother's voice was low. Not that she was trying to be quiet, but because she was probably just as sad as I was.

"I really messed up, Mom."

"Do you love her still?"

With a slow nod, I replied, "I never stopped loving her."

Taking me by the arm, she turned me to face her. "Then please explain to me why you have a ring on that woman's hand when I know damn well she is not who you want to spend the rest of your life with. If she is, then I don't know my own son anymore."

I turned my gaze back over to Daphne. I guess she was happy now that Emylie and Mason had walked off. She was back in a conversation with another person.

Meeting my mother's stare, I knew what I was about to do was going to both disappoint and upset my parents even more. "I need to talk to you and dad."

Her head pulled back in surprise. "Okay, we can talk tonight."

I shook my head. "I need to talk to you now before I end up leaving town and telling you on the phone."

She wore a concerned expression. "Let me go get your father. Lilly's store is open. We can talk in her office."

I blew out a deep breath and followed my mother.

I was going to tell them everything and I had no idea how they would react, but I knew it wasn't going to be good.

CHAPTER 9

Emylie

MASON AND I walked along Main Street in silence. I hadn't told him yet what Holden had told me yesterday about Daphne. My heart still ached as the words bounced around in my memory.

"Talk to me, Em."

Sighing, I stopped walking and faced Mason. Those blue eyes of his held a piece of my heart that would always belong to him. He was not only my best friend, but the man who helped pull me out of a darkness I was sure I'd never climb out of.

"Holden told me what happened. The real reason he broken things off."

His eyes widened in surprise. "Do you want to talk about it now?"

Becca walked up and glanced between us.

"What's wrong?" she asked with a concerned expression.

"Holden told her why he broke up with her."

Her mouth fell open. "Your mom is playing with Sage, let's go behind the stage. We can talk there."

I followed Becca and Mason as we made our way through the crowds. I felt so numb. My feet were moving, but I wasn't sure how.

The knowledge of what Holden had done continued to hit me over and over, right in my heart. Each time I heard his words replay in my head, my heart broke a little bit more.

He cheated on me.

He broke my heart.

Destroyed my dreams.

Got another woman pregnant.

The knowledge of it pounded me again. This time harder. Burying my face within my hands, I sobbed uncontrollably. Mason quickly pulled me into his arms.

"I'm here, Tink. I'm here."

Knowing Becca was with us, I needed to start pulling myself away from my vice. Taking a step back, I looked at Mason and shook my head.

"I know. I know, Mason."

He gave me a funny expression before turning to Becca. It was then he realized what I was doing.

I wiped my tears away and blew out a deep breath. "He said he cheated on me over the Thanksgiving holiday. With Daphne."

Anger moved across Mason's face and was replaced by a look of confusion. Becca shook her head and mumbled, "Damn fucking cheaters."

Mason shook his head in confusion. "But he came home that Christmas break. He told me he was going to ask you to marry him on Valentine's Day."

The strong intake of air almost made me choke. *Holden was going to ask me to marry him?* My heart instantly ached as the life we had planned together flashed through my mind.

Both Becca and I said, "What?"

Wiping the tears away, I said, "You never told me that."

"Why would I? Em, he broke up with you not a week after going back to California. When he was here, he showed me the ring and said he was planning on asking you on Valentine's Day. He seemed so happy and excited. When he broke up with you, I was confused and couldn't figure out why. I even called him demanding he tell me what was going on. Why would I hurt you more by telling you he planned on asking you to marry him? The whole damn thing seemed so off."

My stomach turned. What if that was the ring Daphne now wore? The thought sickened me.

"Wait. I'm royally confused here. He cheated on you how many times?" Becca asked. I knew how much this had to hurt her as well. Her own husband had cheated on her, and now one of our very best friends was a cheater.

Holden. Cheated.

I closed my eyes. "I guess he'd met the bitch before. She had flirted with him a few times. He said he got drunk and Daphne started flirting. He thought someone had slipped him something because he said he felt high. He woke up the next morning in her bed."

Mason shook his head and whispered, "Fucker. Why would he come back home and act like everything was okay?"

With a shrug, I replied, "He said he wanted to forget the mistake he made that night. But when he got back to LA, Daphne told him she was pregnant."

With a shocked expression on both their faces, Mason and Becca gasped. "Holy shit, what?"

I nodded. "Yeah. Daphne was carrying … she was pregnant with …" My voice shook as I attempted not to start bawling again.

Becca nodded and said, "I'm so confused. If she was pregnant, why didn't they get married?"

"She lost the baby."

Mason scrubbed his hands over his face. "If she lost the baby, why the fuck didn't he leave her? Why didn't he tell you what happened?"

"I don't know if I would have forgiven him for cheating, and I'm positive he knew that."

Mason shook his head and said, "So she lost the baby. What was his reason for staying in California then? He must have felt something for Daphne if he stayed with her all of this time. After all, he asked her to marry him."

That was the cruel reality I had been dealing with ever since he told me yesterday. Why did he stay with her?

"Yeah, I've been thinking that too. He said it was a mistake, yet when Daphne lost the baby, he chose to stay with her. That's what hurts even more than him cheating and getting her pregnant." I could feel the tears stinging. "Maybe he thought he wanted to marry me, but he found something he liked better in her."

Closing my eyes, I felt the tears fall. I needed to accept the fact that Holden had found someone who he wanted to be with more than me. It was time for me to move on.

Becca walked up and took me in her arms. "For what it's worth, he doesn't look at her like he looks at you, Em."

Crying harder, I felt Mason wrap his arms around both of us.

Debbie and I moved about the kitchen in silence as I helped her prepare for tonight's dinner. My mind was racing as I tried to figure out how I was going to react when I saw Holden and Daphne. Of course, I still had a few hours before I had to deal with them since they weren't staying at the ranch. Something that really pissed Debbie off. She hadn't seen Holden in a few years and Daphne was still keeping him away from his family.

The air in the room instantly charged and I knew he was there before he even spoke a word.

"Good morning, ladies."

I froze in my place at the sound of his voice. Spinning around, I about choked on my own spit.

My lower stomach clinched as I stared at his sweat-dampened T-shirt clinging to his chest and abs. The way he took me in had my cheeks burning. He was taking me in like I was taking him in. With desire.

"What are you doing here?" I asked when I found my voice.

He lifted his brow and tiled his head. "It's my house."

I was momentarily stunned for a moment. Mentally preparing myself that I wouldn't see him until later, I fought to find words to speak.

"Ah, I thought you were staying at the cabins. I wasn't expecting to see you this morning."

His half-grin faded and the corners of his mouth dropped into a frown. "I've been away long enough that it didn't make a lick of sense to be staying at the cabins. I came home to spend time with everyone. Not hide out."

Did I detect some hostility in his voice? Things must not be so great between the happy couple. It was a childish way for me to think, but I didn't care.

Deciding not to let it go, I pressed him for more information.

"Hide out? That's an odd way to describe spending time with your fiancée."

Holden stared at me so intensely I shuddered.

With a panty melting smile, he asked, "What are you doing for lunch, Em?"

Whoa. That came out of left field.

"Probably helping Debbie."

"Nonsense. You need to eat lunch," Debbie quickly injected.

My head snapped over to her as I shot her a *what-in-the-hell* look.

"Please let me take you to lunch, Em. I really want to talk to you alone. We need to talk."

My stomach dropped. What in the world could he possibly want to talk to me about?

"Okay, I have to run home in a bit to pick up the lights for the back porch. I forgot to grab them. Did you want to meet in town?"

His face lit up and he smiled at me. "No. I'll pick you up at your place at eleven. That way we can be back in plenty of time to help Mom and Dad."

The only thing I could do was say, "Okay. Sounds good."

Oh. My. God. He drops a bomb on me that he cheated on me. Got the girl pregnant, and now he thinks I'm going to drop everything and have lunch with him?

Wait. I totally just dropped everything to have lunch with him.

Holden gave me a wink and grinned from ear-to-ear. I didn't want to admit how it made my stomach flutter. Or how the idea of spending some time with him alone thrilled me more than it should. But it did.

Chewing on my lip, I turned back to peeling the potatoes.

Debbie cleared her throat. "He still loves you."

My hand stopped moving and I stared at the potato. "He's engaged to another woman, Debbie. I'm pretty sure he doesn't love me."

"That's not what he told me and Sam last night."

I glanced over my shoulder and gave her an inquisitive look.

"He told us everything."

I lifted my brows and asked, "Everything?"

She nodded. "Yes. We told him he needed to talk to you, to let you know how he truly felt and to tell you the *whole* story."

The whole story? What did she think I knew? I was pretty damn sure I knew the whole story. Maybe I didn't.

Anger rushed through my veins like ice water. "It doesn't matter, Debbie. He made his choice. If he truly loved me and wanted this life, he'd have come back home when Daphne lost the baby."

Debbie gave me a knowing look. "I'll let him explain everything to you, but keep an open mind, sweetheart."

I dropped the peeler into the sink and set the half-peeled potato down. "It's in the past. He has a future with her, and I have my own future."

"With Mason?"

For a brief moment, I was stunned. "I'm not sure what my future holds."

Debbie turned away. "You're each other's crutch is what you are to each other. You both think you can forget your pain by being together, but you can't. Neither of you would be happy together. You're better friends more than anything else."

Now I was really pissed. Ripping off the apron, I tossed it onto the counter.

"You don't know anything about what Mason and I have together or how we feel about each other."

Crossing her arms over her chest, she nodded. "You're right. I don't. But what I do know is the way you light up when you see Holden. The way your breathing changes when you're near him. I see the same thing in him, and what I don't see is either one of you looking at Mason or Daphne the way you look at each other. Emylie, my darling, I'm going to tell you what I told Holden last night. The two of you were made for each other."

Tears collected in the corners of my eyes as I turned away. "I'll be back this afternoon to help you."

Deep in my heart I knew she was right. The only thing I wanted to do was get home and figure out what I was going to wear on this lunch date with Holden. When really I should be telling Holden to go screw himself.

No. Lunch meeting. I certainly was not going on a date with an engaged man.

Walking out to my car, I pulled out my phone and sent Mason a text letting him know what was going on. His only reply was a simple, "*good luck.*"

As I got in my car and drove off, I glanced back to the house. Daphne was standing on the porch staring at me.

With a forced smile I waved.

I wasn't surprised when she didn't return the gesture.

CHAPTER 10

Holden

"**W**HERE ARE YOU going?"

I was about to walk out the door when Daphne's question stopped me.

Turning, I forced the corners of my mouth up into a smile. "I'm heading into town for a lunch meeting."

"Really? A lunch meeting with who?"

There was no sense in lying to her. "Emylie."

Her hands crossed over her chest and she huffed. "Why? Why in the world are you having lunch with your ex-girlfriend? You should be taking me out to lunch or to a spa so I can prepare myself for the onslaught of your family."

Damn if I didn't want to roll my eyes at her.

"I need to clear the air with Em about a few things. That's all."

Her upper lip snarled. "Oh, cute. Em. What would Mason think if he knew *his* Em was having lunch with you?"

The thought of Emylie and Mason together still boiled my

blood. Every time I looked at the guy who I thought was my best friend, all I wanted to do was punch the living hell out of him. But then I'd come to my senses and realized I pushed the two of them together in the first place, and I couldn't blame either one of them.

"I'm sure he is fine with it since it's simply lunch, nothing more."

She stomped her foot like a child. "What in the hell am I supposed to do while you're off having lunch with that slut?"

Balling my fists together, I quickly walked up to Daphne. "Don't you dare call her that."

She narrowed her gaze and glared at me. "Why not? She's sleeping around with Mason, yet going off and having lunch with you."

"And that makes her a slut?"

She shrugged. "Maybe. Have you noticed the way she eye-fucks you? It turns my stomach. Then she goes off with her arms around your best friend." Lifting her chin, she smirked. "So yes. I'm going to say she is a slut."

"I'm warning you, Daphne. Don't call her that."

Her face dropped and tears formed in her eyes. "If I didn't know any better, Holden, I'd think you still loved her. Don't you even care that I'm carrying *your* baby?"

I shook my head. "For Christ's sake, are you really going to pull this shit with me? You're the one with the ring on her finger and here to meet my entire family. What more do you want from me, Daphne?"

A tear slipped down her cheek. "I want you to not go to lunch with your ex. I want you to want to be with me ... the woman carrying your baby. The woman you intend on marrying. I'm pregnant for fuck's sake!"

Something in me snapped. It was like a dam broke. I couldn't hold back all the words I'd been dying to say.

"Let's be real here, Daphne. This thing between us has been

built on a one-night stand and you getting pregnant."

Her mouth fell open. "Well you certainly cared enough to stay after we lost the baby."

"Because you had a breakdown, Daphne! Did you really think I'd leave you when you were suffering? You could hardly get out of bed."

Her chin started to tremble. "So what you're really saying is you're with me out of pity?"

"For fuck's sake, I don't want to do this with you again."

She buried her face in her hands and started crying. I wasn't in the mood for her dramatics.

"I don't have time to deal with one of your tantrums, Daphne. I'll be back in a few hours. In the meantime, why don't you go sit by the pool and relax?"

"How can you say such cruel things to me?" Her crying grew stronger.

I knew I was being a first-class dick right now, but I didn't care. Heading to the front door, I pulled it open.

"Holden!" Daphne cried out. "Don't you dare walk away from me. Holden!"

She followed me out to the porch. I didn't bother to look back until I heard her make a groaning sound.

"Oh God! Not again!" she cried out.

Stopping, I turned to see her on down on her knees with her arms wrapped around her stomach.

"The baby, Holden you hurt the baby."

Quickly rushing back up the stairs and onto the porch, I cried out, "Daphne!"

I lifted her in my arms and carried her back into the house. "It's okay, I'm sorry if I got you upset."

She buried her face into my chest and cried.

"What happened?" Mom asked rushing out from the kitchen.

"We got in a fight and something's wrong. I think I need to take her to the hospital."

Daphne jerked her head up. "No! No the last time they started poking around I lost the baby. No, I don't want anyone touching me. I need to lay down and not be stressed. That's all."

The instant guilt felt like I had walked into a brick wall.

Walking faster, I said, "Let's get you up to bed."

My mother stopped at the bottom of the stairs. "Maybe I should at least have a doctor come out and make sure everything is okay."

Daphne stared into my eyes with fear. "No doctors, Holden. Please."

"It's okay, Mom. I don't want to stress Daphne out. Let's let her rest."

By the time I got Daphne up to my room, she was somewhat calmed down, but still complaining of cramping in her stomach.

"Daphne, I'm worried if we do nothing, something bad will happen."

"No, I only need to rest. Please don't leave me, Holden. Please."

Not wanting to add any additional stress, I crawled into bed next to her and pulled her into my arms. It didn't take long for her to fall asleep.

I was suddenly overcome with exhaustion. I figured once she was in a deep sleep, I'd sneak out and meet Emylie for lunch. Fighting to keep my eyes open, I let them close for just a few moments.

"Holden, baby wake up."

Jumping up, I quickly looked around. Daphne was standing in front of me with a smile on her face.

"How do you feel?" I asked.

"Better. I think I needed the rest and having you next to me helped even more."

She was changed and had her hair up and her make-up done. "Wait. How long have you been up?"

With a tilt of her head and a smug smile, she replied, "I woke up at two. You seemed so tired, I thought it best to let you sleep. Especially with how you acted toward me earlier this morning. You were not yourself, Holden."

Glancing at the clock, my heart stopped.

Four-thirty.

"Emylie."

Her smile faded. "Her again?"

I shook my head. "Daphne, I never called to tell her I couldn't make it to lunch, that's all."

She put her hand over her mouth and gasped. It was so fake I was actually surprised how terrible it was. I thought she was a better actress than that.

That's when it hit me. Earlier today was nothing but a show. A way to keep me from meeting Emylie. "There was nothing wrong, was there?" I questioned.

Staring at me with a stunned expression, she replied, "I can't believe you would accuse me of such a thing. Why in the world would I lie about something like that?"

My hand raked across my head. I had no idea of she really had cramps or if it was all a lie. She was so devastated from the last pregnancy loss I knew she wouldn't do something like that with this one, or would she?

There was no way I could really know, so I played it safe. I needed to make sure she stayed calm and had no stress. Walking up to her, I pulled her into my arms. "You're right. I'm sorry. I'm in a weird place right now and I'm not sure what I'm thinking or saying anymore."

"Cleary," she mumbled.

Pulling back, I searched her face. I had tried so hard to feel something for this woman, but I just couldn't. There was no way I was going to be able to live a lie. It wasn't fair to me or Daphne.

"Let's go find my mom."

She nodded and gave me a weak smile.

We left the room and headed downstairs to the kitchen. Pulling my phone out, I started to text Emylie. I'd rather call her, but I couldn't with Daphne next to me.

Her laughter filled the air and my heart began to race. Emylie was here. Turning around the corner, I stopped dead in my tracks. It was my mother, Emylie, and Mason. Mason had his arms around Emylie as she tried to get away from his hold while he tried to make her eat something.

Feeling the heat build, I said, "Well don't you two look cute?"

Mason and Emylie instantly stopped what they were doing and stood there. Mason took one look at me and shook his head. Walking up to me, he gave me a push.

"You motherfucker. Why do you keep insisting on hurting her?"

"Mason!" my mother and Emylie cried out.

I gave him a push back. "Stay the fuck out of it, Mason." Turning to Emylie, I pleaded with her, "Em, I can explain what happened."

Giving me a distant and cold stare, she barely said, "Don't bother. Your mother already told me what happened with Daphne."

Emylie's gaze drifted over to where Daphne stood.

The doorbell rang and before I knew it, there was an entire film crew surrounding us.

I needed to talk to Emylie but the commotion of the camera crew and Daphne talking a million miles a minute, had me fighting to even get over to Emylie.

A mic was shoved into my face. "So Holden, what do you think about Daphne's father flying in for the engagement dinner?"

Everything stopped. My mother stood frozen in her place, as did Emylie and Mason. My father walked in right about then and said,

"What engagement dinner?"

Turning to Daphne, I took her by the elbow and guided to the dining room.

"What in the hell is going on, Daphne?"

She gave me an unsuspecting look. "What do you mean?"

"I told you this wasn't an engagement dinner. Did you even bother to tell your father to call off the crew?"

Her focus drifted over my shoulder. "Well, it was a tad bit too late since the film crew was already on its way here. I thought maybe we could pretend the dinner was our engagement dinner. You know, maybe have your mom and dad give a small speech about how happy they are for us and then let Daddy speak."

My mouth hung open in shock. "In the middle of our family reunion dinner? You want them to stand up out of the blue and give a fucking speech?"

"It only has to be something short. Five minutes or less."

"No!" I shouted. "This dinner is *not* about you, Daphne. I know you find that hard to believe, but this is not … about … you."

My body came to life when I felt her hand on my shoulder. Turning, I saw Emylie standing there with a worried look on her face. "I think you two need to take this somewhere else." She motioned to the film crew all pinned in on us.

Daphne let out an evil laugh and stepped between me and Emylie.

"This dinner is for family, and you are clearly not family. So back off, bitch."

Emylie stared at Daphne with a stunned expression. Heat immediately raced over my body.

My mother was now standing next to Emylie with a very pissed off expression on her face. "Daphne, you have no right speaking to Emylie that way. She is very much a part of this family and has been for a number of years. Now there was a misunderstanding, sweetheart, and I can see you're upset. This dinner is a yearly tradition that kicks off our family reunion. We did not plan an engagement dinner in your honor, and I'm sorry if you're hurt by that. I'm sure we can work something out for your ... father if he needs to have something filmed."

Daphne's hands went to her hips. I figured she would back down now that my mother had said something to her and thrown her a bone to chew on for a while. Little did I know Daphne was about to try and take down the entire night.

"I'm sorry. I guess my hormones are a little crazy."

My head snapped over to Daphne. She wouldn't. My mother and I stared at each other, each with a horrified look on our faces.

"Let's grab something to eat, Daphne." I said, trying to pull her away.

She wouldn't budge as she stood firm, glaring at Emylie.

"I'm not hungry, but I should probably eat for the baby."

When her hands went to her stomach, I watched Emylie's face. Taking a few steps back, her head jerked over to look at me. There was nothing I could do now. I wanted to tell her myself today at lunch how I had been planning on coming home when Daphne told me about the baby. How unhappy I was and that I still loved her. A part of me was ready to walk away and fight for joint custody. Now that I was home and saw Emylie, I knew I would never be able to go through with marrying Daphne.

Never.

Taking a step toward Emylie, I softly said, "I was going to tell you today at lunch."

Her head whipped back and forth between me and Daphne.

With a smirk on her face, Daphne turned to me. "Baby, I think I could use something to eat after all."

Daphne stepped around me and walked up to the camera crew. She started spouting off orders as my mother followed.

I took a step toward Emylie but she shook her head. Covering her mouth, I watched as a tear slipped from her eye. My entire world felt like it was turning black and I instantly felt sick.

"Em," I whispered.

Dropping her hand, she forced out the air from her lungs.

I hated myself.

I hated Daphne for blurting out about the baby. But worse of all, I hated that I had hurt Emylie yet again.

"Excuse me, I need some air."

I reached for her arm and pulled her back to me. "Em! Wait."

"Please let me go, Holden. *Please*."

The sound of her voice nearly brought me to my knees. "Em, if we could go somewhere to talk."

She pressed her lips together and shook her head.

"I can't. I can't do this."

Panic filled my chest. I couldn't lose her again. I wouldn't lose her again.

Turning quickly, Emylie rushed out the door, leaving me standing there feeling like the world's biggest fucking dick.

I dragged in a deep breath then forced it back out. My gaze drifted over to where my mother was attempting to get the camera crew out of her house. Leaning against the wall, Daphne stared at me with a smirk on her face as she took a drink of ice tea.

She pushed off the wall and walked my way. Stopping right in front of me, she started talking. Her voice sounded cold and distant. "It's better she knows about the baby, Holden. Maybe now she'll stop sniffing around what's mine."

My entire body began went rigid. I'd never hated Daphne as much as I hated her right then. Leaning down, I pressed my lips against her ear.

"I'm not yours. I never have been and never will be."

CHAPTER 11

Emylie

SOB AFTER SOB escaped from my lips as I ran to the barn. I could tell someone was following behind me and I hoped like hell it wasn't Holden.

Finally making it into the barn, I stopped and inhaled deeply.

"Em?"

Mason.

Turning, I gasped when I saw Becca at his side. Why I was surprised I had no idea. Once Mason and I called it quits on what ever it was we had together, he started talking more to Becca.

"Do you want me to leave?" Becca asked.

I felt like the world's biggest bitch because I wanted more than anything to tell her yes. Yes, I wanted her to leave. Yes, I wanted to fall into Mason's arms and use sex to forget what I had heard.

No.

No, I wouldn't use Mason as my crutch anymore. And I wouldn't stand in the way of my two best friends finding their way to each other. Even if nothing came out of it, at least they had the chance to find out if there was something there.

Shaking my head, I forced a smile. "No, Becca. Please don't leave."

"What in the hell happened, Em? What did Holden and that witch say to you?" Mason asked walking up to me. I took a step back, making sure he knew I didn't want any physical contact. So far we had been able to keep the need to touch each other to a minimum. For two years, I had allowed myself to fall into his arms every time something upset me.

No more.

It was over. I needed to learn to be on my own. Deal with things the right way.

Wiping my nose in the most unladylike way, I forced the words out. "She's pregnant."

Becca covered her mouth. "What?"

With a quick nod, I let out a fake chuckle. "Yep. Imagine my surprise when she blurted it out like everyone in the world knew."

"Was that what Holden was going to talk to you about at lunch today?"

I shrugged. "He said he was going to tell me today, but really what does it matter? I don't mean anything to him. He owes me no explanations."

Becca walked up to me and pulled me into her arms. I didn't start crying again until she said, "It does matter because Holden still loves you, Em."

Tears streamed down my face as I squeezed my eyes shut. Barely shaking my head, I whispered, "No. If he loved me, he would have tried. He would have given us a chance."

Wrapping her arms around me tighter, Becca said something to Mason I couldn't understand, I was crying too hard at that point.

It was over. What we had was really over.

Mason placed his hand on my back and softly spoke. "It's okay, Em. I promise it's all going to be okay."

I pulled back and quickly wiped my tears away. "It's not going to be okay. Don't you see that, Mason? I've been trying to get over him and I can't. He was my everything and now … now I know it's really over."

"You can find someone else, Em."

My chest ached as I glanced between Mason and Becca. "I don't want anyone else, Becca. I wanted him. I *want* Holden."

A tear slipped from her eye. The only way I could even attempt to move on was to leave. I didn't have Mason to fall back on anymore and I didn't want that anyway. Maybe that was my problem this whole time. I had been holding on to the past and I didn't even realize it. Being with Mason was the closest thing I could get to being with Holden. *How messed up is that?*

Pushing my shoulders back, I took in a deep breath. "It's going to be okay. I had a moment of weakness, and I'm okay. Maybe I just needed a good cry." I let out a chuckle and Mason narrowed his eyes and stared at me. He knew me too well. Probably better than anyone, even Holden. We had grown close the last few years. All he had to do was look at my body language and tell I was lying.

"Do you want to go back up to the dinner?" Becca asked.

With a nod of my head, I replied, "Yeah, I'll be up there in a few minutes. I need some time by myself to get my head straight."

Tucking a piece of my brown hair behind my ear she gave me a weak smile. "For what it's worth, sweetie, I really don't think Holden is happy with her."

The knife in my chest went deeper. If he wasn't happy with her, why did he stay after she lost the baby? All the unanswered questions caused me even more confusion.

I gave her a reassuring nod. Mason walked up to me and placed his hands on my arms. "You're not okay, Em."

Forcing back the sob that wanted to escape, I whispered, "I will be."

Mason leaned in and kissed me on the forehead and said, "Don't be long."

I swallowed hard. "I won't."

I somehow managed to slip away from the dinner without being noticed. Racing into my place, I grabbed a suitcase and began packing up a few things. I knew deep in my heart I wouldn't be able to face Holden or Daphne again. The idea that she was carrying his child … again … turned my stomach. They were only in town for a few more days, and I could just act sick. But I saw the look in Holden's eyes. He would come after me if he knew I was hiding. He was hell-bent on talking to me about this.

No. What I needed to do was to get away and figure some things out, and the only way I could do that was to leave all the memories behind. I needed to clear my head.

If only I could get the look of regret I saw in his eyes out of my memory. A part of me knew he still loved me. I could feel it when we were near each other. The pull was too strong to deny it.

I sat on my bed and buried my face in my hands and cried.

"Why? Holden, why did you destroy us? There is nothing left but pieces and parts of our life."

Dropping back, I stared up at the ceiling as I thought about the last night Holden and I were together. I wasn't dreaming when I felt the love between us. It was there.

It. Was. There.

Holden wrapped me up in arms as he ran his fingertips lightly across my back.

"What are you thinking about?" I asked.

His body stiffened for a quick moment before relaxing again. "How much of a mistake it was for me to leave you. How stupid I was thinking I needed something different in my life. You're all I'll ever need, Em."

Lifting my head up, I watched as he stared up at the ceiling. "We only have a year-and-a-half of school left."

"Unless I transfer to A&M and finish up there."

My heartbeat picked up. The last thing I wanted to do was pressure Holden into doing something he didn't want to do.

"That would be nice, but we've made it this long. We could last a bit longer. Besides, what about the team? You don't want to walk away from your football scholarship, Holden."

He turned and looked down at me. I winked at him and he frowned. "Em, I need you to remember something."

I lifted some and captured his gaze with mine. "Okay."

"No matter what happens. I love you. I've always loved you, and I will never love anyone like I love you. Please never forget that."

Smiling, I crawled on top of him. Leaning in closer, my lips brushed against his. "I'll never forget it. I promise."

Tears pooled in my eyes as I let the memory of that night wrap around me. The signs were there. If I had looked hard enough, I would have been able to see the guilt in his eyes. He was trying to tell me then what was about to happen. If only I hadn't been blinded by love.

My phone dinged. Rolling over, I pulled it from my back pocket.

Mason: Emylie, where in the hell are you? Holden is freaking out.

I let out a gruff laugh. Like I gave a fuck what Holden was doing.

Me: Tell him to focus on his pregnant fiancée.

Jumping up, I quickly gathered up some clothes and put them in the suitcase. Heading to the bathroom, I grabbed everything I would need to stay with Jamie for a few weeks.

After getting everything packed up, I sent a few text messages out.

Me: Hey Momma and Papá, I need to get away for a bit. I'm going to go stay with Jamie. Please don't tell anyone I'm there. I really need some space to clear my head.

It didn't take my mother long to text back.

Momma: Emylie. Running is not going to help anything. Mason told us what happened. Please come back to the dinner. We can help you work this out.

I rolled my eyes and sighed. The last thing I wanted was to go back and work out anything. There was nothing to work out. Holden was having a baby with that evil witch. They were getting married. Mason was moving on. Becca was moving on. Everyone was moving on but me. The only way I could was to get some distance.

Me: Momma, please don't argue with me, and I'm asking you to please not tell anyone where I am. As your daughter, I'm asking you for this. I'm driving up there and I'm leaving now.

Momma: Now?! Emylie Sanchez! You won't even wait to say goodbye to us! And you know I would never betray your trust, but I think you're making a huge mistake.

Of course she did.

Me: I'll check in often. I love you, Momma. Kiss Papá for me. Thank you for understanding.

I knew she didn't, but I thought I would attempt to sugarcoat the situation.

Momma: Be safe, darling. We love you. Your daddy is going to be mad at you.

I shook my head as I let out a soft laugh.

Me: I love you too. Tell him I'll make it up to him.

Wiping a tear away, I sent out the next text.

Me: Hey Jamie. If you don't mind a last minute house guest ... I'm headed your way tonight. Driving up and thinking of staying a week or two if that works for you.

Me: I know you won't understand, but I'm going to be leaving town for a couple of weeks. I'll call Debbie and Sam tomorrow. If they want to let me go, I'll understand, but I really need to be alone for a bit. I love you, Mason. Please don't worry, I'll be okay. I need to figure out how to stand on my two feet and find the girl I know is in here somewhere.

Me: I'm heading out of town for a bit. Don't be angry with me, Becca. I need to find some peace within and I can't do it in Brady. Especially with Holden and Daphne here. I'll check in when I get to where I'm going. I love you, Bec. Please explore this thing with Mason. Kiss my princess for me.

I slipped my phone into my purse, grabbed my suitcase and headed out to my car. It was less than a minute and my phone started going off.

Ignoring it, I started my car and headed out of town. I thought the further I drove, the better I would feel. It was the opposite.

With each mile marker I passed, I felt my heart break a little more.

CHAPTER 12

Holden

"WHAT DO YOU mean she's gone?" I asked Mason as he stared at me.

Becca cleared her throat. "She sent a text saying she needed some space and will be gone for a couple of weeks."

My hand pushed quickly through my hair as I sighed.

"Fuck. I never got a chance to talk to her."

"Because you talking to her would make it better," Mason bit back.

Balling my fists, I knew he was only concerned for Emylie. Quickly glancing over my shoulder, I saw Daphne deep in conversation with her father.

"Let's head outside, I need to talk to you both."

"I need to make sure Sage is okay first," Becca stated.

Mason looked at Becca and then me as he said, "Sam took her out to the barn to see the horses with Debbie. I think they needed a break from your future wife and father-in-law."

Letting out a frustrated groan, I replied, "Same."

Becca shot me a dirty look and I knew she was about to unleash on me. "Let's go outside and you can bitch me out all you want, Becca."

"Oh. I intend to, you jackass."

Placing my hand on her lower back, I guided her through the kitchen and outside. Mason was following behind me. I could see the worry in his eyes. This wasn't like Emylie to up and take off without saying anything to anyone.

The second the back door closed, Becca turned and slapped me across the face.

"What the fuck?" I said, rubbing the sting out.

"I've been wanting to do that since you showed your face back in this town. How could you, Holden? How could you hurt her like that?"

I shook my head. "Let's head to the other side of the pool, in case Daphne searches for me."

Becca spun on her heels and marched across the deck and down the steps. Turning to Mason, my eyes widened in surprise. "How long as she been itching to do that?"

He laughed. "Probably since the moment she met you."

"Haha," I mumbled.

Plopping in a chair, Becca folded her arms and lifted her left brow. Waiting for me to explain myself. There was nothing to explain. I fucked up. In a big way. More than once.

"Before you slap me again, let me start from the beginning. Then you can let loose on me."

She flashed me a smirk as Mason sat next to her.

"So, you think you can try and explain your dickness away?" Becca asked.

I frowned as I took a seat. "The week I decided to stay at school and not come home was probably the biggest mistake of my life."

"Ya think?" Becca spat out.

"Becca, he'll never get through this if you keep interjecting your thoughts."

She rustled around in her seat. "Fine. Talk."

Pulling in a deep breath, I let it out. "I got drunk, and I'm almost positive someone slipped me something. I don't really remember much of that night. I remember Daphne being there. I had met her before at a few parties and she had flirted big time with me. I never paid much attention to her before that party, though. I can't lie and say I didn't like the way it felt to have someone so completely different from my life here give me a bit of attention that night. I must have been feeling lonely, knowing I wasn't going to be seeing Emylie and my family. I never would have acted on it. No matter how drunk I was getting. I knew the flirting was getting too much, and I pulled back."

Becca opened her mouth to say something, but Mason cleared his throat and she snapped it shut again.

"Like I said, I started drinking pretty heavily, and the next thing I knew I was in bed with Daphne next to me. I immediately jumped out of the bed and started getting dressed." Closing my eyes, I felt the sickness building like I was standing in that bedroom again. Looking back at Becca and Mason, I kept talking.

"I'll never forget the look on her face. It was almost evil. She knew I had a girlfriend. I had talked about Emylie before. Even when she would come on to me, I would remind her I was with someone."

Becca leaned forward. "Are you sure that baby was yours?"

Staring at her, I pinched my brows together. "I'm not that stupid, Becca. The moment Daphne told me about the pregnancy, we arranged to have a DNA test done. They can do a non-invasive procedure."

"And?"

"Well, of course it turned out to be mine. I wouldn't have stayed if the baby wasn't mine."

She sat back and sighed.

"Anyway, once she agreed to the DNA test, I knew she wasn't lying about the baby being mine. It was then I called Emylie and told her I had met someone. I didn't have the guts to tell her what really happened. If I could go back and change how I handled it all, I would."

Mason cleared his throat. "Why did you give up Emylie, though? Why not tell her what happened and see where things went? She would have been hurt and pissed. But I think she loved you enough to have maybe have tried to work through it."

I lifted my eyebrows. "I knew how much Emylie hated cheaters. I knew the moment I told her, we would be over. And how would I make it work with a baby in California and me in Texas? I wasn't about to ask Emylie to give up her own dreams because of my stupid-ass mistake. I cheated on her and got a girl pregnant. She would have kicked me to the curb, I'm sure."

"She would have," Becca said. "But she would have made her way back to you, that I don't have any doubt. She loves you, Holden. Even now, she loves you so much she had to leave."

My head dropped. "Well, we'll never know because I didn't tell her the truth when I should have. Daphne had a hard pregnancy from the get go. She was terribly sick and bled some. She was stressed, and I guess a part of me didn't want to stress her anymore by saying I was going to try and make things work with Emylie. I did what I thought I should do. But then she ended up losing the baby and she fell into a serious depression. So much so she ended up leaving school. She would lay in bed for days without getting up. Her parents were no help. Good ol' daddy dearest wanted to keep it on the down-low. Heaven forbid that it gets out that his daughter had gotten knocked up in college and then lost the baby. Worse yet, she was depressed because she lost the baby. Daphne's father told her the day she had the miscarriage it was for the best. She could now focus on a career in the movies."

Becca covered her mouth. "How terrible."

I nodded. "Yeah. It was, and I did everything I could to help her through it. I knew I was to blame."

"You? Why?" Mason asked.

I felt my chest squeeze as I thought back to the day she lost the baby. "We got in a fight the day she lost the baby. I came home from class and she was there in my apartment. She was changing everything around. Then she informed me she was moving in. I had been honest with her and told her I didn't have the same feelings for her that she did for me. I told her I loved Emylie. That she was the love of my life. The only thing she kept saying was I would forget Emylie and fall in love with her. Once the baby was born, I'd grow to love her." My hands scrubbed down my face as I thought about what happened next.

"What happened?" Becca asked.

"I got pissed she was moving my furniture around. Honestly, I was still reeling over losing Emylie. The last thing I wanted was for Daphne to move in. She started getting upset and asking why I didn't love the baby. It all kind of hit me at once. I yelled at her. Told her I didn't love her and I never would. That the only reason I was with her was out of obligation to the baby she was carrying. I know it was a terrible thing to say, but I had reached my breaking point. She got upset and started crying. Then she started cramping. She went to the bathroom and started screaming. I ran in and stopped when I saw her. There was a lot of blood."

Closing my eyes, I thought back to that moment. My voice trembled. "So much blood."

Becca dropped in front of me and took my hands as I looked at her. "Holden. I'm not trying to place blame, but was she moving large pieces of furniture around?"

I stared into her eyes, the haze over my brain lifted. "Um, yeah, she had been moving the sofa and coffee table around. She said she liked the arrangement better. It was what set me off."

"Holden, moving the heavy furniture could have caused the miscarriage. It's a possibility. You can't blame yourself for that. It could have been a number of things that went wrong."

A heaviness moved across my body. "I know, but I still can't help but feeling responsible. It didn't help matters any that Daphne fell into the depression. By then the guilt had torn me apart and I couldn't even begin to think of leaving her or trying to reach out to Emylie. I was truly worried Daphne would take her own life."

"So you decided you'd stay with a woman you didn't love while the woman you did love was barely making it."

I glared at Mason. "I wouldn't say that. After all, you two seemed to fall right into place."

Mason stood and made his way over to me, but Becca jumped up and stopped him. "This isn't going to help any with you two fighting." Turning to me, she pointed. "You have no right to say anything to Mason. He was there for Emylie when she needed him. You didn't hear her crying for days on end and asking both of us why over and over again. Your only reason was that you met some-one and fell in love. Then, being the coward you are, you stayed away so you didn't have to face the cold truth of what you did to her."

My eyes filled with tears. Clinching my jaw tightly to keep my emotions in check, I replied. "You're exactly right. I'm sorry, Ma-son."

The anger on his face was something I wouldn't soon forget. No matter how much he and Emylie claimed there was nothing between them, there was something there. Even I could see it.

"So you stayed with her and what, decided to bring a child into a loveless relationship?"

"It's not like that, Becca. I truly care about Daphne and would never want to see her hurt, but I don't love her. I tried to love her. Tried to give *us* a chance. We started drifting apart and we would go weeks without even sleeping in the same bed. It was almost like she could tell when I'd grown tired of it, and she would spend the next few weeks being someone totally different. I mean it was her, but she did things like go camping and take hiking trips. She really put an effort into the relationship, but in the long run, I couldn't make myself fall in love with her."

Shaking her head, Becca regarded me with pity. "Holden, that's not a relationship, it's a prison. You've stayed with this girl out of guilt."

"A few months back I called my boss. Told him I was thinking of moving back to Texas. Daphne must have heard me because that night she talked me into going out. We drank, had a good time with a few other friends, and she did all the right things. We ended up fucking in the bathroom of the restaurant. I hated myself because the only way I could get through it was to think of Emylie and that tore me even more apart. Here I was staying with a woman I didn't love because I was too much of a coward to face the woman I did. Then, being with Daphne and thinking of Emylie the whole time made me feel like a real dick. We hadn't slept together for months before that night. A month later I was so miserable I knew I couldn't do it anymore. I told Daphne I was leaving, and that's when she told me she was pregnant again. It was the night we were together in the restaurant. The night I pretended it wasn't her I was with … but Em."

Becca slowly shook her head. "That's some serious fucked-up shit right there, Holden. I'm not going to lie. Like, if I hadn't known you for as long as I have, I'd probably tell you to take your ass back to California and that Emylie was better off without you."

My stomach felt sick. I knew she was right. It was more than fucked-up. "I keep fucking up. Every time I say I'm going to leave her, I mess up. I really don't even know how she got pregnant because she was on the pill. She said the doctor told her these things happen."

"You didn't go with her to the appointment?" Mason asked.

With a shrug, I turned away. "No. As much as I want to be excited about this baby, I can't. I feel nothing." Turning to my two best friends, I felt the tear slip from my eye. "How much of an asshole does that make me that I can't even feel joy for my own child? All I feel is a void."

Becca leaned forward. "How far along is Daphne?"

Mason let out a frustrated groan. "Who really cares. I think what we need to be talking about is Emylie and the fact that she left. She's gone y'all, and we have no idea where she's heading."

Becca stood. "I care, because I have a really weird feeling something is not right here." She shook her head before turning back to me.

"How is the morning sickness?"

"Um, she hasn't had any this time around."

"Mood change? Is her body changing? Are breasts getting bigger?"

I shrugged. "Not that I can tell, but we're not that intimate."

"No condom?"

Mason gagged. "Gross. Why are we talking about this?"

Becca held her hand up to Mason and said, "Shush. This is important, Mason. You don't understand women. I do. Some of them will go to the ends of the earth to keep something they think is theirs."

Daphne's words replayed in my mind.

"Maybe now she'll stop sniffing around what's mine."

"I've always worn condoms. Even when she was on the pill, except for the night in the restaurant. It was unplanned and I didn't have one. The other night at the cabin we got in a fight because I wanted to wear a condom and she said it was pointless because she was pregnant."

"Ugh," Mason said as he walked to the other side of the pool.

"Did you wear it anyway?" Becca asked.

"Yeah and it caused a huge fight."

An evil smile moved across Becca's face. "Not trying to be personal here, Holden, but why are you still wearing one?"

Shaking my head, I answered her truthfully. "I don't know. Something tells me I need to."

She looked at me with understanding. "I may be really off here, and you may be really upset with what I'm about to say, but I've been watching your future wife. Did you know she has been sneaking in alcohol?"

My stomach lurched. "What? That can't be good for the baby."

Mason laughed. "You daft son-of-a-bitch."

My chair knocked over as I stood. "What is your fucking problem, Mason?"

Walking up to me, he gave me a push. "You. You are my fucking problem. You walk back into our lives and expect everything to be fine. It's not fine. You made Emylie run. You caused her to leave and none of us know where she is. You are my problem, Holden."

Becca walked between us. Her expression seemed like a mix of sad and angry. "We are all upset here, Mason. You're not the only one. But I have a hunch, and I think you caught on to it."

He nodded and turned to Holden. "Too bad you can't open your eyes a bit more and stop feeling sorry for yourself. Maybe then you'd see Becca is trying to say Daphne probably isn't even pregnant. She's playing you."

My head jerked back as my breath caught in my throat. A sudden coldness hit my core and everything began running through my mind. Everything about this pregnancy was completely different. Maybe I didn't want to see. Maybe deep down, I knew.

"Holy shit," I whispered.

"What?" Becca and Mason asked at the same time.

I shook my head and pushed both hands through my hair in frustration. "She never wants me at the doctor appointments. I asked her about the sonogram and she said the machine was broke and they'd do it next time. She keeps doing things like she forgets she's pregnant. They announced her in a film that they start filming in two weeks! I asked her about the pregnancy and she told me to let her and her father worry about it."

Pacing back and forth, it all hit me when I thought back to the other night in the cabin when she got so pissed because I wanted to wear a condom.

Stopping, I glanced between Mason and Becca. "She's trying to get pregnant."

Becca pinched her brows together. "What do you mean?"

"If she isn't pregnant, then she's trying to get pregnant. The other night she said there was something wrong with the condom I wore. She said there must have been a small tear in it. When we were together before we came to Texas, the same thing happened. I even questioned her where she was buying the damn things if they kept breaking. But now I know, she's doing something to the condoms."

Mason shook his head and held up his hands. "Wait. She's doing something to the condoms? Okay, now both of you are talking crazy. I can maybe see her lying about being pregnant, but going so far as fucking with a condom so she can get pregnant? That kind of shit only happens in movies."

Becca laughed. "Let me show you something, Mason. I'm about to enlighten your world to the lengths women will go to when it comes to keeping a man."

Pulling out her phone, she started typing away on it. A minute later she showed something to Mason. He read it and looked at her. "Is this for real? Like, women are selling these?"

"Yes!"

"What? What is it?" I asked.

Taking her phone and practically shoving it in my face, Becca showed me an ad on Craigslist.

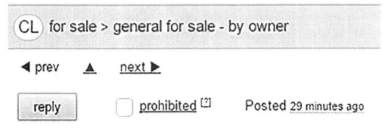

◀ prev   ▲   next ▶

reply   ⬜ prohibited [2]   Posted 29 minutes ago

☆ Positive Pregnancy Test – $30

For sale. Positive Pregnancy Test. Can't get him to pop the question. Have a fake baby. I'm five months pregnant and will pee on your test for $30.

- do NOT contact me with unsolicited services or offers

"You've got to be kidding me," I whispered as I looked up at the two of them.

"I saw it on the news. Let me guess. I bet Daphne showed you a pregnancy test that said positive."

"Yeah, but she carried the box into the restroom with her and did it."

Mason cursed under his breath. "She might have already had the positive test in the bathroom and then opened the box like she was doing it. Did you see her physically take the test?"

Slowly shaking my head, I answered him with a resounding, "No."

Dread coursed through my veins and bile moved to the back of my throat.

Could I really be that stupid? That naïve?

Was Daphne faking her pregnancy?

CHAPTER 13

Emylie

Three days later

S ITTING ON JAMIE'S front porch, I took a sip of coffee and looked out over the dark mountains. I had called my parents who both begged me to call either Becca or Mason. The only person I called was Debbie. It was one of the hardest phone calls I've ever made.

"Emylie! My goodness, where are you? Everyone is worried sick, including Holden. He isn't himself right now at all."

My heart felt like someone was squeezing it. "Debbie, I needed some time alone. I understand that I up and left you without so much as a notice, but the news of the baby threw me, and honestly, I need to get my head back in the right place. The last two years I've been leaning so much on Mason and everyone around me, I forgot what it felt like to be strong. If I don't have a job when I come back, I totally understand."

"Don't be silly. You have job here no matter how long you're gone. Honey, you have to know that running away isn't going to help things."

I was tired of everyone telling me that. Becca. Mason. My parents. Even Holden sent me a text message begging me to call him and to not run away. I texted back telling him he got to run away so now it was my turn. I hadn't heard from him since.

"Debbie, I have to go. I love you and Sam."

"Will you not tell anyone where you are?"

I knew I shouldn't say anything, but I trusted Debbie. "I told my parents and they know where I am. I've got to run. Bye, Debbie."

Before she had a chance to say anything else, I hung up. I knew even if she did ask my mother, she would be tight-lipped. The two of them had been going after each other the last few days. With Holden coming back home, he caused chaos in more than one way.

"Penny for your thoughts?" Jamie asked, taking the seat next to me.

"It's chilly here at night," I replied, not knowing what else to say.

Jamie laughed. "Yep. Hot as hell during the day and chilly nights. Makes for snuggling up to someone pretty enjoyable.

Rolling my eyes, I gazed back out over the mountains. "I see why you love it here so much."

She followed my gaze. "Yeah. That and I found a guy who actually knows how to use his stick in the oh-so-right way that makes me all happy inside."

Ugh. Jamie hadn't changed a bit. Even in college she was outspoken and said pretty much what popped into her mind.

"Well I'm glad to know Jax makes you happy inside."

"Girl, he makes me happy inside, outside, in the cold, in the heat, you name it."

Turning to her, I shot her a dirty look. "That's gross. I really don't need to hear about your perfect sex life."

She tossed her head back and lost it laughing. "Did I mention Jax's best friend from college is in town? Perfect timing."

She avoided eye contact at all costs. "Do not even think of trying to set us up."

With an evil smile, she said, "I would never! But, since you're here and Carter's here ... y'all are going to be seeing each other. Especially if you want to see me. Speaking of, we're going out to dinner. A welcome celebration for you and Carter."

I dropped my head and groaned. "No, Jamie! I don't want to go out. I came up here to get away."

Taking my hand, she kissed the back of it. "You came up here because you're hiding from something, or dare I say, someone. While you're here, you might as well have a bit of fun. He's cute. Really cute. Jax even told me the guy is from Colorado. You know what that means."

She wiggled her brows. Oh geesh. Here we go. "No. What does that mean?"

With a shocked expression, she covered her heart and pretended she was hurt I didn't know.

"He's a good dancer."

I let out the breath I had been holding. Giggling, I said, "And here I thought you were going to say something about him sex wise."

"Oh, well everyone knows guys from Colorado have big dicks."

My mouth dropped. "No. Not everyone knows that. I didn't know that."

Standing, she winked and said, "You've been warned. I'll make sure to put some lube in the drawer next to your bed along with a few condoms. Not sure you had time to pack any. Did I mention he's in the Marines?"

"Jamie!" I cried out as she laughed and took off back inside the house. "Oh my lord, that girl will never change."

I took another drink and looked out over the mountains. Chewing on my lip, I wondered what it would be like to have a one-night stand. Just screw a guy for no reason other than him making me come. Nothing said I couldn't. I had no boyfriend. My fuck buddy was gone. My future consisted of nothing but sad movies, hot romance books, and a vibrator.

With a giggle, I pushed the thoughts out of my head.

The back door screen slammed and I let out a small scream.

"Shit! I'm so sorry. I didn't know anyone was out here. Jamie told me to head on out to the deck to see the view."

Wiping the coffee off my blouse, I groaned internally. Great. I didn't pack that many clothes and I just ruined one of my favorite shirts.

Damn Jamie for sending this guy out here. I was going to kill her.

I took a deep breath and slowly turned.

Oh. My. God.

The man standing before me was drop-dead gorgeous. His military buzz cut framed his chiseled face perfectly. The tight black T-shirt showed off how built he was.

Removing my eyes from his chest, I looked at his handsome face. Then he smiled and I knew exactly what Jamie's intentions were. Send a hot guy out here to make me forget all my problems. Well, it wasn't going to work. I used a guy the last time to try and erase Holden. I wasn't about to do it again.

I let my gaze move over him again, this time noticing the tattoos covering both arms.

Shit. I was a sucker for tattoos.

My teeth sunk into my lower lip as I ogled the poor man. Surely he was used to it, I mean look at him.

With a smile, I said, "No worries. You must be Carter. I'm Emylie."

Reaching his hand out, he returned the friendly gesture with a grin that about knocked me back a few steps.

Holy. Hell. The dimples. He went from hot military guy to adorable in two seconds flat.

"Hey there. Nice to meet you. I'm sorry I didn't realize you were out here or I wouldn't have barged on out. Jamie told me I had to come out and see the view."

I rolled my eyes. "Why do I have the feeling she was meaning me?"

Carter laughed. It was a nice laugh. Not too over the top, yet sincere. "Since it's night, I'm going to say you're spot on. But if I may be so forward as to say she was right."

I lifted my brows. "About?"

"The view. It's beautiful."

My chest felt a flutter. It wasn't earth shaking, but it was nice to have a guy flirt with me.

"That's sweet of you to say."

Carter motioned to the seat that was next to the one I had been sitting in. "Please, yes."

We both sat and stared out over the dark mountains. The silence wasn't awkward at all. In fact, it seemed to be welcomed by both of us.

"So how do you know Jax?"

I knew the answer already, but thought it was a good conversation starter.

"We meet in college. First day."

"Really? Same with me and Jamie! I bumped into her and knocked a box out of her hands. We were best friends from that point on."

He let out a soft chuckle. "Jamie's great. I'm happy for Jax that he met someone."

I nodded. "Yeah, she is pretty great."

The silence came back and settled in around us. It was Carter who spoke next. "So where are you from? Utah?"

"Texas. I drove up kind of last minute. I needed a few weeks to try and figure some things out."

He gave me an understanding look. "That sounds familiar."

"Same?"

With a nod, he sighed. "Yeah. When I joined the Marines, my father wasn't very happy with me."

Pulling my head back in surprise, I asked, "Why?"

With a shrug, he answered. "Well, according to him, when he sent me off to college to get a business degree it was so I could take over the family business, not run off to join the military. I'd always told him running a hardware store was not my idea of fun. I wanted to do something more with my life."

"And he didn't support you?"

"No. What he heard was I was joining the military because I didn't want to run a hardware store like my old man. I really do want to run it in the future. I just didn't want to start my life out doing that. I wanted something else. The Marines gave me something else."

"So was he angry with you for a while?"

I could see the frown on his face even in the darkness. "He hasn't talked to me since the day I joined the Corps. My mom called me a week ago and told me my father's health was fading." Turning to look at me, he said, "Cancer."

My heart instantly broke for him. How terrible that must be for him to know he broke his father's heart because he followed his own.

"I'm sorry, Carter. That has to be so hard for you."

"It is. I wanted to go home to see him, but he told me I wasn't welcome."

My chest squeezed. It sounded like Holden and Sam.

"He doesn't mean it. You have to know deep down he doesn't mean it."

His head dropped back against the chair. "I'm not so sure. He's a stubborn man."

"Even the most stubborn man can be cracked."

Carter let out a laugh. "You sound like you speak from experience."

With a friendly wink, I replied. "A little. But honestly, if you don't try to reach out to your father, you'll regret it for the rest of your life."

His face softened and it was in that moment I truly saw the sadness as the light from inside the house reflected in his eyes.

"You're right."

I leaned back and put my feet up on the rail. "Of course I'm right. I'm a woman. We're always right."

My stomach fluttered when I peeked over at him and saw the way he was looking at me. The smile he wore on his face was both sweet and sexy. I wondered how many broken hearts this guy has left in his wake.

Forcing myself to turn away, I cleared my throat. The last thing I needed was another guy in my life.

With a quick slap of his hands on his legs, he stood. "Well, listen, I'll let you get back to enjoying your peaceful evening. Will you be staying here?"

"Yep. You?"

Jamie's house was huge. Six bedrooms and six bathrooms. She had bought it with her parents as an investment and was planning on turning it into a bed and breakfast. When she called to ask advice from my parents, I could hear the excitement in her voice.

For now, though, it appeared it was a place for Carter and I to both figure out what our next step in life was.

"I am. I'm on leave for a month. Figured I'd hang here a few days and then maybe make my way home."

The only word I could come back with made me sound like I was in middle school. "Cool."

With another killer smile, he winked and replied, "Cool. See ya in the morning."

"Sleep well," I said as he nodded and headed into the house.

The moment the door shut behind him, I looked back out over the dark mountains. The emptiness that settled into my chest had me inhaling a deep breath. For a brief moment in time, I forgot about Holden before my reality quickly fell back upon me. I couldn't hold my emotions in any.

The future I had so stupidly kept a tight grip on quickly fell away with every fallen tear.

Closing my eyes, I whispered, "Holden."

CHAPTER 14

Holden

D APHNE AND I were supposed to leave for California yesterday, but I faked being sick. My mother was all over that shit and insisted we had to change our flights. Then my second stroke of luck happened. The second Daphne thought I had a fever, she high-tailed it out of the bedroom we shared.

Grabbing her small overnight bag filled with every face product known to man, she huffed by me. "I cannot believe we are still stuck here. I want to go home and sleep in my own bed. There is so much to do to prepare for the movie. I could have left on the flight but no, your mother gave me that stupid guilt trip. Ugh!"

"And prepare for the baby?" I asked as I sat up in bed and pretended to cough. I'd forgotten how hard it was to fake being sick.

She looked over at me and flashed me a smile. "Yes. And for the baby. We have plenty of time to prepare for that."

For that? She just referred to our child as ... that.

I searched her face as I tilted my head in curiosity. "You never talk about the baby, Daphne. Why is that? The first pregnancy, that's all you could talk about. Now you barely mention being pregnant."

Something moved across her face. "Well, um, can you blame me? I don't want to get my hopes up in case we lose it again."

It.

"Are you spotting? Like before?"

"No," she said quickly.

"Any cramping?"

She shook her head.

"I'd like to go with you to the next appointment."

Her face went white.

I continued on, even though she looked like she was about to freak out. "Mom wants me to video when we see the baby for the first time."

"Well ... I don't think they are doing that at the next appointment."

A thought popped into my head, and I couldn't believe Becca hadn't thought of it.

"Hey, Becca's mom is an OB. I bet she would do one for us so we could see the baby, and she wouldn't charge us. You're far enough along now for us to see the little peanut."

A look of horror passed over her face, and I knew it was wrong, but it felt good knowing I was giving her a taste of her own fucking medicine.

Daphne's mouth dropped before she snapped it shut. "I am not letting some strange woman near me, poking around where she doesn't belong."

"It might be a good idea to have a backup OB. Especially if we're going to be coming to Texas more often to see my folks." The thought of coming back here would drive her insane.

"What?!"

I let out a fake moan. I'd given her enough to chew on for a bit, and I was positive she wouldn't be coming back to the room anytime soon. "I feel like I'm going to get sick."

Covering her mouth, she rushed out the door and yelled, "I'll get your mother. I'm going to the cabin."

Fist pumping when she shut the door, I jumped out of bed. Less than a minute later, Becca and Mason were in my room.

"I just bought us hours," I said.

Becca and Mason stood there with huge smiles on their faces. "I liked the whole bit about my mother being an OB. I wonder what Daphne would think if she knew my mother owned a quilt store!"

Laughing, I shook my head. "Alright, what are we looking for?"

With a deep breath, Becca glanced around. "I have no clue."

"Let's search her suitcase first since she seems to have most of everything packed in when she thought y'all were leaving."

I nodded to Mason. "Good thinking." Picking the case up, I dumped everything on the bed and grinned like a fool.

"Did that feel good dumping her clothes on the bed?" Becca asked in a baby voice.

With a huff, I glanced between her and Mason. "I'm never allowed to touch her stuff. Like ever. It's one of her ... 'rules.'" I used air quotes when I said rules.

"Dude, how in the fuck have you stayed with that monster?"

"Guilt makes you do weird shit."

Mason frowned. "I guess so."

We quickly got to work searching through her clothes, the drawers in the bathroom, and each dresser. Each time, we came up with nothing.

With a frustrated sigh, I said, "We don't even know what we're looking for."

Becca sat on the bed. "Have either of y'all heard from Em?"

Shaking my head, I looked at Mason. "I swear I haven't heard from her."

"Holden, I still think we should text her and tell her what our thoughts are on the pregnancy."

"No. I don't want to jump the gun because there is still a chance that we could be wrong and Daphne is pregnant. She might not be happy with being pregnant. Surely she knows I don't love her. Hell, I told her I was leaving her."

Mason agreed. "I think if we jump the gun and fire off what we think to Emylie and then we're wrong, it will destroy her even more. But, I did talk to her folks earlier. They know where she is."

"Did they tell you?" I asked.

His eyes filled with sadness. "No. They promised her they wouldn't tell anyone. What they did tell me though, was that she was staying with a friend she met in college and that they thought she needed some time alone. Away from all the drama here in Brady. That she said she needed to find out who she was and what she wanted."

My heart ached. I don't think I'll ever be able to win Kim and Mario's trust back. I hurt their daughter in the most unimaginable way.

I scrubbed my hands down my face as I sat in the oversized chair in the corner. "I know where she is."

Glancing up, I could tell by the looks on their faces, they knew too. "Jamie," was all I said.

Becca nodded. "They were super close in college."

Mason agreed. "Yeah, they were. She bought that place up in Park City to turn it into a bed and breakfast."

As much as I wanted to run to Emylie and pour everything out to her, I knew she needed this time alone. With everything happening with me, and by the way Mason and Becca were sitting next to each other and the way he looked at her, I was guessing his fuck buddy relationship with Emylie was over. Not that I wasn't over the fucking moon about that, because I most definitely was.

"Let's let her have the time she needs. If we're right, I'll be here when she comes back and maybe we can work on repairing what I fucked up."

Both of them nodded then Becca said, "You did fuck up, Holden. I'm not going to lie. I still hate you like forty percent."

I lifted my brow. "Why forty?"

With a shrug, she replied. "I guess because in a way, I feel like Karma has come back on you. Twenty-fold."

Mason laughed.

My shoulders dropped as I let out a half-hearted chuckle. "I'm going to have to go see a doctor from all the emotional shit I've dealt with from her."

Becca jumped up. "That's it! Oh my God, Holden! You're a genius!"

Quickly standing, I turned to Mason for some guidance but he lifted his shoulders and looked as confused as I was.

"I am?"

"Yes!" Becca said, slamming into Mason and hugging him. He quickly wrapped his arms around her and I couldn't help but smile. The two of them had always had secret crushes on each other and when Becca got pregnant by that dirt bag ex-husband of hers, I knew it threw Mason into a serious funk.

"Why are you hugging me if Holden is the genius?"

Becca pulled back and winked at Mason. "Because I want an excuse to hug you. With Holden, I need an excuse not to kick him in the balls every time I see him. That forty percent is strong."

I covered my junk and cringed. "Okay, well are you going to at least tell me why I'm a genius?"

"The doctor. Call the doctor she went to before. Surely she would go back to the same obstetrician. Call the office and act like you are confirming her next doctor's appointment."

It was like the idea hit me square in the forehead and caused me to take a few steps back. *Why had I not thought of doing that before?*

"I think we can get even more information. There was a girl that worked in the office who had a special needs brother. He is a huge fan of USC. I got them season tickets for two years. She told me if I ever needed anything to let her know. I wonder if I can get Daphne's medical files?"

Becca frowned. "Shit. You're not married, and there are strict laws about that."

Mason cleared his throat. "My mom could."

Turning to look at him, my heart started racing. "Your mom would do that?"

He smiled. "If I told her why, yes. You are like a second son to her, Holden. Even though you pissed her off, I know she'll do it."

I shook my head. "No. I won't let her put her medical practice in jeopardy. Besides, she's the only decent doctor in Brady."

Becca giggled. "I'll do it. I work there, and if I get in trouble, your mom can fire me."

I held up my hands. Even though I had let my best friends down, it felt good to know they were willing to go to such lengths. Of course, I also knew they were doing it for Emylie more than for me. "No. No one is doing anything. Let me call the girl and see what I can get from her first."

Both Mason and Becca agreed to let me call first and see how far we could get by going that route.

"Hi, yes, this is Daphne Weston's fiancé, Holden Warner. Is Kate available?" Lifting my gaze over to Mason and Becca, I nodded.

Little did I know my entire world was about to be turned inside out with this one phone call.

CHAPTER 15

Emylie

"**G**OOD MORNING, PRINCESS! How'd you sleep?"

I grunted as I walked into Jamie's kitchen. "Terrible."

With a sad frown, she handed me a glass of orange juice. Taking it, I smiled. "Thank you."

"You know what you need? A hike. Get out and move your body and enjoy the air." She glanced at me and noticed I was already dressed.

Placing the glass to my lips, I narrowed my brows before drinking the whole glass. Setting it on the table, I gave her a knowing look. "Is Carter going hiking by any chance?"

Jamie placed her hand over her mouth and gasped. "Why yes! Yes, he is, after his morning five mile run."

My lip snarled as I shuddered while picking up a piece of toast. "Ugh. He's one of *those* types of guys."

"And what exactly are *those* types of guys?"

The toast stopped at my lips as I closed my eyes and died from embarrassment.

Shit.

Glancing behind me, I saw a very sweaty Carter standing there with a drop-me-to-the-floor smile. Damn. He was better looking in the daylight.

Play it cool, Emylie. You are not interested in that.

I flashed him my best smile then replied, "You know, the overly into fitness and eating raw veggies and soy types."

Carter walked more into the kitchen. He wasn't taking his eyes off of me, and I wasn't sure if I liked it or not. One was because I couldn't tell if it was a friendly look or I-want-in-your-pants look.

"Sorry to disappoint you, Emylie."

"Em," I quickly said.

His smile widened and I couldn't deny the way it made my stomach drop a little. "Sorry to disappoint you, Em. I hate soy, I don't eat enough vegetables, and I have a very healthy appetite for exercise."

I hadn't realized I was digging my teeth into my lip until it started to go numb. Turning back to Jamie, I tried to ignore the way she was staring at me. She was giving me that expression that is normally saved when you're out at a club and your best friend is telling you to go for the hot guy hitting on you.

Shooting her a dirty expression, I grabbed another piece of toast and spun around to leave, only to run right into Carter.

My body hit his full on, causing me to stumble back. "Jesus, you're like a brick wall."

He laughed and I had to admit, I liked the way it sounded. His hand came up and held me by my arms. One would think you would feel something when a hot guy grabs onto you and gazes at you with nothing but lust in his eyes, but I felt nothing. Maybe I was reading into it wrong, or I wasn't attracted to the guy.

He was cute. Had a great body, but he wasn't *him.*

He wasn't Holden.

My eyes instantly filled with tears and Carter leaned in closer with a concerned expression on his face. "Are you okay?"

I wasn't sure where my emotions were coming from, but I shook my head and quickly made my way around him and out the door.

My chest felt like someone was sitting on it as I gasped for air.

"Emylie?"

Walking as fast as I could, I headed to a trail, thankful I had put on sneakers before coming downstairs.

"Please wait! Emylie!"

Tears were streaming down my face as I started to run.

I needed to get away.

Stumbling over a log, I fell to the ground.

"Fuck," I shouted as I sat on the ground and buried my face in my hands.

His arms wrapped around me as he lifted me up. My hands, still covering my face as I sobbed uncontrollably. Carter pulled my hands down and placed his finger on my chin.

"Talk to me, Em. Please."

Glancing up, I could see the concern in his green eyes. "He cheated on me." I cried between sobs. "She's pregnant."

It wasn't the whole story. Far from it. But it was enough to get Carter to pull me into his body. I didn't even care that he was sweaty. It felt good to be in a stranger's arms. Someone different. Something different.

Maybe this was what Holden had needed.

Different.

"Oh, hell, Emylie. I'm so sorry."

Burying my face into his chest, I let go and cried. I was slowly coming apart. The reality of everything hit me full force. I was never getting Holden back.

She was his.

Forever.

"Feeling better?"

I nodded while taking another drink of water. "I'm sorry I freaked out on you like that. I guess I needed to break down."

Carter grinned. "We all need to break down every once and awhile. Want to talk about it?"

With a weak smile, I replied, "Want to go on a hike with me?"

His face lit up. "I'd love to go on a hike with you, Em."

Our hike started off in silence as we walked along the trail. It was a cool morning and I was thankful I had on a light pullover shirt. Taking in a deep breath, I slowly let it out. The mountain air smelled so clean and fresh. Almost healing in a way. As if each breath I took was repairing my broken heart. It felt like I grew stronger with each step taken.

With a deep breath in, I started talking. "Holden and I had been together for as long as I can remember. The first time I ever saw him on the playground in elementary school, I was pretty sure we were going to fall in love, go to the same college, work for his daddy's ranch, get married, have kids. You know that whole dream."

Carter let out a chuckle. "And, I take it he had other plans?"

"Yeah. He went to USC on a football scholarship. At first, he thought it was a good idea for us to be away. I guess he needed something different in his life and had to make sure our plans for our future is what he really wanted. Especially when they had really been my plans for us. My dreams. Long story short, we made it all the way to our junior year. He came home for Christmas break, and I knew something was different. I could feel it."

"Was that when he cheated?"

Pressing my lips together, I shook my head and looked away. "He stayed in California over Thanksgiving break. That's when it happened."

Carter didn't press me. We walked another ten minutes while I got my emotions in check. I saw a large rock and walked over to it. Sitting, I pulled my knees to my chest while he sat next to me.

"Not long after he went back to California, he called and told me he met someone and had fallen in love with her. He wasn't coming home again. California was where he was staying. That was all he said to me. It didn't make any sense because a week before that he was all about us and the future. He didn't care about his scholarship, nothing. He said he needed to be by me and then ... then he—"

My voice cracked and I wiped my tears away as Carter put his arm around me.

"Let me guess. He got back to California, found out the girl he cheated on you with was pregnant."

My head snapped over to him. "Yes! How did you know that? I didn't even know until recently. He never told me another reason other than he loved this girl."

Carter shrugged. "Just assumed. Did he cheat on you this one time only?"

Glancing back over the mountains, I answered. "He said it was only that time. He got drunk, claims he doesn't remember anything and that he woke up in her bed. I guess this girl had been flirting with him for a while. He said he was sure someone drugged him. I don't believe him."

"Sounds like she took advantage of a situation."

I looked at Carter. "Are you saying it wasn't his fault he slept with another girl? He had sex with another girl! He cheated. How can you defend him?" My voice got louder as I kept talking.

He removed his arm and held his hands up. "I'm not defending him, Em. I can't stand cheaters. I've been cheated on myself, so I know how deep the hurt goes. I'm playing devil's advocate here."

I lifted my brow and stared at him with a questioning expression. "Well by all means, I'm on pins and needles here to hear your theory."

With a smirk, he shook his head. "You said she had flirted with him before?"

"Yes. At least that's what he said."

I turned away, feeling sick to my stomach.

"Okay, so you got a girl who has the hots for a guy, right? Finds out he stayed in town and was at a party. She goes, he's a little drunk, she flirts, he flirts back, but when it gets too far, he backs off. After all, he has a girlfriend, and I'm going to assume the guy is somewhat of a decent guy. Girl gets pissed because what she wants is in reach. She slips him a little something into his drink, next thing he knows, he's in her bed. No memory of what happened. Mostly likely though, nothing happened because when a guy is that drunk, his dick doesn't work."

My face heated as I glanced down to hide my embarrassment.

"Then, a few months later, girl shows up and claims to be pregnant. The guy freaks, would rather break up with you than let you ever know he did the one thing that makes him sick to his stomach … cheated."

My mouth dropped open. "Wow. You pretty much nailed it. You think he was drugged by her?"

"Totally."

"What makes you so sure?"

His expression turned dark and a look of anger washed over his face. "Because almost the same thing happened to me, but luckily I wasn't dating anyone. I had a girl who had been hounding me for months to hook up. Was at a party getting my drink on and the next thing I know, I'm in her bed. Worse hangover of my fucking life. She, of course, claimed it was the best sex of her life, which I thought was funny because anytime I've ever been drunk, my di—"

Holding up my hands, I shook my head. "Stop talking about your dick and it not being hard. Please."

Carter laughed. "Right. Anyway, a month or so passed and she was at my door. Said she was pregnant. She had everything planned out. We could get married, her parents would buy us a little starter home. It would be hard because I was in the military and would be gone, but we'd make it work."

My hands came over my mouth. "Oh my gosh. What did you do?"

"I laughed in her face. See what she didn't know was, I can't have kids."

Feeling my heart drop, the words were out before I could stop them. "Why?" Closing my eyes, I felt my face heat up. Looking back at Carter, I frowned. "No, wait. I'm sorry that was so rude of me and none of my business."

He chuckled and said, "It's okay. When I was younger I got an infection. I can't produce sperm."

"I'm so sorry, Carter."

Forcing a smile, he replied, "I've come to accept it. It doesn't go over too well with the ladies though, when it comes time to tell them. Can you imagine a man telling you hey, I know you want kids, but I can't help you in that department?"

I reached for his hands. "You can adopt."

"Yeah, I know."

He turned and started walking.

"Wait, when was the last time you talked to your doctor about it?" I asked.

"Ten years ago."

I grabbed his arm and pulled him to a stop. "Carter, you may be producing sperm and not know it. Or, there may be a way from them to extract it if you've had a blockage."

He narrowed his gaze and looked at me. "How do you know so much about this?"

"I took some classes in college. I've always been interested in medical stuff. Not just in animals. Biology is a passion of mine." There was a small amount of hope that shined in his eyes. "Seriously, I can call a friend of mine I went to college with. She's doing her internship at a hospital in Boston and I'm positive she can recommend a fertility doctor for you to see."

We stood there staring at each other before Carter busted out laughing. We're talking a bend-over-gut-busting laugh. I couldn't help but start laughing too. "Why are we laughing?" I asked.

He shook his head and said, "Em, we hardly know each other, and we're talking about my damn sperm!"

Covering my mouth to hide my flaming cheeks, I started laughing again. The situation was serious, but funny also.

Carter grabbed my hand and pulled me down the trail. "Come on, I want to show you something."

I allowed him to lead the way. There was something about Carter that soothed me. I was comfortable around him. I trusted him. It was crazy, and if he wasn't Jax's best friend, I'd have never have gone on a hike with him, or shared so much. But there was something different about this guy.

There went that word again.

Different.

We started climbing up a steeper trail, and I couldn't help but notice that when he placed his hands on my hips to help me up, my stomach dropped a bit. I was positive it was because another man was touching me. I'd only been with two guys my entire life, Holden and Mason. It was kind of nice having another man who I had no emotional attachment to make me feel this way. I needed to feel alive, and Carter was helping me do just that.

"Here, let me climb up first and then I'll help you," he said as he pulled himself up and over a ledge. The idea of not knowing what was at the top was exciting. My heart was racing as Carter leaned over and reached for my hands. With a huge smile, I grabbed onto him and climbed up the rock wall while Carter pulled me up. When I got to the top he pulled me into his arms. For a moment, I thought he was going to kiss me, but he quickly proved me wrong by letting go and turning away. I let out a sigh of relief.

"Check it out. What do you think?"

I turned to where he was pointing. I gasped out loud at the sight in front of me.

"Oh. My. Goodness," I whispered. "I've never seen anything so beautiful."

In front of us was a view of the mountain range with a crystal blue lake in the small valley. The way the reflection of the mountain and sky bounced off the lake was breathtaking.

"It looks like a picture. How did you know this was here?"

"I come to visit Jax a lot when I'm home, and I do my best thinking when I'm out hiking. I stumbled across this old path. No one ever walks it because it appears the trail ends at the cliff wall, but if you look hard enough you see the trail leading up."

"It's beautiful," I repeated as I glanced back at him.

He smiled. "Yeah it is. I'm not the only one who knows about it, though. Unfortunately, I've seen a lot of folks up here. Especially those who hike and fish."

"Oh, I bet the fishing is amazing. That's one of the things on my bucket list."

Carter turned to me. "Fishing?"

With a giggle, I looked at him. "Not just any fishing. But fly fishing up in the Colorado Rockies. I've always wanted to go there."

Something in his eyes changed. "Let's go there. Let's go fishing in the Rockies. I know the perfect place to go."

Tilting my head, I smirked. "You're running."

He returned my own look. "So are you."

I couldn't argue with him on that one. My stomach flipped a little at the idea of running off with Carter and spending a few days in Colorado.

No. What in the hell am I thinking? I don't even know him. But he is a friend of Jax and Jamie seems to trust him.

Turning away from Carter, I began pacing. *Could I do it?* Run off and do something I've always wanted to do with a perfect stranger? My parent's would kill me. Mason would kill me.

My chest ached. I should be doing this with Holden. This was our dream.

I fought to hold back the tears. He has a new dream. A new life. A baby on the way.

The hurt was almost too much to take. I knew I was running away from reality as much as Carter was, but in that very moment, I didn't give two shits. Spinning on my heels, I looked into his green eyes. Squaring off my shoulders, I said, "Let's do it! But one rule. Friends only. No expectations of anything other than friendship."

He jerked his head back in surprise. "Are you fucking insane? Just like that you'd run off with a man you hardly know, Em?"

My mouth dropped to the ground. "Wait. You were the one who suggested it."

"Well I know, but damn, girl. That's dangerous as hell to say yes when a man asks you to run off with him."

Chewing on my lip, I said, "Then no?"

"Fuck yes, we're going!"

I let out a giggle. "You are confusing me, Carter."

He took my hand and led me back over to the ledge. Dropping it, he started down over the ledge. "Slide down and I'll catch you."

"Wait. Where are we going?" I asked as he climbed back down. Peering over the edge, he stared back up at me with a huge smile on his face.

"We're going fishing in the Rockies."

I did a little jump and started climbing down. Carter's strong arms grabbed a hold of me and set me firmly down on the ground.

Butterflies were dancing around in my stomach. Not from Carter's touch, but from the idea of going on an adventure. Mason and I talked about it and it didn't work. Maybe it was because I was supposed to go with Carter. I wouldn't think too much about it. I was just going to do it.

By the time we got back to Jamie and Jax's place, both Carter and I were over-the-moon excited. Running up the steps, I called back over my shoulder. "I'll be packed up in five minutes!"

"Meet you back out here," Carter said, making a pass on my left once we both hit the porch.

As I ran into the house, Jamie and Jax walked out of the living room.

"I'm going fishing!" I called out with a huge smile on my face before running up the steps to the guest room I was staying in.

Before I reached the top, I heard Jamie say, "Oh shit. They had sex."

By the time I packed up my few things and made it back down the stairs, Jamie, Jax, and Carter were all on the front porch. I could hear Jamie talking to Carter in a raised voice. "You are not taking my best friend, whom you just met may I add, off somewhere. Hell no."

Coming to a stop, I tried to get my instant anger in check.

"Now hold on, Jamie, this is my best friend you're yelling at. I seriously doubt he would let any harm come to Emylie."

"Do you know what a fragile state of mind she is in? No. She came here to get her shit together, and you are not dragging her off so you could end up in her pants because I know that's what will happen. Jax talks when he's drunk, and I've heard stories about you, Carter. Do the two of you honestly think you're going to run off and fuck like rabbits and everything will be okay? All your problems solved with a little bit of fishing and fun?"

Carter started talking, but I pushed the screen door open causing it to bang. Everyone jumped and looked at me.

"Is that what you think of me? And for the record, we did not have sex earlier, even though *you* were pushing it. We're friends.

And Carter invited me to go fishing and I'm going fishing! So … so screw you Jamie!"

"Emmie! I was only kidding about hooking up with Carter. I know you're torn up about Holden, but sweetie, running away with Carter is not going to fix anything."

I shook my head. "You don't get it. I want to do this. I need to do this."

Pushing past everyone, I headed to my car. It was then I realized that both Carter and I had our own cars. I didn't want to drive alone. Turning around, I watched as Carter shook Jax's hand and then leaned over and kissed Jamie on the cheek. He whispered something in her ear and she nodded. Her eyes looked sad, and I knew she hadn't meant what she said, but I was pissed. There was no way I was walking back up there and saying goodbye to her.

When Carter walked up to me, he smiled weakly. "You'll follow me, right?"

My old insecurities came rushing back. I didn't want to be alone. "No. I'll leave my car here if that's okay? I can always fly back to pick it up."

With an incredulous look, Carter asked, "Are you sure, Em?"

Peering past his shoulder at Jamie staring at me, I nodded. "Positive. I'll leave the keys in the car if they need to move it."

I quickly opened the door to my car and dropped my keys on the seat. I could feel the weight of Jamie's stare.

"Emylie, I didn't mean what I said. Please don't do this. What am I supposed to tell your parents if they call?"

A feeling of dread swept over my body, and for one brief second, it felt like I was making a huge mistake. It quickly passed when I thought of Holden and how Daphne was carrying his child yet again.

Glancing over my shoulder, I walked to Carter's truck and replied, "Tell them I went fishing."

CHAPTER 16

Holden

STANDING AT THE fax machine, I watched as Daphne's medical records printed out page by page. Becca stood next to me, chewing on her nail.

"She said Daphne hadn't been in since when?"

My stomach felt sick. "Last December."

Mason walked up to me. "Maybe she's seeing another OB."

I nodded and barely whispered, "Maybe."

My chest tightened as the thought of Daphne not being pregnant bounced around in my head. I wanted more than anything for it to be true, but a small part of me mourned the loss of another baby. It wasn't our first baby's fault that he was conceived during a drunken night. He was still a child. My child.

The fax machine finally stopped printing out papers. Gathering them up, I handed them to Becca.

"How do we find out if she's going to another doctor?" Becca asked as she searched through the paperwork.

Letting out a frustrated sigh, I headed to the kitchen. "I need a fucking beer."

"Dude, it's not even noon. Let's hold off a bit longer and go grab something to eat. I know I'm starved."

I gave Mason a small head bob. I knew he was right. Drinking is what got me into this damn mess in the first place.

"Where are you kids off to?"

My mother's voice had us all stopping on a dime and freezing.

"Oh hell. What did the three of you do? Is Daphne okay?"

Turning to look at my mother, I let out a gruff laugh. "Do you really think I'd hurt her, Mom?"

She lifted her brows. "Well, I don't know. You faked being sick in order to stay here longer. I'm not really sure what's going on anymore."

Her gaze drifted to Becca. "What is that you're reading, Becca?"

Before I had a chance to lie, Becca answered her. "The wicked witch's medical records from the OB."

My mother quickly made her way over to Becca. I was ready for her to rip them from her hand and then ground us all for a month. Instead, she said, "Now, now, Becca, it's not nice to call people names. Does it say how far along she is?"

Mason and I both looked at each other with stunned expressions. My mother wasn't freaking out. She wasn't yelling at me for doing something illegal. She was on my side.

"No, she hasn't been in since last December."

My mother tapped her chin. "Interesting. Come on into the kitchen, and I'll make us an early lunch. We can all figure it out together."

Becca mindlessly followed my mother as she kept thumbing through the records.

"Dude, your mother is either one hell of a badass mom, or she really doesn't like Daphne." Mason stated.

With a huge grin on my face, I slapped him on the back and replied, "It's both."

My mother set a plate of pancakes and bacon in front of each of us. I had started to read the notes the doctor had made after Daphne's miscarriage but I had to stop. I slid them over to my mother as she sat down next to me.

"I can't read these," I mumbled. Trying to find my appetite, I forced myself to eat a bite of the pancakes.

"The only thing I can think of doing is calling every OB in LA and seeing about confirming an appointment for Daphne."

"That would be crazy," my mother said as she narrowed her stare and read something.

"Becca, where are the notes from Daphne's first appointment, where she first found out she was pregnant?"

Rustling through some papers, Becca pulled a few out and handed them to my mother.

"Here they are. I didn't read over them since it was the first pregnancy."

We all ate in silence as my mother read the notes. After eating half the pancakes, I pushed my plate away.

"You not going to eat those?" Mason asked.

I rolled my eyes and motioned for him to take the rest of my uneaten food.

Burying my hands in my face, I wanted to cry. I hated that we were even doing this. It was an invasion into Daphne's privacy, and I was about to tell my mother to forget it when she asked, "Were you in the room when the doctor told you Daphne had lost the baby?"

I dropped my hands. "Yeah. Why?"

"When you were there, did the doctor ever mention how far

along Daphne was?"

"She was almost fourteen weeks."

Shaking her head, my mother peered into my eyes. "Did anyone other than Daphne ever confirm to you how far along she was in the pregnancy?"

I thought back at the one time I went to the doctor with her. The next day is when she had the miscarriage. "Um, no. Come to think of it, the doctor came in, did an exam and said everything was going well."

A heaviness settled into my limbs. I could tell by the way my mother was looking at me, she was about to say something I wasn't going to want to hear.

"You couldn't have been the father of that baby, Holden."

Becca and Mason froze. I was pretty sure I stopped breathing.

Forcing myself to speak, I asked, "Why?"

My mother glanced back at the paperwork as she pursed her lips together, then looked directly at me. The sadness was almost more than I could take.

"Because she was almost seventeen weeks pregnant. That means she was pregnant already when you slept with her. If you even slept with her."

Becca gasped and said, "No!" The sound of Mason's fork hitting his plate caused me to jump.

"What?" I barely said. "Maybe she didn't know she was pregnant."

Shaking her head, a single tear fell from my mother's eye before she quickly wiped it away.

"I don't think so, sweetie. It has the date she had her last period. It says the doctor told her the date she most likely conceived and when her due date would be, which is not the same due date you told your father and I when we talked the other night. Holden, she lied to you. She was indeed pregnant, but not with your child."

I jumped up, causing my chair to crash onto the floor. "No. Oh

God, no. Please God no. I hurt her for nothing. For nothing!"

Becca was around the table and had her arm around me. "Let's sit back down, Holden. Please."

Mason was now on the other side of me.

"Emylie. I hurt her for nothing. The baby wasn't even mine. I told her I had fallen in love with another woman because I didn't want to tell her I was a cheating bastard. If I had only been honest. She might have forgiven me."

My hands pushed through my hair as I squeezed my head and screamed out, "Why?! Why did you do this to me?"

Mason grabbed onto my arm. "Come on, dude, let's at least step outside to get some fresh air.

I pushed him away from me and took a few steps back. "No. I'm going to talk to Daphne."

"Ah fuck," Mason said under his breath as my mother walked toward me.

"You will not, Holden Warner. You are angry and now is not the time to confront Daphne."

I let out a short blunt laugh. "You're goddamn right I'm angry. I want to rip her fucking head off. She lied to me, Mom. She ruined my life. If she lied to me then, how do I know if she is lying to me now?"

"You don't, but you're not going to solve anything by going over there angry like this."

Becca touched my arm, causing me to jerk away before she squeezed it. "Holden, your mom is right. If you go in blazing mad, it's not going to help the situation. She could honestly be pregnant. If she lost another baby, do you really want that on your conscience?"

My head was spinning and my entire body felt as if it was buried in sand. I fought for each breath like it was my last one. I had so many different emotions tumbling around in my mind, I didn't know which way was up or down. Disbelief. The feeling of loss all over again. Disappointment. Anger. Hatred. It all swirled together into one big fucked up mess.

Mason walked up to me with a serious expression on his face. "Let's put at least one thing into perspective here. We wouldn't even be standing here if you hadn't slept with her."

I went to say something when he lifted his hand and continued. "I honestly think she drugged you that night, Holden."

My mouth partially opened, but nothing came out. I'd had a feeling all along that someone had slipped something in my drink. "The last thing I remember is I was flirting pretty heavy with Daphne and realized what I was doing. I backed off, said I was heading back to my place, and she got upset with me. Then I was in her bed."

Mason closed his eyes and shook his head. "Dude, I really wish you would have been up front and honest with us."

Stabbing my hand into my hair, I nodded. "You and me both."

My heart dropped. If I had been honest with Emylie, she might not have fallen into Mason's arms. The thought of them together still made my skin crawl. I needed to get to her. Tell her everything we found out. The only way to do that was to finally get the truth from Daphne.

With one deep breath, I slowly exhaled. "I'm going over to the cabin to talk to Daphne."

"Maybe we should come with you, Holden," Becca said as she glanced between me and Mason.

With a gruff laugh, I shook my head. "I'm not going to do anything stupid."

Lifting her brow, she smirked. "Well your track record shows differently. The first thing we're going to do is stop and buy a pregnancy test. It's time to nip this shit in the bud." Becca's eyes filled with tears and her voice cracked. "I want my best friend back."

Mason walked up to Becca and wrapped her in his arms. "We all want her back," he whispered as he kissed the top of her head.

I turned to my mother. She blew out a long sigh and slowly shook her head. "This is so surreal. It's like watching a movie play out right before me. I'm honestly stunned and trying to figure out why this girl lied to you about being the father of that baby."

Walking to my mother, I stopped and glanced down at the papers spread out on the table. "That's what I'm about to find out, Mom." My gaze lifted and met hers. "I'm so sorry I stayed away like I did. I'm sorry I didn't tell you what was going on in the first place. I knew once I did, you and Dad would be disappointed in me."

She dropped the papers in her hand on the table and walked into my arms. I held her tight before she pulled back and studied me. "We've all made mistakes in our lives. This will not be the last one you make. I can promise you that. The key to it though, is learning from them. The one thing you have in this world is family and friends, Holden. Your strength grows from our strength. Your love from our love. You may falter with the trust, but that can be earned back."

I turned away. "I'm not sure if I'll ever be able to earn back Emylie's love or trust again."

Placing her hand on the side of my face, I peered back into her green eyes. "Oh, sweetheart, you never lost her love. I can promise you that. Why do you think she left?"

"Because I'm an asshole who came back to town with the girl I cheated on her with, stood her up for lunch, then allowed Daphne to hurt her again by telling her she was pregnant."

Becca cleared her throat. "I'd say that about sums it up."

My mother looked over at Becca and frowned slightly.

Becca shrugged. "What? If the shoe fits, put it on and own it."

Leaning in, I kissed my mother on the cheek. "Mom, will you get rid of this for me? I don't want Daphne to see any of it. I need her to tell me the truth without her thinking I know."

With a quick nod, she replied. "I'll take care of it now."

I turned to head out when she took me by the arm. Glancing back at her, I smiled. "I promise not to mess this up, Mom. I'm going to the get the truth from her, then I'm going to get Emylie and bring her home."

She pressed her lips together and smiled. "I think you need to make one more stop before you set off for Emylie. There are two more people who you need to speak with first."

I knew who she was talking about. With a wink, I took her hand and squeezed it. "I love you. Will you catch Dad up on everything?"

"Yes, of course. Please remember to keep calm." Peeking over to Mason and Becca, she pointed to them both. "I'm counting on you two to make sure he does just that."

Becca quickly walked up to my mother and hugged her. "We will. I promise."

Turning to face me and Mason, Becca slapped her hands together and smiled. "Let's get this bust going. I've got to pick up Sage in three hours!"

Mason chuckled. "It's not a drug deal, Becca."

With a wink, she walked up to me and wrapped her arm around me. "No, but it sure feels good to all be back together again. And together, we're taking this bitch down."

CHAPTER 17

Emylie

"WE'RE ALMOST TO Rifle," Carter said with a huge smile on his face. "The fly fishing there is amazing."

I could feel the giddiness bubbling up as we drove across the state line a few hours ago and into Colorado. Carter and I had talked nonstop since we took off. Of course, the first thirty minutes he wanted to make sure I was okay leaving my car behind and how he knew Jamie didn't mean what she had said. The subject was finally changed and the conversations flowed flawlessly. It was nice to be with someone so completely different from Holden or Mason.

"Penny for your thoughts."

With a light-hearted chuckle, I glanced his way. "Just excited. I googled and saw there is a fishery close by the town. Would it be possible to stop by?"

"This is your bucket list trip. We'll do whatever you want to do."

I couldn't help but smile. And it wasn't lost on me I hadn't thought about Holden in a few hours. For the first time in awhile, I felt free. Light. Hopeful that life would continue on. Maybe not like how I wanted it to, but it would keep going on."

"How did you know about this place?" I asked.

"Grew up here."

My mouth dropped open. "Shut up! Really?"

He laughed and took a quick peek at me. "Yep. My granddaddy was the one who taught me how to fly fish. Our family has a place up in the mountains a little way out of town."

"Is that where we're staying?" I asked.

Carter's jaw tightened. "If you want. Or we can stay at my folks' place."

"So you really weren't running?"

He slowly shook his head. "No, but you've been one hell of a good distraction. Plus, if you're with me, my father can't be too much of an asshole toward me."

I let out a soft chuckle and looked out the passenger window. "You've been a good distraction too."

"Are you sure you don't want to call him, Em? Just let him know where you are. I know if I were him I'd be going insane."

Snapping my head back to him, I glared at him. "What for? He's getting married and having a baby, Carter. There is nothing there for me. Nothing."

"The whole story maybe? You said he was wanting to meet you for lunch. Maybe he was going to explain everything to you."

My mind drifted back to me sitting there waiting for Holden to pick me up. After an hour, I got up and went back into the house and changed. My heart felt like it had been ripped out yet again knowing he had stood me up.

"Well, we never made it to lunch because his pregnant fiancée came first, so let's change the subject. I really don't want to talk about Holden." I sighed as I closed my eyes and counted to ten.

Opening them, I forced myself to forget about everything back in Texas. "I'm starving."

"I know a place I bet you'd like."

Peeking over to Carter, I took in his features. Strong jaw line. Beautiful green eyes that I swear sparkled when he was excited. I didn't really know him all that well, but what I did know was that he really wanted his father's forgiveness. It was evident and reminded me of Holden and Sam.

A few miles down the road, Carter pulled off an exit and headed into a small town. "Where are we going?"

"To eat. You said you were hungry. I know the perfect place to take my new Texas friend. You'll feel right at home."

I stared at him with a suspicious smile. "Why am I all of sudden second-guessing this little trip we're taking?"

Tossing his head back in laughter, Carter looked at me and winked. "Trust me."

With a smile, I stared straight ahead. Carter pulled into a parking lot of what looked to be a bar.

"A bar? You're bringing me to a bar for lunch? Is this what I can expect when we go fly fishing? Disappointment?"

Placing his hand over his heart, he pretended to be hurt. Then he pointed to me and said, "You'll be saying you're sorry to me in less than ten minutes. I promise."

"And if I don't?"

"I owe you a fancy dinner."

I wiggled my brows. "I like fancy dinners."

"Somehow I picture you as a picnic kind of girl."

He had me there.

Carter jumped out of his truck and jogged around the front, reaching my door just as I slid out. He shut the door and placed his hand on my lower back, guiding me to the entrance of the bar.

I didn't want to admit I liked having his hand on me. The feel of him guiding me, yet letting me lead the way was nice. It was almost like he could read my mind.

The second we stepped inside the bar, I knew I had lost my own bet. With a deep inhale through my nose, I moaned.

"That smells like heaven."

Leaning in closer to me, Carter placed his lips up to my ear and whispered, "It's beyond heaven."

I smirked as I looked at him. "I'll be the judge of that."

Carter winked and took my hand, leading me to the bar.

He didn't let go of my hand as he slapped the bar and said, "Jeff Fucking Roberts."

The bartender turned and smiled big when he saw Carter.

"Holy shit. Look what the cat dragged in, and he has a beauty on his arm."

My cheeks burned as I grinned and took a quick look around. This was far from being a bar. It was a bar, restaurant, and they had a huge dance floor. I wasn't the least bit surprised to see a few families sitting at tables eating.

The music was playing and a few people were on the dance floor dancing. Peeking back over to Carter, I listened to him and the bartender catching up.

"Jeff, this is my friend, Emylie."

Reaching his hand out, I shook it and leaned in closer so he could hear me over the music. "Nice to meet you, Jeff."

"What in the hell made you hook up with this crazy ass Marine?"

Carter rolled his eyes.

"He promised me good fly fishing."

Jeff laughed. "Is that all he promised you?"

"All right, that's enough," Carter said.

I chortled and glanced back at the dance floor. I was itching to get on it.

I had one week. One week to forget my past and move on. I already knew Carter was going to play a role in helping me do just that. Only as a friend. I wasn't interested in hooking up and using sex to forget, and I truly felt Carter was on the same page. We connected, but not in a sexual way.

"We'll each take the Texas plate."

Snapping my head back to Carter, I raised an eyebrow. "Texas plate, huh?"

He nodded and replied, "I promise it will be the best you've ever had."

"Drunk Drunk" by LoCash started and a glanced back at the dance floor.

"You want to dance?"

Turning to look back at Carter, a wide grin spread across my face.

"You'll really seal the deal of this friendship if you tell me you can two-step."

Snarling his lip like I had insulted him, he said, "Girl, please, I put the meaning in two-stepping."

Before I knew it, we were gliding across the dance floor. My body pressed against this man I only met yesterday. I'd done things in the last three days I'd never done before and it felt freeing. Being in Carter's arms actually felt the most freeing. He wasn't looking for anything from me and I wasn't looking for anything from him.

The song changed and Carter spun me around as I laughed. This was the beginning of what I suspected was going to be a great friendship. If only he danced a bit better.

CHAPTER 18

Holden

MASON HAD PULLED up a little way down from the cabin and parked. I pulled up behind him and got out of my truck, making my way to the driver's side window.

Becca leaned forward and asked, "Are you calm?"

With a nod, I replied, "I am."

"Liar," she said with a wink.

"I'm trying."

Her grin faded and her expression turned sad. "I know you are."

My body felt fatigued. Like two years of unhappiness hit me full force all at once. A grim expression appeared on Mason's face. "Holden, you can't change the past. All you can do is look toward the future. Do you want Emylie in your future?"

My chest felt like a vice was squeezing it. "I've always wanted Emylie. I've always loved her."

"Then don't push. Get the answers you need, and then we'll take it from there. I know how you're feeling and I know you. I'm honestly surprised you didn't turn north and head to Utah when you got in your truck."

I gave him a weak smile. "I thought about it."

"It's all going to work out."

Reaching in, I grabbed his shoulder and said, "Thank you. Both of y'all. I know how much I hurt y'all too, and the fact that you're here supporting me ... well it means a lot."

Becca reached over and I placed my other hand in hers. "Holden, you and Emylie were made for each other. We've all known that for years. You'll get her back. I promise."

My chin trembled and I cleared my throat. "Right. Well should we do some kind of chant like we used to before we would play tag football?"

Mason and Becca laughed.

"On three. One. Two. Three!" Becca called out.

At once, all of us shouted, "Give 'em hell!"

Taking a step away from the truck, I gave them one last reassuring nod, and headed back to my truck.

Two minutes later I was walking up the porch. Opening the door, I walked in. The rental car was parked outside so I knew Daphne was here. She was probably napping.

I made my way into the kitchen and saw she was standing there reading the directions on one of those microwave meals.

"You should really lock the door, Daphne."

She screamed and jumped. "You scared the piss out of me, Holden. Jesus. What are you doing here?"

I tossed the truck keys onto the table. "I feel better."

Just looking at her made my skin crawl. Knowing she had lied to me. Caused me to destroy my future with Emylie. I truly hated this woman.

With a forced smile, she nodded. "That's great. Maybe we can head home tomorrow then?"

"Sounds good. What are you making?"

Her stiff posture relaxed some. "Um, one of those heat-up meals."

"We can go out to eat if you want."

"Sure. If that's what you want. Will there be anything decent in this town?"

With a short laugh, I replied, "Probably not for you, but if you wanted to make the drive into Austin, I guess we could."

"We should find out what time the flights leave."

I nodded.

"Mom found something in our room when she moved your suit-case."

Daphne swallowed hard. "Wh-what was it?"

Reaching into the duffle bag I had brought in, I pulled out the pregnancy test. Becca and I had gone in to Walgreens together to buy it. It only took me two seconds to find the same box that Daphne had carried into the bathroom when she told me she was pregnant.

Her eyes widened in shock.

"Were you worried about something, babe?"

The way her gaze flickered from the test to me had me wondering if she actually had a fucking test stashed in her case.

"Um. Well, you know I've been so um … I've been so ah … stressed and worried. It's become compulsive to keep checking."

I tilted my head. "I don't want you stressing yourself out like that."

Walking up to her, I took her hand in mine and led her to the bathroom. "Where are we going, Holden?"

"We're going to take one last test. Then you're going to put your mind at ease."

It couldn't have worked out more perfect. I hadn't even needed to come up with an excuse for her to take the test. She gave me one.

"No. I need to stop now and not even do it."

I stopped and searched her face. "I'm worried about the other day, when you were cramping. It will put my mind at ease as well. I won't leave your side the entire time."

Opening her mouth to protest, I narrowed my stare at her. "Are you worried about something?"

Her mouth snapped shut, she shook her head. Closing her eyes, I wondered if she was praying the last time we had sex I got her pregnant.

Daphne slowly walked into the bathroom and turned to face me. She lifted up her dress and pulled her panties down. Once she sat on the toilet, I ripped the box open and opened the test.

"Do you need water?"

She shook her head no. When I handed her the test, she took it with shaking hands.

I watched her carefully as she peed onto the stick. Taking a piece of toilet paper, I held it out and set the test on it. With each second that ticked on the clock, her chest rose and fell at a faster pace.

Setting the stick on the counter, I stared at it while she stood and pulled up her panties.

"You know, sometimes they will give false readings," she softly said.

"There are two in here."

She went to talk, but her voice cracked. Clearing her throat, she replied, "That's right."

My heart pounded so hard in my chest I was sure it would break from my ribcage.

Then it happened.

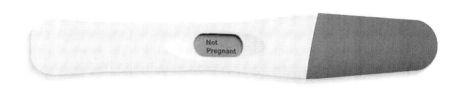

The breath I was holding whooshed from my lungs, and I wanted to scream out, "Yes!"

I could hear the sobs coming from beside me. She was going to pretend she lost the baby, and I needed to prepare myself for her new lie.

When I turned to face her, she shook her head. "I'm so sorry I lied."

All the air in my lungs left at once. I reached out for the counter to help me stand up.

"What?"

She quickly wiped her tears away. "You were going to leave me again for her. I couldn't let you do that. You're mine, Holden. I knew from the first moment I saw you. When I overheard you telling your boss you were leaving, going back to Texas, I freaked out. I knew I had to get you to have sex with me. The only way I could get pregnant was to take you off guard when I knew you didn't have a condom. But it didn't work. So then I cut small tears in all of your condoms."

The room started spinning. Holy fuck. She was admitting to it.

"You did what?"

More tears fell. "I told Daddy, and he told me to tell you I was pregnant and then he started to pressure you into asking me to marry you. We would just plan another miscarriage. I wasn't sure I could fake one ... the last one was so terrible. Daddy assured me I could."

I slowly shook my head and leaned against the counter. *Was I dreaming? Is any of this real?*

The only thing I could say was, "Why?"

"The moment I saw you, Holden, I knew I had to have you. Then, you mentioned your girlfriend and kept ignoring me."

Scrubbing my hands down my face, I hoped like hell Mason and Becca had snuck into the cabin, because I was so stunned I was positive I wouldn't remember half of what Daphne was saying.

"What are you saying, Daphne?"

She walked up to me and placed her hands on my chest. "I'm saying you and I were meant to be together. I knew it the first time I saw you on that football field. The way you smiled at me when you walked back to the locker room. I saw it in your eyes."

"Holy fuck, you're insane."

She laughed. "For you! I'm insane for you."

"You don't even touch me! We hardly even sleep in the same bed, Daphne. Why in the hell would you want to be married to a man who is in love with another woman?"

She took a step back. "You're not in love with her. You think you are, but you're not. Don't you see, Holden? I've been giving you space. Think about when we fuck." She reached down and grabbed my dick. "It's so good. I know you like it when I wrap my lips around that thick cock of yours. It throbs with desire. I knew that first night I brought you back to my place that I could make you want me. The only reason you passed out was because I slipped you a little too much of the drug."

Jesus H. Christ. She's fucking admitting she drugged me. I looked at the bathroom door. It was partly open and I saw Mason standing there with a stunned expression on his face. They were listening to ever crazy ass thing this nut case was saying.

"Did we even have sex that night?"

She jetted her lip out. "No. You couldn't get it up no matter how many times I sucked you off."

Sick. I felt sick.

"The baby. It wasn't mine?"

A look of shock moved across her face as she covered her mouth and took a few steps back. "I'm so sorry, Holden. I never meant for you to find that out. I went to such lengths to keep the truth from you. Daddy paid the doctor and the nurse to lie to you about how far along I was. He would do anything to make me happy, you know."

"Did you know you were pregnant the night you drugged me?"

She nodded. "Rich told me you were planning on staying home over Thanksgiving. It didn't take much to convince him to throw the party and get you there."

Pushing both hands through my hair, I wanted to scream. It was an overload of information I was looking for, but wasn't prepared to hear. "Who ... who was the father?"

Her eyes looked sad. "He told me he loved me. He promised we would have a life together. So the night he showed up at my apartment, I thought maybe things would be different. After all, you had your precious girlfriend. I could have Chuck. He made love to me all night. We made that baby. Things were going to be different, but when I woke up the next morning, he told me he thought he could do it, but he couldn't. He left me all alone, but what he didn't know was I was pregnant. His baby was growing inside of me. I'd have a piece of him forever."

"That's why you were so depressed when you lost the baby. It was because you lost a piece of this guy?"

Tears fell from her eyes. "I couldn't do it alone. When I found out I was pregnant, I knew I had to somehow make you believe the baby was yours. I thought it would be hard, but you made it so easy. You totally broke things off with Emylie and ran to my side."

Pushing off the counter, I paced back and forth. "Wait. The DNA test."

"It was altered. Daddy paid to have it done."

No wonder her father was so pissed. He had gone above and beyond to help her with this scheme.

"Jesus Christ, this is fucking insane. You're insane, Daphne. Do you realize you fucked up my life because you wanted me to help you raise some other guys kid, but you made it so I would think it was mine? You belong in the nut house."

She shot me a dirty expression. "It would have all worked had you not brought us back to this God-forsaken state. I knew I had to keep you from her because the moment you saw her, you would know how much you loved her. But you needed time to love me."

Disgust filled every inch of my body. "You're sick. You need help, Daphne."

She shook her head. "No. I know if you work harder on us, we can make this work."

"I can honestly tell you I would have never fallen in love with you. The only woman I have ever loved and will ever love is Emylie."

Burying her face in her hands, she cried. "Don't say that, Holden."

"I think you need to get your shit from my house and leave. Don't even think of going back to our place in LA. If you do before I get there and retrieve my things, I'll let the news know about your crazy little stunt. I'm sure that won't be good PR for Daddy's new movie."

"No one will believe you," Daphne said with a short, evil laugh.

The bathroom door pushed open and Becca walked in with her phone in her hand. "Oh. My. Gawd! I'm pretty sure I could get on *Entertainment Tonight* with this stuff!"

Daphne glared at Becca. If looks could kill, Becca would be flat on the ground.

Turning back to me, Daphne narrowed her eyes and gave me the evilest look. "You tricked me. You knew I wasn't pregnant."

I slowly shook my head. "No, I didn't know."

Her mouth parted open, but nothing came out.

"The pregnancy test? You had me take it."

"I had a suspicion, that was all. You pretty much confessed to everything, Daphne."

She shook her head. "Why would you trick me?"

"Why did you lie to me?"

A look of pure hate washed over her face. "I don't need you. I've never needed you. I should have known that little bitch was going to come between us."

"It was never going to work because I never loved you. All you wanted was a puppet to boss around. Not anymore, Daphne. It's over."

Squaring off her shoulders, she shot me the most hateful look I'd ever seen. "Fine. If this is the way you want it, but I promise you, Holden, you'll regret this day. I promise you that."

"I doubt it."

She smirked and said, "You turned out to be a terrible fuck anyway. It took everything I had to get through each time we were together."

With a slight laugh, I shook my head. "If you're trying to hurt me with your words, it's not going to work."

Pushing past Becca, Daphne left the bathroom. I dropped my hands to my knees and dragged in a few breaths. Leaning over to talk into my ear, Becca whispered, "How does it feel knowing you lived with a psychopath? Dude, you had sex with that?"

I frowned as I lifted my gaze up at her. "Seriously, Becca?"

Standing, she shrugged. "I don't know about you, but I'm thinking a restraining order is the first thing I'd be doing when I got back to Cali."

"The first thing I'm doing is getting my boss to change the locks on my apartment, and then putting Daphne's ass on a plane and out of Texas."

"And then?"

Standing up straight, I stared her in the eyes and smiled. "Then I'm going after Emylie."

CHAPTER 19

Emylie

THE RIVER MEANDERED alongside of us as Carter drove. It was the most peaceful sight I'd ever seen.

"It's beautiful here," I softly said.

"Yep. Growing up here wasn't a hardship, I can tell ya that."

With a lighthearted laugh, I glanced over to him. "Are you nervous?"

"More like scared shitless he's going to slam the door in my face."

Reaching over, I took his hand in mine. "He won't, Carter. You're his son and he loves you."

He forced a smile. "It's been awhile since I've been home."

My stomach lurched. It sounded almost exactly like Holden. Except Carter had stayed away because he joined the military. He didn't get some girl pregnant.

Turning down another road he drove for a bit more before stopping at a long driveway. "This is it."

His voice sounded shaky.

"Let's get out of the truck for a minute. Stretch our legs and take some deep breaths."

He nodded and followed my lead. It didn't take long before Carter was pacing back and forth. His hand running over his buzz cut more times than I could keep track of.

"This is stupid. I shouldn't have come back."

I leaned against his truck and let him get it out of his system. Another truck pulled up and came to a stop. A blonde jumped out and yelled out Carter's name. Spinning, he came to a dead stop. If I thought he was scared before, now he was just plain frightened.

Smiling, I watched as the girl ran and jumped into his arms. I tilted my head and watched the scene play out.

"Tori! What are you doing here?" Carter asked when they finally let each other go.

"I moved back home! As much as I swore I couldn't wait to get out of here, something was pulling me back. I'm working at the hospital."

"Nurse?"

She nodded with excitement. "Yes! I'm loving it."

I knew she hadn't seen me and the moment she did, she would get the wrong idea. Clearly these two had a past together with the way they were looking at one another.

Carter stared at her in the most loving way. It made my heart drop.

Well, I might as well get this over with now. Pushing off the truck, I walked up to the two of them. They were completely lost in one another.

Carter's gaze drifted up as he saw me approaching. With a smile, he looked back at Tori.

"Tori, I'd like to introduce you to Emylie."

She spun around and forced a smile. Okay, I could see it all over her face, she had a thing for Carter. I was going to question him about this Tori girl.

"Hi, Tori. It's a pleasure meeting you."

She nodded and seemed to be trying to find the words to speak. "I'm a friend of Carter's. He offered to taking me fly fishing. I hear this is the place to be for that."

With a nervous chuckle, she said, "Um, yeah. We have some great fishing here."

I smiled bigger. "That's awesome. I'm looking forward to it."

"I'm so sorry, I didn't know you had someone with you. It's just I saw you and was surprised and had to say hi. I'll let ya go."

Peering up at Carter, I waited for him to clear up that we were only friends. He just stood there, like an idiot.

"Oh heck, you don't have to leave on my account. I had a cramp in my leg and Carter stopped to let me stretch it out."

He lifted his eyebrows in surprise. I hadn't thought that one through since he had been the one pacing when she pulled up.

"Carter is a great friend. I have a degree in Agriculture and life science and also in wildlife and fisheries science. So I'm in heaven right now. It's an open classroom!"

Tori chewed on her lip as she looked between us. "Are you in the Marines as well?"

Throwing my head back, I let out a roar of laughter. "God, no! Our best friends are dating. That's how we met and became friends. Just *friends*."

I was hoping she would catch on to the stress I put on the word friend. I gave her a look that asked if she was picking up what I was hinting at. She smiled bigger, and I was glad to see she was.

"Oh, I see."

She turned back to Carter. "How long are you in town for?"

"I'm ah … I'm not sure."

She pressed her lips together and began rubbing her hands over each other. "I see. Well, I hope maybe we can grab a cup of coffee or something before you leave."

I wanted to scream out, "Yes! He will grab coffee, lunch, dinner, whatever you want."

"That would be awesome."

Tori's face lit up. Oh yeah. This girl had it bad for Carter, and he seemed to be at a total loss of words. "Cool."

"Cool," Tori replied as she turned back to me. "It was a pleasure meeting you, Emylie. I hope to see you again before you leave."

"Same here, Tori."

As she headed back to her truck, I looked at Carter and hit him on the arm. "Do you have her number?" I asked in a whispered voice.

"What?"

Giving him a what the hell look, I asked again, "Her number, Carter? Do you have it to call her?"

"Um ... I think."

"Tori!" I yelled, causing her to come to a stop.

"Yeah?"

"Carter lost his phone." Glancing over my shoulder at him, I said, "And it appears his voice. He needs your number again."

"Oh! No problem." Reaching into the truck, she grabbed some paper and quickly wrote her number down. Walking up to us, she handed the paper to Carter. "I put my work number too, just in case."

Taking it from her hand, he nodded. "Great. Perfect. This is good. Okay."

My eyes widened as I stared at him.

Who is this man?

Tori giggled. "Okay. See ya later."

"See ya soon. Looking forward to it." Carter said with a drop-me-to-the-ground sexy smile.

Ah. There he is.

Taking a few steps back, the poor girl attempted to pull her stare off of him. Glancing over at me, she gave me the sweetest smile. "Thank you, Emylie."

With a knowing expression, I said, "Call me, Em."

She reached for my hand and gave it a squeeze. Good, she realizes I'm not a threat.

I watched as she practically skipped back to her truck. When she drove off, I turned to see Carter watching her drive down the road.

"Holy shit. That was some serious eye-fucking going on between the two of you!" I said with a laugh. Carter looked back at me and rolled his eyes.

"Shut up."

I pointed to him and shook my head. "You totally have it bad for her. Who is she? Did y'all date before? The way she ran into your arms I'm going to say there is serious history there."

He glanced down at the number before folding it and putting it in his pocket.

"Yeah. There's history there. Come on, let's get this over with."

My hands dropped to my side, and I was pretty sure my jaw was on the ground.

"Wait. You seriously are going to leave it there? That's it? No history lesson on you and Tori? Carter! I saved you back there. You were going to let her walk away and I got her number for you." Walking up to him, I wiggled my brows. "If you're lucky, you may be getting lucky."

He rolled his eyes and shook his head. "You don't understand, Em. That's all water under the bridge. The past."

A lump formed in my throat. "Was she the girl who cheated on you?"

"No. She was the girl I thought was my future. But life doesn't always go by our script. You of all people should know that."

"But we have the ability to re-write the script, Carter. If we want to."

He let out a fake laugh. "Do you want to? Because if you did, you wouldn't be here."

My hands went to my hips. "That is why I'm here. To try and

153

re-write mine. I have no idea of knowing what lies ahead of me, but I know what I just saw. Two people who clearly have feelings for one another. What I felt between the two of you wasn't in the past. If I felt it, I sure as hell know you did too."

"Not now, Em. Let's tackle one problem at a time. Please."

The sadness in his eyes reminded me of Holden. It was the same look he gave me after Daphne said she was pregnant. His eyes were filled with so much regret and sadness.

I nodded and softly said, "Okay. Let's deal with your dad first."

"Then fishing."

Heading back to the passenger side of the truck, I jumped in and buckled up. Without looking at Carter, I waited for him to turn down the driveway.

"Right. Dad. Fishing. Then we'll talk about Tori."

With a frustrated groan, Carter hit the gas and went faster. I knew he wasn't in a hurry to see his dad. He might be to go fishing. But I had a suspicious feeling he wanted to dial that number on the piece of paper in his pocket.

Smiling, I started figuring out the plan in my head.

When we pulled up to the log cabin, I caught my breath. It was beautiful. It wasn't too terribly big, but it was large. The landscaping around the house was simple. A few flower beds with bright flowers planted in each. Tall pine trees surrounded the house all all sides.

"What an adorable house," I said as I went to open the door. Carter grabbed my arm.

"Wait. I don't think I can do it."

Glancing back at him, I smiled. "Yes, you can. Take a deep breath and get out of the truck and start walking toward the door. I'll be by your side. I swear."

It was strange to think two days ago I had no idea Carter even existed. Now, it felt like we were all we had to help each other through the craziness of our lives.

Fate brought us together, there was no doubt about that at all.

"Where did you come from?" Carter asked with a smile.

Winking, I replied, "Texas."

With a laugh, he got out of the truck and I followed. We met each other at the bottom of the steps. Reaching out, he took my hand in his.

"Let's get this over with. The sooner he tells me to leave, the sooner we'll get up to the cabin and get some fishing in."

I knew he didn't mean what he said. He would be devastated if that happened. With each step I prayed that his father wouldn't turn him away.

By the time we got to the door, my heart was pounding in my chest. I couldn't imagine how Carter must have been feeling.

He dragged in a deep breath and went to knock.

"Wait!" I said. Pulling my hand from his, I smiled. "We don't want to give them the idea we're together."

Pinching his brows together, he stared at me for a second then looked back at the door and gave it three quick knocks.

Less than ten seconds later, the door opened and an older version of Carter stood before us. His eyes instantly filled with tears.

"Hey, Dad."

Carter's father stood there staring intently at him. I wasn't sure what was about to happen. I could see it though. He was glad Carter was here.

"I um ... I wasn't sure if you would want to see me or not."

I heard a gasp and glanced over Carter's father's shoulder. An older woman stood there with her hands covering her mouth. Tears rolled down her cheeks. Pushing past the dad, she wrapped Carter up in her arms and cried harder.

Not realizing I was holding my breath, I slowly let it out. When

Carter's mom stepped back and looked him over, she shook her head. "I'm so glad you're home, baby."

All eyes landed on Carter's dad. I was stunned by what I saw next.

He closed his eyes. When Carter's father looked back at him, he held his arms open while a few tears rolled down his cheeks. "You're finally home."

When they embraced, I covered my mouth and tried to contain my sobs.

His mother embraced both of them as she cried harder. "My baby! You're home! Carter's home!"

I took a few steps back and walked over to the rocking chair on the front porch. Carter didn't need me. He was already on the path of re-writing his script.

Smiling, I wrapped my arms around my body and closed my eyes. Holden invaded my thoughts. Pulling my phone out, I pulled up his name and typed out a text.

It was time to start working on my future. The first thing I had to do was admit that a part of my past would never truly be let go. Not a love that strong. I could still see the love in his eyes before I walked away from him a few days ago.

I might not have the future I dreamed of, but I'll always have a piece of him in my heart.

Holden's words from the last night we were together rushed into my mind.

"No matter what happens. I love you. I've always loved you, and I will never love anyone like I love you. Please never forget that."

Me: You're probably back in California, but I wanted you to know I never forgot what you said to me, Holden. I've always loved you too, and I will forever love you. You will always own my heart.

156

I hit send but an error message came up.

Damn. No signal.

I saved the text and made a note to myself to send it when I got back down into town.

"Em?"

Glancing up, I smiled when I saw Carter sandwiched between his parents.

"Mom, Dad, this is a good friend of mine. Emylie Sanchez. Em, these are my parents. Ron and Carrie Davis."

Reaching my hand out, I said, "It's a pleasure meeting you Mr. and Mrs. Davis."

Mrs. Davis smiled warmly. "Please, call us Ron and Carrie."

With a nod, I replied, "Ron and Carrie it is."

"Carter told us you'd like to do some fly fishing?"

Smiling as big as my cheeks would let me, I answered Ron, "Yes, sir. I don't have a rod with me, but Carter promised to let me use one of his."

Carrie turned to Carter and Ron. I could practically see the happiness flowing from her body. "How about I pack up some food and supplies and we head up to the cabin for the day?"

Carter looked at his father. "You feeling up to it, Dad?"

Ron grinned from ear-to-ear. "There is nothing more I'd rather do than that, son."

My eyes misted over as I watched Carter and his father. Whatever had happened in the past was truly buried there. I hardly knew this family, but somehow I felt like I could relate to them.

"Carrie, please let me help you get things ready."

With a nod, she replied, "Yes, please. It's so nice to have another woman to talk to."

With a giggle, I followed her into the house. After a quick tour, we headed to the kitchen and got busy making sandwiches and packing up snacks.

As we filled the two large picnic baskets, Carrie moved from small talk to hard core.

"Emylie, I want to thank you for being here with Carter. I know it was hard for him to take the chance and come home. I had a feeling the moment Ron saw his son, he would get over the silliness of being angry about the Marines."

With a gentle grin, I replied, "Don't thank me too much, Carrie. The moment Carter gave me an excuse to run a little further from my own reality, I jumped on it. My father would be pretty upset with me if he knew I took off in a guy's car whom I'd only known less than twenty-four hours."

Her mouth dropped. "You did what? Oh Emylie, do you know how dangerous that could have been? Thank goodness it was Carter, but don't you ever do such a thing again."

Placing her hand to her heart, she gasped. "I mean to say, if I was your mother I'd put you over my knee right now!"

I couldn't help but giggle, but the moment she shot me a look, I stopped and began chewing on my lower lip in a nervous fit.

"I don't normally do that kind of thing, it's just Carter is best friends with Jax, and I know Jax and I felt safe with him and … well … I um."

That's when it hit me. I slowly sank down in the chair. "What was I thinking?"

My heart started pounding and my hands were so wet from sweat I had to run them over my shorts.

What in the hell was I thinking? And why did it take me this long to realize how stupid I was?

"Emylie, darling look at me."

My gaze lifted and I saw the most beautiful gray eyes staring back at me.

"Whatever it is that made you run off, it won't get any better, sweetheart, the longer you're gone."

I nodded my head. "I'm sure he's gone now. Back to California with his fiancée."

"Oh. I see. Love is a crazy thing, isn't it?"

I nodded in agreement. "May I ask you something, Carrie. It's about Carter."

"Of course."

"When we were down at the end of the driveway, a beautiful girl pulled up. Her name was Tori. You could feel the chemistry between her and him immediately."

Carrie's face lit up as she smiled. "Tori and Carter dated in high school. I'm not sure what happened between the two of them, but they broke things off. From what I could gather, it wasn't something either of them wanted. I never pried and asked Carter why, but I see regret in Tori's eyes every time I run into her."

"I wasn't meaning to stick my nose where it doesn't belong, it's just, the connection between the two was unmistakable. But I think I'm the only one who caught it."

Laughing, she stood. "Oh, I believe that. Sometimes what's right in front of our eyes is the hardest thing to see."

My heart dropped as I took in her words.

Holden breaking up with me. Staying gone for all that time. The way he looked at me.

He was trapped and unhappy, and I saw it the moment he gazed into my eyes that first day he was back.

"He doesn't love her," I whispered.

"What was that, sweetheart?"

Jerking my head to look at Carrie, I shook it. "Nothing. Just talking to myself."

Carter walked into the kitchen with eyes bright as the sun. "Who's ready to get their fishing on?"

I couldn't help but simper. Carter was re-writing his future, and I was about to be a co-writer for part of it.

CHAPTER 20

Holden

I PULLED UP the address to Jamie's house again as I stood in the National Car Rental line. Emylie was less than an hour away from me. My heart sped up in my chest as I thought about seeing her again.

I had stopped by her parents' house yesterday. Not really knowing what to expect, but knowing I needed to be truthful with them.

Telling Mario and Kim everything, I still didn't expect them to welcome me back into their world, let alone their daughter's world with open arms. But they did just that.

My chest felt light as I thought back to what Mario had said to me.

"We all make decisions, thinking they are the right ones at the time. Sometimes they are, and sometimes they send us into a tailspin of bad choices. It's life. It's lessons. It's the way we learn."

I didn't deserve their forgiveness or love. They were like second parents to me, and I vowed to do whatever it was I needed to do to not only win back Emylie's trust, but theirs as well.

They didn't tell me where Emylie was. I told them I knew she was with Jamie. They had tried to call Emylie with no luck, but when they called Jamie she told them Emylie had gone fly fishing and probably had no signal. I was going to ream her ass for going alone.

"Sir? Do you have a reservation?"

Pulling me from my thoughts, I flashed a grin to the girl behind the counter. "Sorry, was deep in thought."

She chortled and said, "I see that. Reservation?"

"Yes. For Holden Warner."

"Here it is. I show here you'll be dropping the car off at our location in Park City."

With a nod, I replied, "Yes, if that's okay. My girlfriend ... I mean ... a friend of mine has her car up there and I'll ride back with her."

Lifting her brow, she gave me a funny look.

"She used to be my girlfriend, then we broke up. I'm trying to get her back. You know, all that win her over by flying-up-to-Utah-to-tell-her-how-much-I-love-her stuff."

"Right. Well good luck with that, Mr. Warner."

I couldn't help but chuckle. "I need all the luck I can get."

Once I got the keys in my hand, I set off for Park City. My hands were shaking and my heart was racing. The faster I got to Emylie, the better. The sinking feeling of dread in my gut was becoming harder and harder to ignore.

Driving up to Jamie's place, I grinned when I saw Emylie's car parked there. She was still here.

Thank God.

Getting out of the car, I started to make my way up to the house. A guy came walking around the side of the house wearing a kind smile.

"Hey there. How can help you?"

Before I could say anything, the screen door on the porch opened and Jamie came out. I'd met her a few times when I came to Texas A&M to surprise Emylie.

When her face turned white as a ghost and she stopped walking, my heart dropped a little.

But I didn't start to panic until she said, "Oh holy fuck. Holden."

"What? This is Holden?" The guy said as he gazed between me and Jamie.

Jamie lifted her brows and nodded. "Yep. This is Holden."

The guy looked back at me and said, "Shit."

I let out a gruff laugh. "Seems like everyone knows me, but I'm not going to lie, y'all are freaking me out a bit with the holy fucks and the shits."

Snapping out of his moment of shock, the guy walked up to me and reached his hand out for mine. Shaking it, he said, "Sorry, dude. So sorry. I'm Jax, Jamie's boyfriend … no wait … fiancé." He lowered his voice so only I could hear. "I recently asked her and I keep forgetting."

I nodded and laughed. "No worries. I'm Holden. But then again, you know that."

He gave me one of those *oh shit you're about to get bad news* looks. "Yeah, I got that. Why don't we head on in and get some tea? It's hot out here."

As we walked toward the house, Jamie swallowed hard and then quickly turned and hurried inside.

Was Emylie hurt? Something was wrong. What in the hell was going on here?

The screen door shut and Jax motioned for me to head on into the kitchen.

"Have a seat, I'll get some iced tea for us."

"Thanks," I said as I looked directly at Jamie. "What's going on? You seem nervous as hell, Jamie."

"Um. Well." She let out a nervous chuckle. "I wasn't expecting to see you. I, um … it's great seeing you. I think. Well you're here, which I think is good."

I shifted on the stool. "I hope it is too."

"You're here for Em … right? You came for her? Like to tell her you love her. Please tell me that's why you're here?"

With a smile, I nodded. "That pretty much is why. I need to ask her to forgive me for some stuff first and hope like hell she does. Then I have some serious making up to do."

Jamie covered her heart and tilted her head. She gave me one of those looks women usually give to a puppy when they see it.

"Oh my gosh, that's so sweet! Isn't that so sweet, Jax?"

Jax, on the other hand, gave me a *you're fucked dude* look. "Yep. So sweet."

Taking a drink of the iced tea, I set it back down. "Um, where is Emylie?"

Panic washed over both of their faces. "Where is she?" Jamie asked.

She was stalling.

"Yeah. Is she around?"

Jamie glanced over to Jax. "Um, Jax?"

He looked at her with a stunned expression on his face. "Don't 'um, Jax' me. This one is all yours."

She placed her hands on her hips and shot him a dirty look. "Me? How is this all on me? He's your best friend."

He?

"She's your best friend and left with him!"

Left with him?

Standing, I glanced between the two of them. "Wait. Emylie left

163

with someone?"

Jamie turned to me. "She's with Carter."

My heart dropped and I felt sick to my stomach.

Glancing back over to Jax, Jamie pointed to him. "Hey, I tried to stop her."

I reached for the counter as the room spun.

"Where are they?" I demanded.

"You didn't try hard enough. The only thing you did was piss her off and practically forced her to get into Carter's truck."

Holy fuck. Emylie's with some strange guy and it's all my fault.

Mario and Kim are going to kill me.

My head was pounding as Jax and Jamie went back and forth arguing whose fault it was.

"Can y'all stop arguing and tell me where in the fuck they went?!" I shouted, getting both of their attention.

Jamie jumped and Jax stared at me.

"Sorry. Um. Well hell, I don't know where to start," Jax said as he took a seat at the bar.

"The beginning would be nice."

"Carter is my best friend. We went to college together. He comes here often when he's on leave."

I arched my brow. "On leave?"

"Yeah, he's in the Marines."

"Wait. Emylie is with some guy she doesn't know. He's in the Marines. And he's your best friend from college. What in the fuck was she thinking leaving with a guy she hardly knows?"

Jamie sat next to Jax. "Well, they met the first night Emylie was here. Then the next morning they went on a hike together. Emylie had broken down on the trail and Carter brought her back here. They talked for a bit more and went on another hike up to the lake. Then they got the bright idea to go fishing. Carter was heading home to see his parents. His father has cancer and they were at odds with each other. I really think Emylie went to get further away from whatever it is she's running from. Or … whoever."

Okay, I deserved that one.

"Where did they go?"

Jamie glanced down at her hands.

"Jamie, I love her. I at least deserve the chance to tell her that and try to get her back."

Jax cleared his throat. "I don't think they're *together* together. Carter called me and said they were at his parents' place. He talks about Emylie like she's just a friend. More like a sister."

My hand ran through my hair and I took in a deep breath. This was my Karma. It wasn't the hell Daphne put me through, it was the knowledge that Emylie could very well meet another man and move on without me. That's probably what she deserved. All I ever did was bring her hurt.

Jamie walked up to me and put her hand on my arm. "I can see the wheels turning in your head, and if you think for one second you should go back to Texas, I'm telling you that is *not* what you should do. I'm not going to lie and say I don't think you are the biggest ass-hole on the planet, but I also don't know the whole story. I'm guessing since you're here, this other girl is out of the picture? What about the baby?"

I shook my head. "She wasn't pregnant. It was all a lie."

Jamie gasped. "What? She lied about being pregnant?"

Nodding my head, I replied, "There is so much more to the fucked-up story. But yes, she knew I was planning on going back to Texas and she came up with a sick plan to try and keep me with her."

"Wow," Jamie and Jax said at once.

"But, maybe if Emylie is with this guy, I should back off."

"Or you fight for her because you love her," Jax said with a grin.

My phone beeped in my pocket. Pulling it out, my stomach twisted when I saw it was a text from Emylie.

"It's a text from Emylie," I said opening it up.

Em: You're probably back in California, but I wanted you to know I never forgot what you said to me, Holden. I've always loved you too and I will forever love you. You will always own my heart.

Jamie hit me on the shoulder and giggled.

"I think you have your answer, Holden."

Glancing up from my phone, I looked between Jax and Jamie and landed my gaze on Jax. "I'm going to need to know where this Carter lives."

CHAPTER 21

Emylie

"IS THAT BACON I smell?"

Glancing over my shoulder, I grinned when I saw Carter. "It is."

He walked up and opened up the refrigerator and took out a Gatorade.

"What are you cooking bacon for?"

"BLTs," I answered, glancing up at the clock.

He pushed off the counter and walked up next to me. "So, did you send the text?"

My chest tightened as I thought about how Holden would react to my text. "Yes. But I haven't had a signal since. I was going to see if your mom was heading into town later so I can check my emails and such."

With a simple nod, he smiled from ear-to-ear. "Did you have fun fishing yesterday?"

I chucked and replied, "Yes. Your parents are amazing, Carter.

I'm really happy you and your dad got things worked out."

He sighed. "Me too. A huge weight has been lifted off my shoulders. I also decided on something."

I took the bacon off the stove and put it on a paper towel. I was cutting it close getting everything ready in time. "Oh yeah? What's that?"

"I'm not going to re-enlist in the Marines."

The flutter in my chest caused me to gasp. Turning to him, I couldn't help but grin. *Oh, this is perfect! Yes, this works nicely with my plan!*

"Really? That's amazing!"

"Well damn, if my mom is half as happy as you are with that news, I'm in for my favorite dessert since I'm already getting my favorite lunch."

Carrie walked into the kitchen and gave me a slight nod. "Everything is ready."

My heart dropped. This could go two ways. One, Carter would be super pissed at me for sticking my nose in his business, or two, Carter and Tori would realize that they are both still hot for each other. It didn't take me long to figure out what had happened between them when I *accidentally* ran into Tori in town last night. When I saw her walking across the street into a book store, I told Carter I was in desperate need for a book.

"Ready for what?" Carter asked, taking a bite of an apple and ripping me away from my thoughts.

Pulling it from his hand, I shook my head. "I'm making an amazing lunch. Don't eat an apple."

He frowned. "It's like we've known each other our whole lives." Glancing over to his mother, he asked, "Is she like a long-lost sister or something?"

Carrie shrugged which made both Carter and I look back at each other and then back to his mother.

"This is where you say no, Mom. Not leave it open like you had some kind of affair or something."

She rolled her eyes and huffed. "Ha ha. Trust me, there are no long-lost brothers or sisters. You've been lucky enough to stumble into a wonderful friendship. They're hard to come by, so cherish it."

Carter looked back at me and winked. "Today is going to be a great day."

My heart jumped with both excitement and nervousness. "I hope so." I dragged in a deep breath and pushed it out. "Now go change."

He glanced down and then back to me. "Why?"

"Because, you're still wearing what you ran in earlier."

Pinching his brows together, he stared at me. "And because we're having BLTs and potato salad, you need me to be dressed differently?"

Without looking at him, I answered. "Yes. At least take off the smelly shirt, you never know who you're going to be hugging."

"What?"

"Go change, Carter!" Carrie cried out.

Lifting his hands in surrender, he shook his head and backed out of the kitchen.

Once he was upstairs, I spun around. "How does it look?"

Carrie's face lit up. "Beautiful. Now, Emylie, are you sure this is the right thing to do?"

After placing lettuce, a fresh tomato, basil and the bacon on the fresh bread, I cut it in half and stuck the toothpicks through each side.

"Did you put basil on that?"

My eyes snapped up to Carrie. "Oh my gosh yes. It's heavenly."

Screwing up her face, she shuddered and whispered, "Gross."

"And to answer you, I know I've only known Carter a few days, and honestly this seems so crazy, but I really feel like we've grown close. He's shared some things with me, and after running into Tori last night and what she shared, I know this is exactly the right thing to do."

"What did Tori say to you last night? You were on a mission after talking to her."

Once I plated the sandwiches, I added some fresh fruit. "I have no idea what made her open up to me, but she pretty much shared with me how when they were together she got spooked knowing Carter would never be able to have kids. She admitted it was a stupid excuse to break up with him, but they were both going off to college and she was scared. She used it as an excuse, and she regrets it every single day. Then, when Carter went into the Marines, she figured she had lost her chance for good."

Carrie stood there with a stunned expression on her face. "She told you that?"

"Yep."

With a slight shake of her head, she asked, "What is it about you that people just spill their guts out?"

With a laugh, I shrugged. "I don't know, but this is going to sound crazy. I feel like God crossed Carter's and my paths for a reason. If you were to tell me a month ago I'd take off with a guy I hardly knew, I'd tell you no way. Not going to happen. But the moment we met, we connected in a way I can't explain. I really want to see him happy."

Tears filled Carrie's eyes. "He said almost the same thing about you earlier. What I think is even better, is you're both clueless to what the other is doing."

"What do you mean?" I asked as I pinched my brows together.

"She's pulling up!" Ron called out as he walked through the kitchen and toward the front door.

"Oh my gosh! This is it," I said while clapping my hands

Carrie covered her mouth. "I hope you read this right, Emylie."

Now I wasn't as sure as I was last night when I came up with this plan. Doubt filled me to the core as I put everything on two trays and motioned for Carrie and Ron to each grab one. "If y'all can take this out, I'll bring Carter out."

With a quick glance at the clock, Carrie laughed. "This is going to be interesting. Very, *very* interesting."

Waving her off, I jetted upstairs. "Carter!" I yelled out as he came running out of his room.

"What? What's wrong?"

"You took a shower? That fast?"

"I'm in the Marines, Em. I can eat, shit, and shower in less than five minutes if need be."

Scrunching my face up in disgust, I shook my head. "That information I could have gone the rest of my life without."

Carter's phone pinged. He lifted it and smiled.

"How are you getting service out here and I'm not?" I asked as we headed back down the stairs.

"If I told you, I'd have to kill you."

I stopped walking, causing him to bump into me. Turning, I gave him a dumfounded look. "What?"

"It's a joke. You know because I'm in the military and all of that."

With a roll of my eyes, I started back down. My heart was pounding as we got closer and closer to heading outside. "I thought we would eat outside since it's so beautiful."

"Perfect. Damn, that works out perfectly."

Stopping again, I turned and held my hand up. "Do you know?"

His face fell. "Do you know?"

"Do I know what?" I asked.

He narrowed his gaze at me and said, "I don't know. What do I know that you don't know?"

With a curious expression, I replied, "What do I know that you don't know that you think I know?"

Carter pushed his hands through his wet air and let out a frustrated sigh. "What in the fuck are we talking about?"

"Well, you tell me Carter because you asked if I knew. Are you hiding something?"

"Are you hiding something?"

"You know!" I cried out.

"No one knows anything! Will the two of you please get out here!" Carrie called from the front door.

Carter and I stood there for another few seconds pinning each other in place. Leaning in closer, I stared into his eyes.

"You don't know."

With a frustrated look, he replied, "I'm beginning to feel like I don't know anything. And I'm questioning how smart it was of me to drive alone with you in the car, you freak."

Laughing, I shot him the finger and headed toward the door. I could see past Carrie and smiled when I saw Tori.

"Carter, please don't be mad at me," I said glancing back over my shoulder.

He chuckled. "That's funny, I was about to say the same thing to you."

As we both stepped out onto the porch, Carter came to a dead stop.

"Tori?"

"Hey, Carter. It's good seeing you again."

"Um, you too. What are you doing here?"

Tori glanced over to me and I grinned. "Well, Emylie invited me to have lunch with you guys."

"Oh, I won't be joining y'all for lunch," I said. I could feel Carter's eyes on me and I risked looking at him. He looked confused. "I think y'all have some reacquainting to do." I pointed over to a large spruce tree that had a table and everything set up for their lunch.

Carter and Tori both looked in the direction I pointed. "How? When? I mean…"

I walked up to Carter and placed my hand on his arm. "Ask me later, get over there before your dad eats the BLTs."

Laughing, Carter turned to me and stared into my eyes. "Thank you," he whispered. I leaned up and kissed him on the cheek. "Good luck."

He glanced at his phone and said, "You too." Giving me a wink, he took off down the stairs and headed over to Tori. They both started walking over toward the little picnic we had set up for them. I knew I had butted into their lives in a big way, but my heart felt happy. Then Carter's words replayed in my head.

You too.

"What did he mean by that?" I asked as I watched them make their way over toward Ron who was guarding the food. Tori kissed Ron on the cheek as Carter pulled out the chair for her. As Ron walked away, I could see Carter quickly getting lost in Tori.

Fist pumping internally, I knew this was going to work. Now I had to convince Carter about this whole no baby-making thing.

The crunching of a car driving on the gravel pulled my stare from Carter and Tori. Turning, I shielded my eyes from the sunlight beaming straight at me.

When the car got closer, my stomach dropped. It was my car.

"Oh shit … please don't be my parents," I mumbled.

Carrie walked up and took my hand. "He called Carter last night. Told him he was on his way here for you."

He? My father.

"How did my father get Carter's number?"

Jamie! She ratted me out to my parents. I'm so going to get her back for this.

Carrie giggled next to me as she squeezed my hand. When the car door opened, I blocked the sun and tried to think of what good excuse I had for leaving with a total stranger and coming to Colorado.

Temporarily insane. He's Jax's best friend. Jamie knew where I was. A broken heart makes you do stupid things.

My breath hitched when I saw him, and I was pretty sure my heart stopped as well.

"Holden," I whispered.

With a smile that sent tingles through my body, he walked toward me. A million different things ran through my mind. I was feeling every emotion possible.

Confusion.

Sadness.

Anger.

Happiness.

Lust.

The way he looked in those jeans and that tight red T-shirt. Not to mention the cowboy hat. God, how I loved Holden in a cowboy hat. My mind was going to mush watching him walk my way with that crooked smile.

Placing my hand over my stomach, I tried to find my voice. When he stopped at the bottom of the stairs, it was then I noticed Carrie was gone. Leaving me alone to deal with Holden standing before me.

Carter knew. Somehow he was a part of this and that was what he was talking about earlier.

My eyes stung with the threat of tears. He wasn't looking at me like he was mad or upset. I'm not sure if I would ever be able to describe the way Holden was gazing up at me.

"Hey, Em. I got your text."

My stomach flipped as a sob slipped from my lips and I covered my mouth.

"I'm so sorry for the hell I put you through. I'm not sure if I deserve a second chance, but I pray to God you'll give me one. I never meant to hurt you. I was stupid and did some pretty stupid things. Some damn stupid things."

My chin trembled as I let his words penetrate into my brain.

"You're my world, Em. I can't live another day without you. I... I. Damn it."

Holden's voice cracked as he wiped a tear from his face. My

whole body ached and I wasn't sure if it was from holding myself back or because I was shaking so badly.

Walking up the steps, he stopped in front of me. "You once told me we were made for each other. No words were ever so true. The last few years I've been so lost, Em. I love … I love you so much. I'm … I'm so s-sorry."

His head dropped and I watched as his body shook. He was crying. Holden was standing before me crying.

My heart pounded so loudly in my ears I could hardly think.

He came for me.

Holden came for me.

Holden

MY BODY LIT up when I felt her hands touch me. Emylie had always held the power to make my body come alive. Lifting my gaze to meet hers, she wiped my tears away.

With a bright expression, she softly spoke. "You came for me?"

Her words were clouded with confusion. Everything about this whole situation was fucking confusing. Me, Daphne, Emylie taking off with a complete damn stranger. I was still pissed she pulled that stunt, but that could wait. Although I talked to Carter for some time last night while driving to Colorado. The guy seemed like someone I could become good friends with. He was concerned about Emylie, that was obvious. He didn't seem interested in her romantically, but I was still on guard.

"I'm sorry it took me so long, baby."

Drawing her head back, she searched my face. "What about ..."

I shook my head. "It's over. She went back to California."

Her brows pinched together. "What ... what about the baby?"

"She's not pregnant."

With a sharp intake of air, Emylie whispered, "What? Did she have a … I'm so confused."

With a slight smile, I dropped my gaze to her lips then back to her eyes. "I'll tell you everything, but first I really need you to kiss me."

The golden flecks in her eyes shined as her stare fell. She pressed her lips to mine, and for the first time in a long time, everything in my world was right again. Her hands came up to my chest as she moaned softly into my mouth. I wanted to deepen the kiss. Show her how much I had missed her. Needed her. Knowing people were around us, I fought like hell to keep my control.

When her hands moved up and around my neck, I pulled her closer to me. Letting her feel how much I had missed her. How much I desired her.

Slowly pulling back, I took off my hat and leaned my forehead against hers. "Em, we need to talk."

Nodding, she replied. "I know. Please tell me this isn't a dream, Holden. The amount of nights I've prayed for this moment, I really need to know I'm not dreaming."

My finger lifted her chin so she could look directly at me. "It's not a dream."

She searched my face before catching my stare again. I could see how lost her eyes were. As much as we both wanted to get lost in each other, I knew I was going to have to earn her trust back.

As if she was reading my mind, she said, "I'm so happy you're here, but I can't just pick up where we left off."

With a quick nod, I answered, "I know."

A voice cleared from behind us, causing both of us to let each other go and take a step back. Emylie's cheeks burned as she attempted to find her voice.

"Carrie, Ron, um, this is Holden. Holden these are Carter's parents."

I reached my hand out and shook both their hands. "It's a real pleasure meeting you both."

"Pleasure is ours."

Two other people walked up about then. "I'm sorry, I didn't mean to interrupt anything," I said, looking at them.

The guy held up his hand as if to say it was okay. "Hey, Holden, I'm Carter."

My heart stopped for a moment as I took him in. The fucker was built, and I could tell he wouldn't have a problem picking up any woman he wanted. This was the man Emylie up and got into a car with it. The thought made my blood boil.

Sticking my hand out, I shook his with a firm handshake. "Nice meeting you, Carter."

He turned and looked at the girl standing next to him. "This is Tori." She extended her hand toward mine as Carter kept talking. "Tori, this is Emylie's ah … her um … what exactly are you guys?"

With a chuckle, I glanced over to Emylie and winked before saying, "We're still trying to figure that all out."

Carrie stepped forward. "Well, it looks like we have two couples who are trying to figure things out."

Emylie turned back to Carter. "Y'all get back down there and eat before something like a bear comes and gets those BLTs!"

Laughing, Carter replied, "Well, we wouldn't want to waste good food." He took Tori's hand and led her back toward what looked to be a picnic set up. I was curious as hell what that was all about.

When I glanced back to Emylie, she was holding Carrie's hand. "I think my plan is going to work. Did you see the way he took her hand?"

Carrie chuckled. "I saw. You're very sweet for doing this, Emylie."

With a quick look in my direction, she said, "Will you give me a few minutes to grab my bag?"

"You're leaving?" Carrie asked.

"Just into town. Maybe stay at a bed and breakfast or something. Holden and I have some things we need to talk about. I promise I won't leave without saying goodbye."

"And dinner! I want to throw a big cookout before you leave. You kind of snuck in here and captured our hearts, Emylie."

With misty eyes, Emylie hugged Carrie and softly said, "Thank you, Carrie."

Drawing back, Carrie glanced between the two of us and smiled. "Go. Talk and figure it all out."

I didn't know these people at all and neither did Emylie. Something I fully intended on talking to her about. But at the same time, I could see how caring they were.

Emylie grinned and kissed Carrie's cheek before rushing into the house.

My heart hammered in my chest and my hands were wet with sweat knowing I was fixing to be alone with her. Would she be able to forgive me? Could she ever trust me with her heart again? Closing my eyes, I silently prayed the answer to both questions were yes.

I had to admit it, Rifle, Colorado was an awesome little town. The perfect place to escape to and figure shit out.

My phone beeped as I waited outside the CVS for Emylie to run in and find out how in the hell we were so lost. With a quick look, I saw it was Daphne.

Daphne: I would like to get my shit from our place. If you don't let me in to the apartment, I'll have Daddy get his lawyers involved.

With a heavy sigh, I typed out my reply.

Me: Really? I'm sure your Dad wants this kept as low key as possible. My lawyer contacted yours this morning. If you checked your phone messages, you would see they are trying to set up a time for you to go pick up your shit. You can have everything in the apartment that isn't mine. I don't want any of it, but you won't be in there alone.

Her response was immediate.

Daphne: Fuck you, Holden. I hate you. You're going to regret this.

Me: The feeling is mutual, and I don't think so.

"You ready?"

My head snapped up. "Yeah. Sorry. Taking care of some bullshit."

Her gaze glanced down to my phone. I wasn't about to hide anything from her, but she needed to hear everything from start to finish.

"It's Daphne. Bitching about not being able to go into the apartment without my lawyer."

She nodded her head. We had agreed to wait until we got to the bed and breakfast before we talked about everything. Most of the conversation was about how Emylie met Carter, how she had met Tori and found out why Carter and Tori had broken up. Basically, Emylie was playing cupid.

"The bed and breakfast isn't too far. Maybe ten minutes. We took a wrong turn."

Pulling back onto the road, I headed in the direction she said to go.

"Okay, turn right here and it's down this road."

I made the turn and stared in awe at the mountains ahead of us. "Holy shit. It's beautiful up here."

"It is beautiful. I feel kind of guilty for leaving Jamie like I did."

With a quick look over at her, she was chewing on her nails. "I have no idea what came over me and why I left like that."

Reaching for her hand, I kissed the back of it. "It all worked out. Like you said, maybe it was fate that brought you and Carter together."

She shrugged. "Maybe."

We both took in a breath of air and said, "Wow," as I pulled up to Four Mile Creek Bed and Breakfast.

"This place is stunning," Emylie said with a huge smile. Pointing to the large log cabin, she added, "There is the office over there."

After parking, we walked in. The smell of pine engulfed me and I couldn't help but remember the times I'd come up to Colorado to fish with my father and Mason. Those were some of my best memories with my father. For a brief moment, I thought about Carter and his dad. I really hoped everything worked out for them. I especially hoped his father beat his fight with cancer.

The door dinged when we walked in, bringing a woman who looked to be in her mid-forties to the desk.

"Hello! You must be Emylie and Holden. Carrie called ahead and said you'd be needing a place to stay. She wasn't sure for how many nights though."

Emylie and I exchanged looks. "Two at the most?" I asked. I couldn't read Emylie at all. If I hadn't known any better, I would say she seemed disappointed.

With a weak smile, she glanced back to the woman. "Two nights please."

"I have a lovely room upstairs with a king size bed that I think you'll love."

Emylie rocked back and forth on her feet. Something she did when she was nervous. "Um, is the suite room open? The one with two bedrooms," she asked in a soft voice.

Ouch. If that wasn't making a clear statement, I don't know what would.

The lady glanced between the two of us with a confused expression on her face.

"Are you not together? Well what I meant to ask is … oh my, never mind. I'm walking on a thin line of none-of-my-damn-business."

All three of us laughed as I pulled out my credit card and handed it to her.

"Well, at any rate, you're going to love the red barn suite. It's located in the milk room and the tack room of our historic barn. Very romantic and … oh, and well I mean, if you're looking for romance, but even if you're not, you will like it."

I stood there staring at her as she tripped over her words. Someone really needed to put this poor woman out of her misery.

Clearing my throat, I said, "Romance is exactly what we need. But a little space as well."

I could feel the weight of Emylie's stare on me. Not daring to chance a look at how she reacted to my comment, I took my card back, smiled, and headed back out to the car. "I'll grab our bags," I called out over my shoulder.

The sooner I got Emylie to the room, the sooner I could finally tell her everything and we could start over again. Something I prayed like hell she wanted to do.

CHAPTER 23

Emylie

MY HEAD SPUN chaotically as I listened to Holden tell me everything from the very beginning. I finally knew the truth as to why he stayed with her after she lost the baby.

"I thought she would kill herself she was so depressed."

I couldn't even bring myself to feel sorry for her.

"Becca and I came up with the plan to have her take the pregnancy test. When she took it and it came up negative, it was like someone switched something on inside of her because she started confessing to everything. Becca and Mason heard it all too. She confessed to drugging me that night, that the first baby wasn't even mine, that she had been trying to get pregnant ever since she found out I wanted to leave and she told me she was pregnant."

My stomach lurched. She lied about both babies and came up with a scheme so crazy insane she actually believed it would work.

She ripped the one thing I loved from me because she was a psychotic bitch.

All I could do was listen and stare at him. Every now and then I would nod so he would know I wasn't in total shock.

"I don't know how I was so stupid, Em. How I let her manipulate me like she did. I've been going over everything in my mind. I hate myself for what I let her put you through."

I sat on the sofa with a stunned expression. My mouth must have opened five times to speak, but nothing came out. Holden had laid a whole lot of shit on me, and I was attempting to process it all.

"She ... she cut holes in the condoms?"

With a nod of his head, he whispered, "Yes. She was never pregnant, and if she couldn't get pregnant, she was going to say she lost the baby."

I pressed my fingers to my temple. "This is so crazy."

All the lies.

The wasted time.

"I can't tell you how many times I wanted to leave her. Tried to leave her."

My head snapped up as I looked into his eyes. I fought to keep the bile down.

"She would somehow suck me back in. I hated every moment I was with her, Em."

I felt as if I was being split in half. I was so relieved to know the truth. To know that Holden hadn't cheated on me, really. That he had been tricked and that he wasn't marrying that witch after all. The other side of me was still hurt that he didn't trust in our relationship enough to tell me the truth in the first place. I wasn't sure how I would have handled it, but I at least deserved the truth. Not some made-up version.

"I'm so sorry to dump it all on you like this, but I needed you to know everything. If I could go back and do it all over again, I would have done it so differently."

Staring into his eyes, I mumbled, "But you can't."

He slowly shook his head. "No, baby, I can't. All I can do is try to prove to you how much I love you and to earn your trust back."

Finding everything out that had happened didn't make the hurt any less. The fact was, Holden thought he had slept with another woman, then lied to me to cover it up. He broke me so badly I wasn't sure I would ever really heal.

My body jumped when he took my hands in his. The feel of him touching me was almost too much to take. I wanted him to take me in his arms and tell me all of this was a bad dream. That none of it had happened.

"Em, your silence is scaring me. Please say something. Anything."

My eyes stung as I fought to keep my tears back.

"I … I don't know what to say to be honest. I'm glad she's not pregnant and that you're not marrying her. She's evil times ten. But, the sting of everything else still hurts. You didn't trust what we had enough to tell me the truth, Holden. Instead, you tore me in half."

He shook his head. "I did it because I thought at the time it was the right thing to do. That's why I never came back home, Em. For one, I was too much of a coward to face you knowing what I did. And the other, I knew the moment I saw you, I'd want you in my arms. Your lips on mine. What I thought was the right thing to do was the exact opposite. I will never be able to tell you how much I wish I could go back and change the fact that I didn't come home that Thanksgiving. Or that I didn't tell you what happened and let you make the decision about us. I've lived in hell with the bad choices I made."

A tear slipped free and slowly made a trail down my cheek. Holden lifted his hand and gently wiped it away.

"I've never stopped loving you. I never will stop loving you. I can't breathe if you're not with me."

The pain in my heart hurt even more. The fact was he had asked her to marry him. He was trying to give their relationship a go and he brought her home for me to see. "You seemed to do fine before. You brought her home because you were marrying her. You worked at that relationship more than you gave ours a chance."

His wore a pained expression. "No, Em. I brought her home because I knew I would never be able to marry her until I saw you. Told you the truth about everything. That day I wanted to meet you for lunch, I was going to tell you everything. I didn't know the whole truth at the time, but what I did know, I was going to tell you. I wanted to ask you if there was any way you'd ever forgive me. If you said we had a chance, I was prepared to do whatever I had to do. The only true thing holding me to her was that I thought she was carrying my baby."

My head was spinning. What was he saying?

"So wait. When you still thought she was pregnant, you wanted to know if we had a future? What were you going to do, Holden?"

"If I thought I had a chance with you … that you would forgive me … I was going to leave her. Figure out custody after the baby was born. I couldn't marry her, Em. Deep down inside of me, I knew I would never marry her. Then, I found out about you and Mason and I was confused. I wasn't sure if I should let you go so that you could move on with your life, or if I should tell you the truth and fight for our love."

My stomach dropped and for some reason, guilt flowed through my veins. Holden's eyes turned sad. "When I saw y'all together, I thought maybe the right thing to do would be to let you live out your life with him. I only had myself to blame for you being with Mason."

"It was never like that with Mason. Ever."

The corners of his mouth rose into a smile that had my insides shaking. *God how I love his smile.*

"I didn't know that at first. The insane amount of anger and jealousy I felt was over the top. All those times I talked to Mason on the phone and he never once mentioned the two of y'all."

"No one knew, really. We used each other to forget. It was that simple."

Holden's gaze fell as he looked at the ground. "I have no right to be angry, but I won't lie to you and tell you I wasn't angry. Because I was fucking furious."

A small chuckle slipped from my lips. "Imagine how I felt seeing you with Daphne."

Throwing his head back, Holden laughed. I loved the way the sound rumbled through my body. When his muscles flexed under his shirt, I sunk my teeth into my lip. I watched as his throat moved as he chuckled more. The memory of moving my lips over his skin hit me. They tingled as if I had actually just done it. The pulse between my legs grew and I had to press my thighs together in an attempt to ease it. I hadn't felt like this since … since the last time Holden touched me.

When he lifted his gaze and caught mine, his breath hitched. He saw it. Surely he felt it. There was no way he couldn't. The energy in the room instantly changed. My body came to life for the first time in months. Years. And it was because of this man.

The intensity of our gaze only grew stronger the longer we stared each other down. My heart pounded so loudly in my ears I barely heard anything else.

"Em," he whispered before drawing away from me.

I reached out and grabbed his arm. The only thing I could do was look down at his mouth. I wanted it on mine. Needed it like the air I breathed.

He had been kneeling on the floor in front of me, trying to read into my response.

"I don't know how this is going to go, Holden. You hurt me and my trust feels like it has been shattered."

When his eyes glassed over, my heart squeezed in my chest. *Could I do this? Would I be able to forgive Holden and start over?*

I wanted to.

More than anything.

The nights I laid awake thinking about him. Dreaming for things to be different.

Well, things certainly were different now, and I had two choices. Walk away from the only man I've ever love, or mend the hurt between us.

"There isn't a day that will go by where I won't prove to you how sorry I am. How if I could take back what happened—"

My fingers pressed against his lips as I dropped to my knees.

Tears fell freely as I swallowed hard and shook my head. The fear in Holden's eyes was evident. We needed to start the healing by being completely honest with each other.

"As much as I want you, I need to move slow. My heart has to heal, and I truly believe the only way for it to heal is with you … with your love. But I'm wounded, Holden. The scars are going to take time to heal."

His hands cupped my face and I watched the man I love openly shed tears. It was more than my heart could take.

The way he searched my face before he pinned me with the intense stare. "I don't deserve you, but I'm greedy."

His lips pressed against mine. Rediscovering each other was going to be both amazing and gut wrenching. I truly believed that if we fell into bed right then, it would do more harm than good.

My hands gripped onto Holden's forearms as we both moaned into each another's mouths. The feel of his unshaven face against my skin was both painful and delicious.

Holden's hand slid up into my hair as he gripped it, tugging slightly back, opening my mouth to him. The move turned me on as I struggled to maintain my control. When Holden bit down on my lip and deepened the kiss, I felt a little bit of my resolve slip. I had forgotten how much of a hold this man had over me. His kisses were like crack, and I was in desperate need of a fix.

My body shook as every emotion possible rushed through my veins. Love. Desire. Fear. Hurt. All of it swirled around pulling me deeper into him. When his other hand wrapped around my waist, drawing me flush against his body, I whimpered. The feel of his own need pushed into my stomach. I was two seconds from begging him to make love to me.

Then his lips were gone.

Our foreheads rested against each other and each breath was a labored chore. My chest rose and fell to the same rhythm as his.

"My God, I forgot how lost I get with you, Em," Holden said between breaths.

With a smile, I wrapped my arms around his neck. His hands snaked around my waist, luring me as close as he could.

"I've missed you," I whispered as I placed soft kisses over his face.

Drawing back, he gave me the same smile I fell in love with when I was five years old. I couldn't help but return it. "I've missed you too."

He lifted his hand and pushed a piece of my brown hair behind my ear. "Do you know what I think we should do?"

I tilted my head and lifted my brow as I asked, "What?"

"Go dancing. I miss having you in my arms."

My heart fluttered at the idea. Dancing was something Holden and I were good at together. Well, one of a few things.

"That would be amazing fun!"

His hand rested on my cheek, and I leaned into it. "You should call Carter and see if he and Tori want to come."

The excitement at the thought caused me to smile even bigger. "Really?"

"Yes! It sounds like you're working hard at getting these two together, so why not give them another nudge."

I kissed him quickly on the lips. "I love you!"

Standing, I went to turn and grab my phone when Holden reached for my hand. He stood and laced his fingers with mine. When his gaze caught my stare, I held my breath. The look on his face was serious.

"You have no idea how wonderful that sounds coming from you. I love you too."

I turned away as I felt my cheeks burn. Not from embarrassment, but from desire. When I felt like I was strong enough to look back at him, I did. "I've never stopped loving you, Holden."

"I'm going to work my ass off to gain your trust back, Em. I swear to you."

Squeezing his hand, I nodded. I wanted to believe that everything was going to be okay, but deep down inside, I knew this was only the beginning of the battle.

Holden

EMYLIE AND I sat on the front porch of the bed and breakfast holding hands as we waited for Carter and Tori.

"So did he say how the lunch went?"

Emylie chewed on her lip. "I think he was happy he got to spend some time with Tori, but he's upset with me because I had a friend of mine refer him to a specialty doctor."

My interest was piqued. "What kind of doctor?"

With a frown, she said, "Promise you won't say anything to him?"

"Of course not."

"Carter got sick with a virus when he was younger. He can't have kids. That's why Tori broke up with him. She got freaked out because she wanted kids."

The ache in my chest for Carter was genuine. "Damn. What about adoption? They could always do that."

Emylie nodded. "Carter hasn't been tested since they originally told him he couldn't have kids. There have been tons of cases where men who have thought they were sterile actually are not. Carter needs to be seen again."

My mouth dropped slightly open. "And you're pushing him to do this?"

She nodded.

"Wait. How in the hell do you even know this about him?"

The jealousy was quickly bubbling up to the surface. Pushing it away, I waited for her answer.

Wringing her hands together, she looked at me. "I was telling him about what happened with Daphne. It was Carter who planted it in my head that you were probably drugged and he even questioned her truth on being pregnant. When I asked him how he could take your side, he told me it had happened to him."

"What? With who?"

With a shrug, Emylie answered, "Not sure. The girl drugged him and said she was pregnant. When Carter told her she couldn't be pregnant with his baby because he couldn't have kids, she confessed to making it all up and drugging him to sleep with him."

My stomach clinched and I instantly felt sick. "What in the hell is wrong with some women?"

Emylie let out a long sigh. "I have no clue."

Before I could say anything else, a truck pulled up and honked. "That's Carter," she said standing. My heart caught fire as we headed to the truck. She never once dropped my hand until she slid into the back seat of the truck.

"Hey guys!" Tori said spinning around and smiling at us. She wiggled her eyebrows and Emylie gave a slight smile in return. "Are you ready to try and keep up with Carter and me on the dance floor?" She looked at Carter who beamed back at her. "It's been a few years, but I'm sure we haven't lost our touch.

With a giggle, Emylie reached for my hand again as she winked then looked at the overly confident couple in the front seat. "Please, you haven't seen dancing until you've seen us on the dance floor."

Carter tossed his head back and let out a cackle. "It's totally on!"

"Winner gets?" I inquired.

Carter smiled bigger. "Mad respect."

Emylie huffed. "And what about the loser, and who is going to judge?"

"Loser, both of them, will have to stand on the bar and sing a song the winners pick out. Don't you worry your pretty little head about who will judge. I know the perfect person and they'll be fair."

Before I could counter, Emylie called out. "Deal!"

"Wait!" I cried out. "Em, you don't even know how good they are."

She leaned in closer to me, sliding her hand along the inside of my thigh, causing my dick to instantly starting fighting with my jeans for room. "Trust me," she whispered in my ear and then kissed my neck.

Jell-O.

I was nothing but Jell-O.

Carter and I sat at the bar and talked about hunting while Emylie and Tori whispered about something. Every now and then they would both peek up at us and smile. It wasn't lost on me that Carter and I were both attempting to win back our high school loves.

"You should really come to my dad's ranch. We'd love to have you. Get you a whitetail Texas deer and check out the amazing stocked tank we have thanks to Emylie."

Carter glanced over to the girls. "I like the sound of that."

I was ready to move on from the small talk. "So what's the deal with you and Tori?" I asked before taking a drink of my beer.

Placing his attention back on me, he shrugged. "High school sweethearts, broke up during college because I couldn't give her the things she wanted."

My gaze drifted over to Emylie. "At least you didn't destroy her by cheating."

His hand gripped my shoulder as he gave it a squeeze. "You're here now, and that's all that matters. And she loves you like mad."

My stomach felt like someone had sucker punched me. "What makes you say that?"

Carter let out a laugh. "The very first time she spoke about you I could see it in her eyes. Hear it in her voice. It doesn't take a rocket scientist to see how much the two of you love each other."

With a huge grin, I stood and slapped him on the back. "And if you think you're not head over heels for Tori still, you're crazy. By the way, she looks at you like she wants to devour you."

His gaze snapped over to Tori while the corners of his mouth curved up. "The feeling is mutual. But I can't help but keep being reminded of why we broke up in the first place."

I wasn't about to let him know I was aware of his problem. "It'll all work out. For both of us."

Emylie walked up with the most beautiful look on her face while Tori followed her. "I think we should get this dance contest started, don't you?"

Wrapping my arms around her waist, I pulled her to me. What I wouldn't give to sink myself balls deep inside her tonight. The thought alone had me aching. "Let's show 'em, babe."

Her eyes lit up and I loved how those golden flecks sparkled.

Vince Gill's "Make You Feel Real Good" started.

Not being able to contain my smile, I winked and pulled her out onto the dance floor. Carter and Tori were close behind us. Once we hit that sawdust floor, I spun her around before tucking her against my body and taking off. If there was one thing I knew we did good together, it was two-stepping. Fuck, we'd been dancing together since we were in seventh grade. A few spins, a couple flips in the air, and I knew we had this thing clenched.

Emylie laughed as her brown ponytail swung around with each spin. Each time I pulled her back into me, I made some kind of face to insinuate something sexual. I didn't know how Emylie was feeling, but I was so fucking turned on I wanted to beg her to let me have one small taste of her.

"Why, Mr. Warner, you haven't lost your touch at all."

My chest warmed with the way she was taking me in. "It's my partner."

Her eyes turned dark as they fell to my mouth, causing me to swallow hard. The song changed and the air between us instantly charged as I held her up against me while we glided across the floor.

"I love this song," she grinned.

"The words, Em. They're so true."

When a tear slipped and trailed down her cheek, I pulled her into my chest and held her tight. "I love you so much."

The lyrics to Russell Dickerson's "Yours" played as I held the love of my life in my arms. Just holding her gave me the greatest high I'd ever experienced.

She was mine. I planned on spending the rest of my life earning her trust and love back.

And if I had to, I'd wait forever for her.

CHAPTER 25

Emylie

MY HEART WAS racing as Holden and I danced. I wanted more than anything to be with him, but we needed to take things slow. Less than a week ago, he was engaged to another woman. Expecting to have a child with her. I needed to make sure my heart wasn't going to be ripped out again when I least expected it.

The song ended and we took a step back from each other. I instantly missed the smell of his musky cologne. He was my weakness; there was never any doubt about that.

"I wonder who won?" I asked with a grin.

Holden surely could see how much I was fighting the urge to be closer to him. At least I prayed he could see it. I knew he was doing the same. Especially when he was the one who stopped our kiss from earlier. Had we kept on with it, I'm not sure either of us would have had the strength to quit.

Taking my hand in his, he replied, "Let's go find out, shall we?"

As we walked up to Carter and Tori, I couldn't help but smile at the way his arm was around her waist. When he glanced over his shoulder to us, he frowned. *Oh gosh. I hope he still isn't mad about the whole doctor thing. Maybe I pushed too hard and stuck my nose in a bit too much.*

My smile faltered a bit as we stopped directly in front of him. "Are we okay, Carter?"

His eyes softened as the corner of his mouth rose slightly. "Of course we are, Em. But we need to talk."

Chewing on my lip, I nodded. Holden squeezed my hip with his hand, sending a rush of desire through my body, making me quickly forget the nerves I felt not a moment ago.

"So. Who won?" Holden asked.

We all looked at the older bartender. Turned out he used to be a professional dancer back in the day and even starred in couple of movies before retiring to Colorado. At first I wasn't so sure he would be neutral, but he assured me he would be.

With a quick laugh and a shake of his head, he pointed to Holden and me. "By a landslide, those two won."

I jumped as I clapped my hands then hugged Holden.

"What?!" Carter cried out. "Billy, how can you say that? I've known you for years."

With a shake of his head, Billy replied, "And over those years I swear your dancing has gotten worse, boy. Those two danced circles around you. They even did a few flips."

Carter turned back and glared at me as I shrugged. "You did flips? Seriously?"

I tried like hell not to laugh. I knew from the other day when we danced that Carter wasn't that great of a dancer. Our chances of beating him and Tori were very good.

Holden laughed then asked, "Now what was it the loser had to do?"

With a quick look of terror on his face before he smiled, Carter walked up to Holden and gave him a slap on the back. "Let me buy you a drink, buddy, and we'll talk about the elk hunting trip you want to take."

Rolling my eyes, I glanced over to Tori. The way she was staring at Carter spoke volumes. The love in her eyes was unmistakable. I hoped Carter would end up at Tori's place tonight.

"Your mind is racing."

Goosebumps raced across my body as the scruff from Holden's unshaven face brushed against my neck.

"Sorry. It was," I replied with a slight chuckle.

"Em, I'm exhausted with the drive and everything. Would you mind if we headed back to the bed and breakfast?"

My breath caught in my throat. Would I be strong enough to resist the urge to keep my distance? I had to be. Falling into bed together would be the last thing to help us get through all of this. It would be nice … but not the right thing to do.

"Of course we can head back. I'm tired myself. Do you mind if I speak with Carter for a moment?"

A look passed over Holden's face before he grinned and replied, "Sure. Not at all."

Making my way over to Carter, I asked if he had a minute to talk before Holden and I took off. We walked around the bar and stood up against the wall. "I'm not mad, Em."

I let out a relieved breath. "I agreed to be tested again."

There was no way I could hold back my smile. "I'm glad, Carter."

He shook his head and smiled. "You blew into my life and turned it upside down, I hope you know that."

Scrunching up my nose, I replied, "But it needed to be tossed about right?"

"It sure did."

Carter pulled me into his arms and hugged me. "It's all going to work for you and Holden, Em. I know it."

Reaching back to look into his eyes, I replied, "I think so too."

"Now get on out of here. Have a good night."

With a wiggle of my eyebrows, I giggled. "You too! Don't behave!"

Carter laughed as he led me back over to where Holden and Tori were talking.

"Ready?" I asked, glancing at Holden.

"Yep." Reaching his hand out to Carter, he flashed him a large smile. "How about you deliver that song tomorrow night?"

With a grin bigger than the Grand Canyon, Carter nodded and replied, "I'm totally down with that. Totally."

"Um, I'm actually pretty tired myself," Tori said with a smile.

After saying goodnight, Holden took my hand and led me to the taxi. He held the door open and went to say something but quickly stopped himself. I wasn't sure how to read things between us right now. Was he struggling with this as much as I was? The need to be with him was almost unbearable. Yet, I couldn't forget everything that had happened over the last few years.

The drive back was filled with small talk, anything to keep from thinking of what it was going to be like pulling up to the bed and breakfast and head to two separate bedrooms.

"Did you enjoy your evening?" Holden asked as he took my hand in his and led me to the door.

With a warm smile directed at him, I nodded. "Very much so. I haven't had that much fun in a long time."

"Not even with Mason?"

My smile quickly faded as his eyes dropped to the ground. "I didn't mean for it to come out like that, Em."

"I was lost, Holden, and so was he. The easiest thing to do was turn to someone who felt safe."

Holding up his hand, he shook his head. "You don't have to explain anything to me. I have no right to even bring any of it up. I was the one who pushed you into his arms in the first place."

My heart hurt as I looked into his eyes. "It was never anything more than sex."

He nodded, but I could still see the regret in his eyes. I hated Daphne even more for what she did to us. The time she stole, the hurt she caused. The only thing I could do was hope that someday her Karma would come back and bite her in the ass hard.

"I should probably get some sleep," Holden finally said, breaking the awkward silence.

The only thing I could do was smile and nod my head. "Same here. Goodnight, Holden."

Taking a step closer to me, his eyes met mine. His hands cupped my face while my tongue traced my lips, anticipating his soft kiss. "I love you, Em."

Swallowing hard, I placed my hands on his chest. My fingers itched to slide up and into his hair, pulling his lips to mine. But the only thing I could do was softly reply, "I love you too. Sleep good."

He leaned over and gently kissed me on the lips. "Night, babe."

My stomach clenched as I whispered, "Night."

And like that, he turned and vanished behind the bedroom door. Leaving me alone in the living room.

This was what I wanted.

Separation.

So why did it make me feel so completely alone and lost?

Slowly turning, I headed to my room as I ran my fingers over my still tingling lips. I stripped out of my clothes and took a long hot shower. Slipping on a T-shirt and a pair of shorts, I climbed into the large king-size bed and pulled the covers up to my chin. It didn't take long for the tears to start falling.

In the darkness of my room, I sobbed, "I hate you, Daphne."

I glanced at the sunlight shining through the window as I rolled over. Panicked, I sat up quickly and looked around.

Where am I?

Closing my eyes, I let out a small sigh escape from my lips as I realized I was at the bed and breakfast.

The smell of bacon filled my nose, and I couldn't help but smile. Pushing the covers away, I made my way to my private bathroom. Quickly brushing my teeth, I pulled my hair up into a ponytail and pinched my cheeks to give them some color.

I slowly inhaled a deep breath then let it out and made my way to the kitchen. I stopped in my tracks when I saw him.

Holy. Shit. My libido just shot out the roof.

Holden stood at the stove with nothing but a pair of low hung sweatpants on. His hair was wet from what I guessed was a shower. He always did like to get up at the crack of dawn and run.

Dear Lord help me, because this man is the picture of sexy.

Squaring off my shoulders, I rolled my neck and took in a few quick breaths. *You've got this, Em.*

Stay strong.

Holden started humming a song and my panties instantly grew wet. His voice sounded like heaven as he sang along with Kenny Chesney.

My mouth opened to say something, but my stupid voice cracked. Luckily, he didn't hear me. Clearing my throat, I walked up to the kitchen island and tried with all my might to sound completely normal. Even though I was far from normal.

"Good morning!"

Spinning around, Holden flashed me that damn smile of his. I gripped the island and held on until my legs stopped wobbling.

"Hey there, beautiful. How did you sleep?"

Like shit. "Good. You?"

He pouted and my heart melted. "Afraid I slept like shit."

"I'm sorry. Was the bed not comfortable?"

With a curt laugh, he shook his head and turned back to the eggs. "No babe, it wasn't the bed."

I wanted to ask him why had he not slept good, but I already knew the answer. "Can I confess something?" I asked was I watched the muscles in his back flex each time he moved.

Moving the eggs around in the frying pan, he answered, "Sure you can."

"I didn't sleep very well either. As matter of fact, I couldn't sleep at all."

Holden turned back to face me. "Why not?"

"Knowing you were in the room next to me ... I ached the entire night."

He tossed the spatula onto the island and moved so fast I gasped when he drew me into his arms. The feel of his bare chest caused my insides to tremble. His lips smashed to mine while my arms wrapped around his neck, pulling him closer to me. The kiss deepened and we both moaned into each other's mouths.

The ache between my legs grew as I felt him press his hard length against my body. "Let me ease your ache, Em."

My body practically caught fire as his husky voice spoke against my lips. I knew if I said yes, neither one of us would be able to stop. I was trembling from his kiss alone.

Leaning my forehead against his chest, I took in a deep breath. "As much as I want to say yes, I know what will happen."

"I promise you, I'll make sure we stop. Let me make you feel good."

My betraying body was starting to win the battle against my head. The feel of Holden's lips across my neck caused my heartbeat to race faster than it as in a long time.

"Please, babe, please let me do this for you."

The walls were quickly tumbling down around me, and I was about to give in when the smoke alarm went off. Holden and I both turned to look at the stove.

Holden took off toward the stove like a lightning bolt. "Fuck! The eggs are burning."

My chest was rising and falling with each forced breath. *Holy shit. That was close.*

I watched as he dumped the burnt eggs in the sink then ran water over the pan. "Damn, I really wanted to make you breakfast tacos." He glanced up. "Who puts a fire alarm right above a stove?"

A giggle escaped from my lips. Like the crazed woman I was, I stood there and watched his body move. "Looks like we're heading out for breakfast."

Snapping his head to look at me, he forced a smile. "Sure. If that's what you want to do."

With a nod, I replied, "Yep. I'll go change. Maybe we should see if Carter and Tori want to join us."

The look of disappointment on Holden's face wasn't hard to miss. "Sounds good, Em."

With a poor attempt at a smile, I turned and headed back to my room. When I shut the door, I covered my mouth and shut my eyes.

I'd never wanted a man as much as I wanted Holden. But was my heart ready for this?

My head told me no, but body was very much saying yes.

CHAPTER 26

Holden

MY DICK HAD been aching ever since Emylie confessed why she couldn't sleep last night. Little did she know, I had to jack off in the shower twice last night because I couldn't get her off my damn mind.

Now we were walking into a goddamn restaurant for breakfast when I could have had her for breakfast. Stupid fucking eggs.

With a tug on my arm, Emylie said, "There they are!"

Oh joy. It was breakfast with Carter and Tori. It wasn't like I didn't like them, but I was fighting a damn hard-on since the kiss in the kitchen.

Carter stood and smiled as he leaned over and kissed Emylie on the cheek. Turning to me, he pulled his head back and pinched his brows together. Then he laughed.

Fucker.

Shaking my hand, he pulled me into him and whispered so only I could hear, "Rough night, buddy?"

I gave him a push as I shot him a dirty look while I replied, "And morning."

His head tossed back in another laugh.

We both sat as Emylie and Tori quickly started their own private conversation. "I take it by the smile on Tori's face you had a good night."

That bastard leaned back and grinned from ear-to-ear. "Best fucking night of my life."

With a roll of my eyes, I lifted my empty coffee cup and motioned for the waitress. She flashed me a smile and a nod.

"I'm honestly happy for you, Carter," I replied quietly.

He glanced back over to the girls. "Did Emylie tell you about the little stunt she pulled with the doctor?"

"Yeah. She did. What are you going to do about it?"

"I made an appointment. I'm going to have to get personal with a fucking cup."

This time it was my turn to laugh. I hadn't known Carter for very long, but it felt as if we had known each other for years. "Dude, that was more information than I needed to know."

He sighed. "I'll be honest, I'm hoping she's right. With me getting out of the Marines soon, I'd really like to start thinking about my future. And my dad being sick and all."

With a look of understanding, I nodded. "Stay positive and everything will work out how it should."

With a slight grin, he glanced up at the waitress as she poured my coffee. "Thank you," I said.

It wasn't hard to know notice how our waitress smacked her gum as she talked. She was balancing three plates in one hand and held the coffee pot in the other. With a wide grin, she replied, "Anytime. What can I get you and the lady to eat?"

"I'll have the garden omelet," Emylie stated with a sweet grin.

Turning back to me, I stated, "The same for me please."

"Two garden omelets coming up."

Carter bumped my shoulder and asked in a whispered voice, "How are things going?"

My eyes landed on Emylie as I watched her mouth turn into another wide smile. Clearly Tori was telling her about her night with Carter. Both of them were blushing like teenage girls.

"I guess as good as can be expected. She doesn't want me touching her. About all I can do is kiss her."

Carter stood, causing both girls to glance up at him. "If you ladies will excuse us, Holden's going to take a look at my truck."

Lifting her brow, Emylie asked, "Why? Is something wrong with it?"

I glanced back to Carter, curious as hell as to what he was going to say. "Nah, he wants to see the engine I have in it."

"Oh," Tori and Emylie both said together. They seemed satisfied with the answer and promptly went back to talking.

I slowly stood and followed Carter out to the parking lot. We walked over to his truck where he lifted the hood and then turned to face me.

"Holden, I see it in your eyes and you're wrong."

With a confused expression, I asked, "What in the hell do you mean you see it in my eyes?"

"You're overthinking why Emylie is keeping you at a distance."

I let out a gruff laugh. "No. It's pretty obvious. She doesn't want me touching her, sleeping with her, hell, I'm surprised she lets me kiss her. Not that I can blame her. I ripped her heart out and then acted like a total asshole. She asked for separate rooms, Carter. Trust me when I say we are acting more like friends than anything."

"You have to give her time. Put yourself in her shoes, dude. How would you feel? Would you be ready to jump back into a sexual relationship if she had recently been engaged to another man and thinking she was going to be having a baby?"

"Yes! Because I love her and she is the only woman I've ever wanted. Will ever want."

Carter rolled his eyes. "Maybe that wasn't the right question for a guy to answer."

I leaned against his truck. "This morning I misread her. I thought she was asking me to … to …"

Lifting his eyes, he asked, "To what?"

With a frustrated sigh, I replied, "I thought she wanted to feel good. I told her I didn't expect anything in return, but she turned me down. Flat ass turned me down."

"You ever stop and think maybe she's afraid?"

"Of me? I've known her my whole damn life. I'd never do anything to hurt—"

Carter's brow lifted. I felt like a complete idiot.

Scrubbing my hands down my face, I groaned. "Fuck. Will she ever be able to trust me again?"

"She will."

I kicked at the dirt. "That's easy to say, but what if we can't move past this?"

"Do you love her?"

I felt my eyes burn. "More than anything."

"She loves you. She told me there would never be another man who she would love like she loved you."

My head jerked back in surprise. "She told you that?"

"Yep. Holden, give her time. It's going to take you earning her trust back. You already own her heart. Just be patient for her to remember that. Right now she is blinded by all the hurt."

"Hey guys?"

We both looked back to the restaurant to see Emylie standing there. "Breakfast is on the table. You done talking about engines?"

My heart ached. I knew Carter was spot on. Damn. I needed to be patient. I'd give Emylie the space she wanted, but there was no way in hell I'd ever give up on her. I'd never stop fighting for her love.

Another night of twirling Emylie and Tori around the dance floor and I was spent. I had talked to my lawyer earlier. We knew Daphne was going to hit us with something, I just didn't know what it was going to be. She remained quiet, which wasn't a good sign. The only communication I had gotten from her since she called the other day was an email begging me to forgive her and come back. Then another one right afterwards that said she was going to get her revenge on me.

The woman was crazy.

Tipping the beer bottle back, I finished it off. I hit the bar and asked for another. "Hey there, cowboy. I've never seen you around here before?"

My eyes glanced down the body of the tall blonde standing in front of me. Her tits were practically spilling out of her shirt, and I swear I couldn't figure out how in the hell she walked in the tight-ass skirt she had on.

Being the polite southern gentleman my momma would want me to be, I replied, "I'm not from around here. My girlfriend is visiting a friend."

With a pout, the blonde replied, "Girlfriend, huh? Serious?"

Grabbing the new beer, I answered, "Very. You're wasting your time with me."

Her shocked expression almost made me smile, but I held it back. *What in the hell? When did women become so damn forward?*

Turning away, I focused on the band playing. They were good and should've been in Nashville and not playing in this small town bar in Colorado.

I felt her before I even knew she was there. My arm caught on fire when she touched it. "Hey there."

I smiled and turned to her as I leaned down and kissed her on the lips. The blonde groaned and went off to find the next poor bastard she was planning on hitting on.

"What was wrong with her?"

Rolling my eyes, I shrugged. "Don't know, don't care. I informed her I was here with you."

Emylie's teeth sunk into her lower lip. "I heard."

What I wouldn't do to have those plump sweet lips wrapped around my cock while I buried my face in her pussy.

"You okay, Holden?"

"What?"

Her face constricted up in a concerned look. "You're breathing heavy. Are you feeling okay?"

No. You cause my body to burn with an aching fucking desire. "Yeah, I think I'm just tired. I think I'll head back to the bed and breakfast. Especially since we're heading home tomorrow. If you want to stay, go ahead. I'm sure Carter can give you a ride back, you look like you're having fun."

She stared at me like I had grown two heads. "Holden, is everything okay? You've been kind of ... distant."

I had been trying to give Emylie her space. Maybe I was trying too hard. Placing my hands on her hips, I dug my fingers into her and pulled her to me. With a brush of my lips across hers, I answered her. "Everything is fine, baby. I'm really tired and dreading the drive back to Texas. I have to leave to head to California the day after we get back."

Her mouth parted open. "Oh. You're going back?"

Lifting my hand, I traced my finger along her jaw. "Only to sign some paperwork for my lawyer to get out of my lease and get my stuff. I shouldn't be gone more than one day. Then I'm heading straight back to you."

The tears building in her eyes about dropped me to the ground. "That makes sense. Having to go back and all."

I kissed her forehead. "You staying here or coming with me?"

She searched my face, as if she was looking for her answer. "Well, I'd rather leave with you, if that's all right."

My stomach dropped. *Thank you, God.* I was scared to death she was going to want to stay here.

Resting my hand against her cheek, she leaned into. "You know I want you with me, Em. I didn't want you to leave if you weren't ready."

She pursed her lips tightly. "I'm ready."

With a smile, I kissed the tip of her nose. "Great, then let's go say our goodbyes."

The ride to the bed and breakfast was filled with chatter and laughter as Emylie and I reminisced about the crazy times in high school. I held her hand and rubbed my thumb across it the entire drive. Anything to have contact with her.

"Do you remember the time you and Mason talked us into going to that old run down house and claimed it was haunted?"

I shook my head and chuckled. "I think we scared ourselves more than we scared you and Becca."

Sirens rang out and I looked in the mirror.

"Shit."

Emylie glanced over her shoulder. "Were you speeding?"

"Nope."

She covered her mouth to hold back her laughter. I was always getting pulled over for every little thing. The first day I got my license I got pulled over because the light on my license plate was out.

Rolling down the window, I waited for the officer to walk up.

"Evening, sir, ma'am?"

I tipped my head. "Evening officer."

"You know why I'm pulling you over, son?"

Glancing at Emylie, I looked to see if she knew. She shrugged.

"No sir, I do not."

"Your license plate light is out. Can't see your license."

Emylie busted out laughing and the officer shined his flashlight in her face. "Why is that funny?"

Dropping her hands to her lap, she turned to him. "This is like the fourth time he has been pulled over for almost the same thing."

The officer leaned forward. "Have you not changed the light?"

I chuckled. "No sir, it's been years between. The first day I got my license I was driving my father's truck and got pulled over for the tail light. A couple years later I got pulled over in my mom's car … same reason. This is um, this is Emylie's car."

Holding her hand up, she giggled again.

"I see. Well, give me your license and registration, and we'll see what we can do."

Giving him what he asked for, I dropped my head back and sighed when he walked back to his car. Turning my head to look at Emylie, she was laughing so hard she had tears rolling down her face.

"It's so not funny, Em."

She nodded. "It is! It really is!"

After giving me yet another warning, I made a mental note to stop at an auto parts store to buy another light bulb. When we walked into the living room of our suite, I headed to the kitchen and offered her a bottle of water. She looked so fucking cute standing there with a smile on her face.

"No. I um … I don't need a water."

Walking up to her, I leaned down and gently kissed her on the lips. "Good night, Em. I'll see you in the morning. Maybe give those breakfast tacos another go-round."

She giggled and placed her hand on the side of my face. Her thumb brushed across my cheek, causing a rush of blood straight to my betraying cock. I couldn't help but notice as she glanced down quickly before piercing my eyes with her. "Night, Holden."

"I love you."

Her eyes filled with those damn tears again. I had no idea how to read them. Were they happy? Sad? Just ask her.

"Em, are you okay?"

She instantly chewed on her lip. "No. I feel like something changed between us today, and I think it's my fault."

Thud. There went my heart. "What? No! God, no."

"Then why are you barely even looking at me? You've been acting strange ever since this morning when—"

Fear replaced the sadness in her eyes. I dropped my bottled water onto the sofa and cupped her face within my hands.

"Look at me, Emylie. I'm not going to lie and say I wasn't disappointed this morning when you turned me away, but I will not force you into anything you don't want or are not ready for. I'm giving you the space you need for me to earn back your trust."

A single tear slid down her cheek. I quickly wiped it away. "Please don't cry, baby."

"I'm so scared, Holden. I want more than anything to be with you. For it to be like nothing has happened between us, but I can't. At least not right now. I may need a bit more space, but I still need."

Pressing my lips to hers, I let my tongue explore every fucking inch of her mouth. Nipping on her lip, Emylie moaned slightly, sending the vibration straight to my dick. Slipping my hand around her waist, I pulled her closer to my body. Her hands laced through my hair as she pulled me even closer to her. The kiss turned needier. The passion between us was clearly not something we had to worry about.

Emylie finally broke the kiss. I leaned my head against hers as I fought to pull in the air I needed to stay up right.

"Sleep with me tonight, Holden."

My heart jumped to my throat. "Wh-what?"

"No sex. But I need to be in your arms. Feel your body next to mine."

Holy fuck. *Could I sleep next to her all night and not touch her?*

Yes. I'd do anything for her. Even if it meant suffering from the worst case of blue balls I'd probably ever have in my entire life.

Taking her hands in mine, I guided us to her room. "I need to get something to sleep in."

There she went chewing on that damn lip. If she asked me to sleep naked, I was going to have to put my foot down.

"Okay. I'm going to wash my face and brush my teeth. I'll meet you in there?"

Jesus, what am I getting myself into?

"I'll be in a couple of minutes." One more kiss on her lips and I rushed off to brush my teeth and see if I could jack off in record time.

CHAPTER 27

Emylie

I STOOD IN front of the bathroom mirror and stared at my reflection. Lifting my hand, I couldn't keep it from shaking.

"Oh God. What did I do?"

My eyes lifted back to the mirror. *You invited Holden into your bed. You idiot!*

Turning, I began pacing across the small bathroom floor.

What was I thinking? I asked Holden to sleep in the same bed with me! The ache between my legs had been throbbing since this morning when he wanted to make me come. I should have let him.

I stopped walking. "No. No, I shouldn't have. I need to be strong."

My cell phone rang, causing me to jump. Quickly grabbing it, I saw it was Becca. "Becca!"

"What? Oh my God. What's wrong? I'll kill him!"

"Who?"

"I don't know. Holden? I'm assuming it's him that has you all freaked out."

"It is! I asked him to sleep with me."

Silence.

"Becca?"

"I'm trying to figure out now if you're excited or freaked out. I'm not really sure how I should be reacting to this."

"Freak out! You should be freaking out. Did you hear me? I asked him to *sleep* with me. No sex, just him in the same bed with me."

Becca covered the phone and said something to someone. Probably Mason. "Okay, so let me get this correct before I interject my thoughts on the whole thing."

I rolled my eyes. "Hurry, he'll be in here soon."

"Right. So you invited him into your bed, but you said no sex. Is that right?"

"Yes."

"First off, why the no sex?"

My mouth fell. "Are you really asking me that? Hello? Were you not present during the last few years of my life?"

"Okay, so you can't forgive him for being a dick. I get that. But he came for you, Em. How romantic is that? Hell, I'd have jumped his built-ass body the moment we were alone."

I leaned against the sink. "You would have?"

"Fuck yes! Oh my gosh, Em. The history you two have. The fact that Daphne did this to y'all, I'd have had that man all over me."

I rubbed my temple. "Becca, it's not like I don't want to have sex with Holden. I do. Believe me I do. It's just, I'm afraid if I open up completely to him, I'll get hurt again."

"Do you love him?"

"Yes. I never stopped."

"Do you see living without him?"

My eyes stun with the threat of tears. "I've never been able to see myself without him."

"Then what's the problem? You don't have … you don't have feelings for, um, Mason do you?"

My heart dropped. "No! Oh my gosh, Becca no. I swear to you there was nothing more between us than sex."

I cringed after I blurted that out. "Shit. I didn't mean to say that."

She chuckled. "It's okay. I know what went on between y'all. Mason has already assured me of his feelings. Listen, I get that you're feeling nervous about everything. Move slow. You don't have to jump right back into having hot sweaty sex. But you sure as hell could play naughty with other things."

"Ugh. Don't say things like that, Becca!"

"Sorry!" she chuckled then went on. "Why don't you take things slow? Like when you first started dating. When you get back, invite him over for dinner, do some heavy-duty foreplay, but take things slow."

"Okay, but that doesn't help me right now. He'll be in my bed! I'm horny as hell and his body is going to be up against mine. I'm going to combust."

"You know what you have to do."

"I can't."

"Yes, you can. Girl, if you want to make it through the night, you have to do it."

It was then I realized I hadn't asked her why she had called. "Hey, why did you call? Is everything okay?"

"Yeah. It's great. I wanted to tell you about my hot sexual escapade with Mason this afternoon."

I pushed off the sink. "No way!"

"Yes way! Oh my God. Why didn't you tell me he was so big! I'm not going to walk right for a week."

I scrunched up my nose. "Gross. Too much information, Becca." For a brief moment I thought it might have been awkward for Becca to be talking about having sex with Mason. After all, we had been fuck buddies for the last few years. Even though I knew Mason still dated and saw other women, he never slept with my best friend. But it wasn't awkward. I could hear the happiness in Becca's voice.

"Sorry. I didn't know who else to talk to about it. But if it's too weird…"

"No! I'm dying to hear more about it, it's just, Holden will be here soon and I should probably go … ah … I should go and …"

"Get yourself off. Jesus, just say it, Em."

"Right. I'll talk to you tomorrow before we leave. And Becca?"

"Yeah?"

I couldn't ignore the warm feeling that spread through my chest. Knowing Becca was with Mason, the guy she had been crushing on for so long, made me happier than I realized.

"I'm sorry about being with Mason. It was a shitty thing to keep doing knowing you liked him."

"Oh, Em. You don't have anything to be sorry about. I was married when y'all hooked up. It wasn't like you did it on purpose. Everything happened for a reason, right?"

I nodded, even though she couldn't see me. "Yeah. I love you, Becca."

"Love you too. Good luck tonight. You're going to need it."

Before I had the chance to respond, she was gone.

With a long drawn out sigh, I set my phone on the sink and glanced down. Slowly slipping my hand down my pants, I softly rubbed my clit. With my eyes closed, I pictured Holden's face between my legs. My hips jerked and I gasped at my fantasy.

My head dropped back more as I lifted my one leg and set it on the toilet. I could smell the woodsy scent of Holden in the room with me and that spurred me to go faster.

A slight moan escaped from my lips as I pictured Holden's lips slowly moving down my body. The closer it came to my clit the faster my hand moved. His name slipped from my lips as my orgasm began to build.

"Holden, oh God."

Then the heavenly feeling vanished.

My entire world came to a complete stop when I felt heat on my wrist and I gazed into Holden's green eyes. They danced with a fire I'd seen plenty of times from him.

He slowly lifted my hand and slid my fingers into his mouth. I almost came when he sucked on them.

Retreating my fingers from his mouth, he reached down and picked me up, quickly carrying me over to the bed.

After he gently placed me on the bed, he crawled on. My breathing was hard and fast. My head screamed for me to stop him, but my body pleaded to let him do what he wanted.

"No sex was the agreement," he spoke in a raspy voice. "But I'll be damned if you're going to get off to a fantasy about me when I'm right here."

The room felt like it was spinning. I'd never been so turned on in my life.

My body jumped as he placed his hands on stomach then slowly moved them down to my panties.

"Lift that gorgeous ass in the air, baby."

I did what he asked. No questions asked.

My entire lower half was exposed to him and I couldn't have cared less. The only thing my horny-ass body cared about was how he was going to make me come.

"Tell me what I was doing in your fantasy, Em."

My face blushed as I shook my head.

He slowly pushed my legs open while my entire body shuddered with anticipation. When he looked down, he moaned. "So fucking perfect."

My hands gripped at the sheets. I needed relief and I was about to start begging him.

Pushing his finger inside of me, I gasped and lifted my hips. "Yes!" I hissed.

"Tell me what your fantasy was and I'll make it come true, baby."

I'd never had my heart pound like it was now. I opened my mouth then shut it quickly.

Holden massaged my inside walls as he leaned up and gently kissed my lips. His other hand pulled my T-shirt up, exposing my breasts. "I remember exactly what to do to make you scream my name. I promise you, no sex. But let me finish what you started baby."

My stomach flipped like I was on a thrill ride. "You … you had your face buried between my legs."

The smile that spread over Holden's face made my heart skip a beat or two. "I was hoping you were going to say that."

The pressure from his finger kept on as he kissed down my chest, stopping to give each nipple their own special attention. When he gently bit down on one I nearly jumped off the bed.

"Jesus! Holden. I'm so close."

"Not yet, baby, we're just getting started."

My eyes rolled to the back of my head as I felt the heat from his lips move closer and closer to my throbbing clit.

"Ohmygod," I panted out when he blew hot air on my swollen bundle of nerves.

"I love how ready you are for me. I'm going to lick every fucking ounce of your sweet cream."

Arching my back, I begged for him to touch me. "Holden! Please make me come. Please!"

Light kisses trailed up my left thigh. I was expecting him to do the same to my other leg, but he buried his face between my legs, causing me to grab onto his hair and pull. That only made him go slower.

His tongue moved slowly from my clit down. Slipping his tongue inside of me, I felt a slight pressure on my back side.

"What … what are you doing?"

He buried his face in deeper as he gently rubbed against that forbidden area. He never penetrated, but the feel of his finger there was turning me on even more. If that was possible.

I was losing all control as I ground my hips into his face.

"More! God I want more!"

And more is what Holden gave me. His tongue flicked against my clit as the buildup began from the tip of my toes to the top of my head.

"Oh God! Oh God!"

With his thumb pressed against my clit, pressing it ever so lightly, he started licking and sucking like his life depended on it. My entire body began to tremble as his thumb pressed harder and his tongue pushed inside of me. The feel of his other finger on my ass sent me over the ledge.

"Holden!"

My screams of pleasure seemed to last forever. It was the most intense orgasm of my life. At one point, I begged for him to stop. He only slowed down enough to give me time to catch my breath and let the light come back into the room.

"Jesus ... I can't ... breathe," I panted as he flicked my clit with his tongue.

"Ohmygod! I can't. Not. Again."

I was wrong. So very wrong. I could. And I did. The second orgasm was almost as intense as the first. My legs shook and I felt it deep within my stomach.

I was mumbling something even I couldn't understand as the intense pleasure began to subside.

The feel of his body sliding up mine was utterly the most amazing feeling in the world. He was completely undressed except for his boxer briefs.

"One. More. Time," he whispered as he pushed his hard length against my sensitive clit.

Impossible.

There was no way he could pull a third orgasm from me.

"Exhausted," I whispered.

His lips explored my body, sending me into another state of euphoria. Then he pressed his hard cock into me more. The feel of him and the fabric caused a friction that quickly sent my body into its third orgasm. My legs wrapped around his body as we moved together. It was as if time never stopped with us. We moved together like we'd never been apart.

"Jesus, Em, I'm going to come."

The idea of him coming simply from rubbing up against me extended my orgasm. The sounds of him softly grunting into my ear had my arms around him. Drawing him closer to me.

When we finally stilled, all that could be heard was our labored breathing. The smell of sex surrounded us, and I loved it. If this was what it was like with no sex ... how would it be like when we actually made love?

I could only imagine.

Soft kisses moved across my jawline and up to my lips. "I need to go change."

With no energy to even talk, I nodded my head and moaned. Holden laughed and pulled my T-shirt back down over my body. A quick peck on the lips and he vanished from my room.

I laid there for a few moments and enjoyed the pure blissful happiness I was coated in.

Rolling over, I sat up. Every ounce of my body felt relaxed as I made my way into the bathroom. Glancing at myself in the mirror, I saw a totally different woman than I did early. My face was flushed with the multiple orgasms. My eyes danced with a happiness that I hadn't seen in a long time. The glow of my skin was unmistakable. I was a woman in love.

With a sly smile, I made a silent vow. Nothing or no one would ever come between Holden and me again.

Especially her.

CHAPTER 28

Holden

MY HANDS GRIPPED the bathroom sink while I pulled in one deep breath after another. I was lightheaded from the experience I'd had with Emylie a few moments ago. Glancing down, I looked at my boxers and the wet stain from my cum and hers. With a smile, I stripped down. Hearing Emylie calling out my name nearly drove me insane. The taste of her sweet juices was enough to make me beg her to let me sink balls deep into her. But that next step needed to be perfect. The right moment and I knew now was not the right moment. I eased her ache and that was all that mattered. I selfishly benefitted as well. Something I was going to have to make up for.

I turned on the cold water and splashed my face. Looking up at myself in the mirror, I smiled. God how I have missed her. Her smile. Her touch. The sound of her laughter. Nothing made me feel happier than Emylie.

My body came to life when I felt her hands on my back. "I just saw these."

Spinning around, I saw her holding the flowers I had delivered earlier. Damn it … I totally forgot about them.

"They're beautiful, but the note is even better."

With a smile, I pulled her to me. "I mean every word, Em."

She glanced down to the card in her hand and read it out loud.

To the woman
I love with all
my heart.
Forever yours,
Holden.

Her eyes lit up as she looked at me. "I love you with all my heart too. I've never stopped. You also drive me crazy wanting you." She winked and pressed her lips together while her cheeks turned a beautiful shade of pink.

I kissed her gently on the corner of her sweet mouth as I let out a light chuckle. "You've always done that to me, Em. Only you can make me mad with desire."

Her cheeks blushed and she turned away. Using my finger, I pulled her chin my way, looking deep into her beautiful brown eyes. The golden flecks seemed to be shining a bit brighter tonight. "I know you wanted to go slow, but I when I saw you getting yourself off and saying my name, I snapped. Then crawling on you like that was my own greedy way of getting more. The only thing I want now is to lay next to you in bed with your body up against mine."

The smile that spread over her face made my knees weak. "Naked?"

"Do you want to be naked?"

She searched my face as she thought about it. "Do you think we can behave?"

With a laugh, I shook my head. "I'm a strong man, babe, but I'm not sure how strong I can be with your fine ass pressed up against my cock."

Her mouth sucked in a quick breath. "I like it when you talk like that."

My hand moved down to her lower back as I pulled her to me. My dick pressed into her stomach. "Do you now?"

With a nod, she licked her lips. "I do. A lot."

My heart pounded so loud I was positive she heard it. "Then I think we need to wear clothes, because I'm really fighting the urge to bend you over this counter and fuck you hard and fast."

"Oh God," she whispered then swallowed hard. "Clothes for sure."

Walking to my bag, I pulled a pair of briefs out and slipped them on. "That means you have to wear underwear too, babe."

With a giggle, she agreed.

Soon we were crawling under the covers. Reaching my arm around her, I pulled Emylie up against me. The feel of her breathing was calming. I hadn't felt this relaxed since the last time I had her like this.

This woman was my entire life. My happiness. The mother of my future kids.

She was my world.

"I'm going to guess by the smile on Emylie's face last night went better than the night before."

Glancing over to Carter, I stated, "I wouldn't disagree with you."

With a slap on my back, he nodded. "Good. I like seeing her with that color in her cheeks."

"So do I," I replied looking back at her. With a deep breath in, I quickly expelled it. "When can I expect you and Tori to visit us in Texas?"

Carter grinned. "I'm heading back to the base in less than two weeks, then I only have a few months left before I'm out of the Marines. We talked about maybe heading your way this winter. Get away from the snow for a bit."

"Em will love that."

The girls both walked up to us and stopped short. "You about ready?" I asked as Emylie and Tori turned to each other. The threw themselves into each other and started crying.

Looking at Carter, he shrugged. "Is this where we hug it out, dude?"

With a chuckle, I pushed my hand out for his. Carter shook it hard and fast. "It was really great meeting you, Carter. Thank you for taking care of my girl."

"Anytime, dude. She's special. I saw that the moment I met her. Take care of her, Holden."

"Hello, I'm standing right here and I'm perfectly capable of taking care of myself."

My little spitfire. From the first time I met her, she wasn't afraid to say what was on her mind. Reaching for her hand, I kissed the back of it. "Let's head home."

Her eyes softened. "Home. That sounds nice."

Emylie was sound asleep as I pulled over into the rest stop. I had somehow managed to pull through the Chick-fil-A drive-through without her waking up.

When I put her car in park, I gently squeezed her leg. "Em?"

She lifted her arms and stretched while letting out a soft moan. My dick jumped when her shirt rode up and exposed her flat stomach.

"Where are we?"

"Right past Dallas."

Looking around, she yawned. "Man, I have to pee! I'm so glad you stopped at a rest stop."

"Why don't you run to the restroom? I grabbed some lunch and will meet you at the picnic table."

She quickly opened the door. "Shit! It hit me! Okay! Table, be right back."

Laughing, I reached to the back seat and grabbed the bags and the bouquet of flowers the guy was selling on the corner. I had to cross the intersection from Chick-Fil-A but it was worth it.

I headed over to the table and quickly set out her sandwich and bottled water. I set the flowers on the bench next to me so she couldn't see them.

A few minutes later, she was heading my way with a huge smile. "We are in Texas! I can't wait to get back home. I miss my bed."

With a chuckle, I handed her some Chick-Fil-A sauce. "Still your favorite?"

She grinned. "Yep."

"Still like to dip your fries in it?"

With a blush, she nodded. I reached down and handed her the pink roses. "They match the color of your beautiful cheeks."

With a gasp, she took the roses and buried her nose in them. "Oh, Holden! They're beautiful. I don't have any water to put them in."

"I got a cup with some water if you want to put them in that. It's in the cup holder in the backseat."

Her face beamed. "You're spoiling me with flowers, you know."

Shaking my head, I replied, "I could never show you enough how much I love you, Em."

She pressed her lips together and smelled the flowers again. We soon got lost in easy conversation. God this felt so fucking right. Unlike with Daphne, it felt like I was already home.

Later that day, I pulled down the driveway leading to my parents' house. Emylie was sound asleep in the passenger seat. I had called my parents when we were about an hour out, so I wasn't surprised when I saw Mario and Kim's truck parked in front of the house.

"Here we go."

Putting Emylie's car in park, I bumped her leg. "Hey, babe, we're here."

"Oh, man! How long have I been sleeping?"

With a smile, I took her hand and kissed the back of it. "You pretty much fell asleep about ten minutes after I pulled out of the rest stop outside of Dallas."

Her eyes widened in surprise. "Wow. I must have needed the sleep. Are we at your—"

She stopped talking when she saw her father's truck.

"Papá," she whispered. "Oh hell."

"It's going to be fine. I think he got his anger out on me."

She turned and stared at me with a look of fear in her eyes. "Don't leave me."

My heart felt like someone was squeezing it. "Never, Em. I swear to you I will never leave you again."

Chewing on her lip, she finally broke the nervous silence. "Let's get this over with."

"Let me get your door."

I jumped out of the car and took a deep breath in as I jogged around to her. The smell of the ranch filled my nose and instantly made me feel happier. Hay. Manure. Leather. All of it swirled into one hell of a great feeling. We were home.

We hadn't even walked up the steps yet and the door flew open. Mario and Kim walked out first. I could see the relief on Kim's face, but Mario looked pissed as hell, and I had only ever seen that man lose his shit a few times in my life. Once directed at me and I'd never want to have that happen again.

He took a few steps forward and stopped. "¿Lo que pensaban que ir con un desconodido?"

"He's really pissed if he is talking in Spanish!" I whispered as Emylie gripped my hand.

Mario looked at me, then back to Emylie. "Mi preciosa, answer me."

Since I could remember he had called Emylie "mi preciosa," which meant *my precious* in Spanish.

"Um ..."

I leaned in closer. "I heard stranger in there somewhere."

She turned to look at me and shot me a glaring expression. "Yes, I heard. He asked what I was thinking going off with a stranger."

"Smart man," I whispered while giving her a wink.

"Papá, he wasn't a stranger. He was a friend of Jamie and Jax's, and I wasn't really thinking."

Mario went to rattle something else in Spanish when Kim hit him in the chest. "Stop yelling at her in Spanish. I have no clue what you're saying!"

Mario gently kissed his wife on the cheek. "I'm sorry, mi preciosa."

"Holden, thank you for bringing her home to us. You're a good man for seeing to her safety."

With a smile, I went to reply but Emylie turned to face me with her hands on her hips. With a tilt of her head and a look that should drop me on the spot, I knew she was wondering how I went from the asshole who left his daughter to the man who swooped in and rescued her.

Kim motioned for us to walk up the steps. "All right, let's go in and talk. Sam and Debbie have some dinner cooked up for you both if you're hungry."

I waited for Emylie to start heading in first before I followed behind her. One reason was it was the gentlemanly thing to do, the other was I wouldn't put it past her to trip me going up the steps. Peering back at me over her shoulder, she sneered, "I think we can safely say he is no longer mad at you."

With a fist pump, I whispered, "Yes!"

She groaned and headed into the house. My mother and father greeted us both with hugs and kisses.

"I'm so sorry I up and left like that, Debbie. I didn't know what else to do."

My mother peeked over to me then back to Emylie. "I'm going to guess by the color on your cheeks, you two made up?"

Emylie blushed and kissed my mother on the cheek before making her way over to her father and mother who had gone into the kitchen.

Walking up to my mother, I shook my head. "Mom, seriously? I just got Mario back on my good side!"

With a wave of her hand, she brushed off my concern. "Nonsense. That man was so upset when he found out his daughter ran off with a strange man."

Her eyes changed and she looked into the kitchen then back at me. I knew what she was thinking. "Nothing happened between them."

"And between the two of you?"

I smiled. "We're taking things slow."

Taking her hand and brushing off imaginary lint on my shirt, she smiled. "Good. I think that's best. You need to earn her trust back, Holden Warner. You do that by courting her."

I lifted a brow. "Courting her?"

"Yes. Dating. You need to swoon her all over again. Don't expect her to fall back into your bed."

My stomach turned hearing my mother say that. "Ugh, Mom. Really? Are you really going to talk about sex with me?"

"It's not like I don't know you've had sex. Please. I knew when you two went off to go ride what you were *really* doing."

"Mom! No! My ears are burning!"

Tossing her head back with an evil laugh, she spun on her heels and headed into the kitchen. I was left alone in the living room. Then I remembered my promise to Emylie and hurried to her side.

Slipping my arm around her waist, I stiffened when Mario looked down at it. I was half tempted to remove it, but decided I needed to make a statement. We were back together. No matter how easy or hard the road would be, nothing was going to separate us again.

"Papá, please don't be mad. I'm home, I'm safe, and I did what I needed to do at the time. Besides, everything worked out as it should. It was good for Holden and me to be together alone and away from everything here at home. It gave us time to start mending and working on us."

His eyes met mine. With a hard swallow, I waited for what he was going to say.

"I'm not mad, mi preciosa. I was at first, and disappointed in your lack of judgment, but I'm not mad."

Emylie chuckled, "Well with the way you rattled off in Spanish, I thought for sure you were angry."

Mario took a few steps closer to his daughter as I slipped my hand out from her waist. "No, I'm just a father who loves his daughter and only wants you to be happy and safe."

"I am happy. I promise."

Now it was my turn to say something. "And safe. I swear I'll never let anything happen to her, sir. Nor will I ever be the cause of her pain again."

Mario pointed to me. "You're damn right you won't. If you do, I'll kick your ass."

Everyone in the room gasped. Mario and Kim never swore, so when they did, it always came as a shock.

My mother clapped her hands to get everyone's attention. "You have to be starving. Let's get you both fed, then you can get settled and we can talk about what lies in the future tomorrow."

Emylie took my hand in hers and replied, "That sounds like a great idea."

After dinner we sat outside and filled our parents in on our trip to Utah and Colorado. Emylie told them about Carter, his parents, and how his dad was fighting cancer. She saved Tori for last. I noticed she left out a few other details, like how she butted into Carter's business about having kids. It was probably best that was left out. No need for everyone to know the poor guy's business.

231

My dad cleared his throat then smiled. "Well I hope you're both ready to get back to work."

The lightness in my chest was welcoming. It was nice to know that I was on a new path with my own father. Things would probably never really be the same, but I intended on making him proud of me. And that meant jumping in and helping Mason with the running of the ranch. I didn't want to take his job, I wanted to work alongside of him.

"Dad, I hope you know I'm not expecting to take Mason's place. He's done a great job for you. My goal is to work alongside of him, together."

My father's face beamed with pride. "You don't know how happy that makes me to hear you say that, son. But you know you're going to have to earn some respect back from me."

With a light chuckle, I nodded and answered, "Yes, sir."

Emylie reached for my hand. Her touch alone sent a rush of energy through my body.

"Emylie, would you like us to follow you back to your place?" Kim asked.

I held my breath as I waited for Emylie's answer. "If it's all right with Sam and Debbie, I'd like to crash here in one of the guest rooms."

Mario turned slowly and glared at me. Swallowing hard, I moved a bit in my seat.

"Of course you can stay here!" Debbie replied.

I slowly let out my breath and silently said a prayer of thanks that Emylie was staying here.

Reaching for her hand, I gave it a quick peck on the back and stood. "I hate to be the one to say goodnight first, but I've got a flight I need to catch tomorrow afternoon."

"I hate that you're leaving," Emylie said with sadness in her eyes as she rose to her feet.

I placed my hands on her hips pulling her in closer, but not too close since her dad was standing right there. "I won't be gone long. I promise. The faster I do this, the faster we can move forward."

My mother placed her hand on my shoulder. "Don't worry, sweetheart. Emylie will be so busy around here, she won't have time to miss you."

Her eyes never left mine. I knew what my mother had said was far from the truth. The two days I would be gone would be torture for both of us. Not only physically, but mentally as well. I wasn't sure what was going to happen when I saw Daphne again. Would she flip out and go crazy again? Try and beg me to stay with her? Maybe she wouldn't care at all.

Here was hoping for the latter.

CHAPTER 29

Emylie

W ITH MY CELL phone firmly in my hand, I stood at the tank and stared off into thin air.

"Haven't heard from him yet?"

Peering up, I smiled at Mason. "Yeah, earlier. He had to go because Daphne caught wind he was back in town. She informed him she was heading to the apartment so Holden had to ask his former boss and another friend to be there when she got there."

Mason shook his head and jumped off of his horse. Lifting his hat, he wiped the sweat from his brow. "I swear I don't think I've ever met anyone as wicked as that woman. Who does that kind of shit?"

A chill ran down my neck. "Crazy obsessed people."

My arms wrapped around my body as I shivered. It was ninety-four degrees out, but the idea of Daphne causing issues was something that weighed heavy on my mind.

"Mason, do you honestly think someone who went to such great lengths to do what she did to Holden would just walk away like she did? She didn't even really put up a fight."

With an indifferent expression on his face, he gazed out over the water. "Do you want my honest answer to that question, Em?"

My stomach twisted into a knot.

No. "Yes. I do."

"No, I don't think she is going to give up like that. I think she is pissed Holden found her out and left her. Especially when she finds out the two of you are back together. With it being so quick, she's going to seek revenge."

"But Holden could take her down with what he has on her. She wouldn't dare try anything stupid."

He shrugged and then turned to look at me. "And would you have really thought Holden would have been drugged, told he was going to be a father, then strung along only to be lied to again with a fake pregnancy?"

Chewing on my lip, I slowly shook my head. "Well, I guess I need to prepare myself for when she does try something. I just hope Holden doesn't ..."

I stopped myself before I said it out loud. I'd thought it and hated myself for even thinking Holden would do anything to hurt me again. I saw it in his eyes this morning when he left. He hated the idea of seeing her more than I did.

Wrapping my arms around my body, I smiled as I thought about this morning. Holden had slept with me last night and held me all night. He woke me with breakfast in bed. There was even a single red rose on the tray. After we ate, he treated me to a massage that left me utterly and amazingly relaxed.

Mason took hold of my upper arms and bent down. "Hey, look at me. Holden loves you, and he's not going to do anything to risk your trust."

My chin trembled. "I know. I hate how weak I'm feeling right now."

"I'd hug you, but maybe that wouldn't be the best thing to do."

Snapping my head up, I immediately took a step back. All those years of falling into Mason's arms and I was about to do it again. Mind you, I wouldn't have fallen into his bed.

"I'm sorry. I can't keep using you as my own personal crutch when things get bad."

With a slight smile, he replied, "I'm your friend, Em. I'll always be your friend."

"I know that, Mason, but with you and Becca together now, I'd never want her to think there was something between us still. Or for Holden to think that. It wouldn't look very good if she, or anyone else for that matter, showed up and I was in your arms acting like a titty-baby."

With a laugh, he agreed. "No, it wouldn't look right. Not any-more."

Taking in a deep breath, I exhaled quickly. "So what did I miss when I was gone?"

He rolled his eyes. "Jesus, Sam has come up with some crazy ideas for this year's Dove season."

"Oh no. Do I even want to ask?"

"No. No you don't. But I did come to ask you if you were in the mood to put your ranch hat on?"

Squaring my shoulders off, I tilted my head and gave him a questioning look. "For?"

"We've got three hundred acres of square bails that need to be hauled off, and two of my summer guys done took off for the sum-mer."

I couldn't help but smile. "I think Becca needs to be in on this one."

With a wink, he replied, "She'll be here any minute."

During the summer months growing up, Mason and Holden used to bail hay and then haul it to earn extra money. Becca and I, of course, offered to help, but we fizzled out a lot faster than the boys.

Then again, we only agreed to helping them because we knew their shirts would be off within an hour and we would have a muscle-fest show for the rest of the day.

"Well, let's see how good of shape I'm still in!" I chuckled. Mason jumped up on his horse and then helped me up. I wrapped my arms around his waist and held on as he rode over to the west pastures where the hay would be.

Once we rode up, I slid from the horse and looked at the endless bales of hay. With an internal groan, I silently prayed I wasn't in that bad of shape.

"Hey y'all!"

Spinning around on the heels of my tan Ropers, I returned Becca's smile. "Please tell me you brought me gloves."

She held up her hand and showed me the extra pair of gloves. "Somehow I knew you wouldn't have any."

I took the gloves from her and then brought her in for a hug. I hadn't had a chance to see her yet since I'd gotten back home.

She giggled and whispered in my ear, "Did you have hot sex with Holden?"

With a laugh of my own, I replied, "No. But trust me, he made up for it in other ways."

Becca pulled back and wore a huge smile. "Oh, girl, I believe it. I haven't forgotten about sitting up in my dad's barn talking about that boy and his ... magical hands."

I felt my cheeks blush as I quickly added before turning and walking off, "And his magical lips."

"Wait! What? Emylie Sanchez, you can't leave it like that."

"Good excuse for a girl's night tonight?" I replied as I peered over my shoulder.

"Hell yes!" Becca shrieked as she followed me over to Mason. Little did we know he would work us right up until sunset and every muscle in our body would be aching.

"My God. Is this what my future is going to be like, cowboy?"

Becca asked as she wiped sweat off her forehead.

Mason walked over to her and wrapped her in his arms. She didn't even protest about how sweat soaked he was. "Kiss me," he growled while taking his hat off.

"With pleasure," Becca purred before pressing her lips to his. I watched as my two best friends quickly got lost in each other. I was glad nothing was awkward between any of us. I was truly glad to see them together.

As if on cue, my phone rang in my back jean pocket. Pulling it out, I saw his name and my heart skipped a beat.

"Hey! I've been waiting for you to call."

"You sound out of breath."

I plopped down on a bale. The smell of the fresh cut grass swarmed my senses, filling my mind instantly of memories of playing hide and seek. "Mason recruited me and Becca to help load the hay bales. The two summer ranch hands took off for the coast or something."

"Fuck," Holden sighed. "I should be there helping, not y'all."

Peeking over to Mason and Becca still sucking face, I chortled. "Trust me, Becca has not uttered one complaint. She is currently in Mason's arms as they swap spit. I'm waiting for them to just drop and have sex right here on a bale of hay with the way they are going at each other."

I dragged my eyes off of the two love birds and looked out at the field. A group of deer where gathered in the middle eating the scraps of hay we left in our path.

"I wish that was us," he barely spoke.

My chest felt heavy as I replied, "Me too. How did it go today? Did you get everything from the apartment?"

"Yeah. Todd and Rich came over and hung out with me since Daphne called and said she wanted to talk."

My heartbeat increased. "How did that go?"

I could hear him sigh and I pictured his hand combing through his brown hair. "At first it was like I expected it would be. She begged me for forgiveness and swore things would be different."

My thumb nail came up to my mouth as I promptly started to chew on it. I never chewed on my nails. "And?"

"And I told her basically to get lost."

"You did?" I knew my voice sounded a bit too happy.

"Yeah, I told her we were back together."

My breath stalled. "You did? Holden why?"

There was silence for a few moments and I swore he muffled the phone and said something to someone. "Holden?"

"Yeah, babe, I'm still here. There was a bit of a situation I had to take care of."

Oh no. That doesn't sound good.

"Holden, maybe you shouldn't have told her about us. You really just broke up with her and to move on so quickly, might ... well it might ..."

"Make her more unstable?"

I swallowed hard and nodded. "Well, I didn't want to say it like that, but yes."

"She kept talking about flying to Texas. Trying to work on things between us. Then she started rambling about the movie she had started."

"The one her dad is directing?"

Holden let out a gruff laugh. "Yeah. That one. She followed me around the apartment like a lost puppy, Em. I didn't know what else to do. So I told her you and I were going to try and work on putting us back together."

Becca let out a small scream, causing me to turn and look at them. Mason was currently chasing her around the truck and trailer while she played keep away. I couldn't help but smile.

"So, how did she take that?"

"It was weird. She didn't say anything. Well, she said something like she understood. Then she said goodbye to us and left."

My muscles tensed and an intuitive feeling that something bad was about to happen caused a prickling of my skin all across my body.

Trying to speak with the instant dry mouth, I forced out the words. "Somehow I think this is just the beginning, Holden. You might have woken the sleeping beast."

"So, what bottle of wine should we open next?" Becca asked as she examined my wine case.

I set the plate of cheese and fruit on the coffee table and gently sat down. "Oh my gosh, it's only been a few hours and I'm already getting sore. Remind me to never help Mason with the hay again."

Becca giggled and grabbed a bottle of Shiraz. "I enjoyed myself immensely this afternoon."

She tried to play it off, but I noticed how slowly she sat down. "Uh-huh. You're not the least bit sore?"

"From my hot sex last night, but not from today."

"Bullshit!" I giggled as I tossed the throw pillow at her.

With a chuckle, she popped the wine bottle open and poured us two glasses of wine. "So what time does Holden fly in?"

"He'll be in at four. I told him I'd pick him up at the airport. I can't wait to see him."

Becca handed me a glass and lifted hers. "A toast. To what should have been that finally is."

My head pulled back with a confused expression. "What?"

"You know. To you and Holden being back together, and me and Mason dating. It should have been this way all along. Now, hopefully it is."

My heart fluttered at Becca's words. After Holden had helped push away my fears about Daphne causing any more trouble, I finally was able to settle my nerves. Of course, having Becca here with Sage helped even more. We had been having a fun girls' night until Sage tapped out and headed up to bed. That left time for the big girls to talk.

"So, would it be weird if we talked about Mason and sex?"

I shrugged. "I don't think so. What are you wanting to talk about?"

Becca's face blushed. "I don't know. I've only ever been with two guys and so have you. So how weird is it that the second guy for both of us was Mason?"

I went to open mouth to say something, but I had nothing. It didn't take long until we were both laughing hysterically and neither of us knew why.

My doorbell rang and I quickly jumped up. "Speak of the devil! That has to be Mason coming to steal you from me!"

"No way!" Becca gasped like a little school girl. She covered her mouth to hide her giggles.

"Well who else would it be this late at night?"

My cell phone rang and I reached for it as I walked to the door. It was Holden.

"Hey, handsome!"

"Em, whatever you do, don't answer your cell phone or talk to anyone."

My hand reached for the doorknob. "What? Why? What's going on, Holden?"

"Listen to me, if anyone calls you or asks you about me or Daphne, you say no comment."

Twisting the handle, I was thrown off by what Holden was saying and I hadn't bothered to check to see who was at the door. Opening it, I was instantly blinded by flashes.

"What the hell?" I gasped.

"Get out of the way! You're trespassing."

My eyes adjusted and I saw Mason pushing people away from

the door.

"Em! Who is that? What's going on?"

"I um … I don't know."

"Are you Emylie Sanchez?"

"Don't answer them Emylie!" Holden yelled.

"Um," was the only word I could say.

Becca walked up and stood next to me. "What's going on?"

"Are you the same Emylie Sanchez that Holden Warner slept with resulting in his break up with Daphne Weston?"

"What?" Becca and I both spoke at the same time.

"Emylie! Shut the door. Where's Mason?"

"Get the fuck out of here before I call the cops!" Mason pushed one of the reporters out of the way and then looked at me. "Get inside, y'all, and lock the door. I'll meet you at the back door."

Slamming the door shut, I stood there in a stunned silence.

"Well, I guess now we know what she did," Becca called out, making her way to the back of my place to let Mason in.

It was then I realized Holden was still on the phone. "H-Holden?"

"Yeah baby, I'm here. I'm on my way to the airport right now. I was able to get on the last flight out to San Antonio."

I couldn't say a word. The only thing I could do was stare at my door and replay what the reporter had said,

"Are you the same Emylie Sanchez that Holden Warner slept with resulting in his break up with Daphne Weston?"

Holden

Earlier that evening

I STOOD IN front of the TV and watched it all play out. Daphne and her father had called a press conference to announce that she was going to be taking some much needed time off for a few weeks.

"Ms. Weston, why the time off? Is everything okay?" A reporter asked. I knew the scumbag. It was a reporter Daphne's father kept on the payroll, the one who knew all the right questions to ask to steer the direction.

"No, I'm not okay. I found out a few days ago I had suffered a miscarriage."

Liar.

"And that same day my fiancé, Holden Warner, broke off our engagement because he had been having an affair with his old high school girlfriend back in Marble Falls Texas."

My heart dropped. "You fucking bitch."

With my lawyer's name pulled up on the phone, I hit his number.

"Troy," was all I had to say.

"I'm watching it. Her father called me right as it was about to start. God knows how much he paid to get this on *E News*."

"It's all a lie. I want to hit her hard with what I've got on her. There is no way she is going to do this to Emylie."

Troy cleared his throat. "You realize if you do this, you're going to look like the bad guy trying to make up an excuse. It wouldn't look good to go after her after she's lost a baby and gotten dumped. That's what the press will see."

"Fuck that! I'm telling the truth. She's lying, that has to count for something."

I heard papers rustling around. "Listen, if I know West, he already has the paparazzi headed to your place in Texas."

My heart slammed in my chest. "Emylie," I whispered as I laced my fingers through my hair. "I've got to go, Troy. I'll call you tomorrow morning."

I hit Emylie's number but it went to voicemail. "Em, baby I need you to call me right away."

Hitting End, I dialed Mason's number.

"Hey dude, what's up?"

I rushed around the hotel room and got the little bit I had unpacked for the night packed back up. "Where is Emylie?"

"Uh, she's at her place with Becca. Girls' night."

"I need you to get over there as soon as you can. Daphne told the press she lost her fake baby and that I cheated on her with my high school girlfriend. If I know Daphne and her father, they've probably already alerted the press back in Texas of the story that was about to break."

"Wait. She went on the air and told people that?"

"Yes! Mason, I need you to make sure Emylie or her parents don't say a damn word to anyone. Don't you even say anything."

Running to the elevator, I hit the down button. "Can you also call my parents and warn them. I've got to call the airlines and see if I can get a flight back home."

"Um, yeah right. Jesus this is fucked up, Holden."

With a roll of my eyes, I agreed. "Tell me about it. Emylie was wrong about one thing."

"What?"

"I not only woke up one crazy-ass beast, but her fucking father as well."

"How is she?"

I could hear the back door open and close. "She's fine, Holden. I've been keeping the TV off. She slept for a bit on the sofa, and then has been in the kitchen with her mother baking since three am."

Hitting the steering wheel with my hand, I cursed. "I hate that this is happening to her."

"To both of you."

With a frustrated sigh, I shook my head. "I don't care about me, Mom. I care about her."

"How is the security on the ranch?"

"Your father has already asked Mason to look into getting things upgraded. We're thinking of hiring a temporary guard at the front as well. We did have a reporter who made it onto the ranch last night. Mason got rid of him and we're trying to figure out how they got through the gate."

"I'll tell you how they got in, Mom, Daphne knew the gate code. She saw me punching it in more than once."

My mother gasped. "How can anyone be so vile and deceitful?"

"I don't know. I'm only about thirty minutes out. I'm sure once I pull up to the house they will try to stop me for a comment."

"What are you going to say?"

"Nothing right now. Troy is working up a statement for me to release. Hopefully that puts this to bed. I hate that this is happening to her, Mom. I've already put her through so much."

"Listen to me, son. Life is going to throw punches at you. All the time. What you have to decide is are you going to duck and dodge those punches, or are you going to let them land and knock you down?"

With a smile on my face, I nodded my head. "Always were the wise one."

"That's right. And don't you forget it. Now drive carefully. She's fine. I promise."

"Love you, Mom."

"Love you too."

I wasn't that far from the house when I hit Emylie's number.

"Hey."

"Hey back. You doing okay?"

With a slight sigh, she replied, "I am, but I'll be better once you're here."

"Have you tried to get some sleep?"

"I've slept a couple of hours. Becca threatened to sit on my chest if I didn't lay down."

She let out a nervous chuckle.

"Baby, I'm so sorry. Damn, I'm so sorry."

"It's not your fault, nor is it my fault. We both knew this wasn't going to be an easy road with how unstable Daphne is."

I was less than ten miles from the house and I saw a few cars here and there pulled over on the side of the road. Damn paparazzi. I hated them. I'd always hated them. It wasn't a very big road and most of them where still halfway in the street. I wanted like hell to honk at them, but the less attention I drew in the better.

"Speaking of roads, I'm almost there. Stay inside, don't come out."

"No."

My hands gripped the steering wheel harder. "What?"

"I'm not hiding, Holden. We did nothing wrong. I refuse to let her do this to us. It's what she wants. She thinks by doing this it will drive a wedge between us, well it's not. It will only bring us closer and in the end ... she's going to lose."

My cheeks hurt from the smile I wore. Hell yes. That was my girl right there. "You never were one to back down from something, were you?"

"Nope. Now hurry up, my lips are craving yours."

One of the ranch hands was manning the main gate, and when he saw me, he quickly allowed me by, stepping in front of a car that tried to follow me in. *Where in the hell were the police and why were these cars not gone by now?*

Speeding down the driveway, I finally made it to the house. Emylie was standing on the front porch and my breath caught in my throat. She was wearing a pair of my old sweatpants and one of my old football T-shirts. I'd never seen her look more beautiful.

I threw open the door to the rental car and stepped out. Shutting it quickly and making my way to her. She ran down the steps and jumped into my arms. Her legs wrapped around my waist as I held her tightly. Her face was buried in my neck and her soft cries about killed me.

I was the cause of this.

The pain that made her cry was my doing.

All because I made one wrong decision.

"I swear to you, I'll spend the rest of my life making this up to you."

Pulling back, she smiled. "I'm not crying because I'm sad, I'm crying because I'm happy you're home!"

CHAPTER 31

Emylie

THREE DAYS HAD passed since Daphne's announcement. Sam and Debbie added security guards at the gate and ended up having to hire more because the press was sneaking onto the ranch. Most of the security team were off duty or retired cops Sam knew.

Carter had called at least once a day to check to see how I was doing. I couldn't help but smile slightly at the memory of him offering to send in the Marines to clear out the press.

I stood on the back porch and inhaled a deep cleansing breath. The smell of leather lingered in the air. Holden and a few ranch hands were cleaning all of the saddles. It was something to keep his mind off of the shit-storm Daphne had caused.

"He wasn't going to listen to us."

Peeking over my shoulder, I smiled at Debbie. She handed me a cup of tea then sat down in a chair.

"No, he wasn't. He was hell-bent on trying to save me from all the bad talk. Troy tried to tell him the press would spin the statement around and make things even worse. Now it's basically she said, he said. The whole thing is a mess."

I made my way to the rocking chair that was next to Debbie and sat down. My mind drifted back two days ago when I stood next to Holden when he held his own press conference.

"Ms. Weston falsely accused me of having an affair, which ultimately led to our engagement being called off. What led to the engagement being called off was the fact that my fiancée lied to me and was never pregnant in the first place."

Gasps filled the air as people started throwing out questions. Holden continued to speak.

"I believe in privacy and I will not drag Ms. Weston, myself, or an innocent party such as Ms. Sanchez into a battle of going back and forth. The truth of the matter is, I never had an affair, Ms. West was never pregnant, and this is not the first time she has lied to me about a pregnancy."

Hands flew up and question after question was thrown at Holden. "Do you have proof of this, Mr. Warner?" "Where's the proof in that accusation!" "How do we know you're telling the truth?"

Holden glanced in my direction. We didn't have any real proof other than Daphne confessing it to Holden.

Turning back to the reporters, Holden took in a deep breath and exhaled it. Before he had a chance to say anything, Mason stepped forward and spoke. "That's all we have to say right now. Thank you for your time."

Holden turned, winked at me, and headed back into the house as I followed. Mason, Sam, and the off-duty police they had hired cleared everyone out. The moment the door shut, I took in what felt *like the first real breath since Holden started talking.*

When our eyes met, I couldn't help but notice how tired he looked. With a frustrated sigh, he said, "I'm afraid we might have made things worse."

"Emylie, did you hear me?"

Snapping out of the memory, I stared at Debbie. "I'm sorry, what was that?"

"It's all going to blow over. You know that right?"

With a nod, I replied, "I know, but when? Just when I felt like I had gotten him back, she still has a hold of him."

"There is only one thing that woman is trying to do and that is to drive y'all apart. Don't let her. Look at me, sweetheart."

Facing her, I fought back the tears that were threatening to spill. "I've always said you and Holden were made for each other. Have I not?"

Nodding, I softly replied, "Yes, ma'am, you have."

"Now for a while there, I was worried things might not go the way I was hoping, but in the end, when I saw the way the two of you looked at each other, I knew."

"What did you know?"

"That nothing would keep you apart. I knew somehow you would end up together. You've been through so much, don't let their lies pull you apart."

The tears spilled from my eyes as I quickly wiped them away. "I wish he had come home. Why didn't he just come home?"

Debbie stood and held her arms out for me. Walking into her embrace, I let the scent of her perfume wrap my body in a warm glow as she pulled me into her, instantly pushing away my doubt and fear.

"Oh, darlin', I'm almost positive Holden has been asking himself that same question since the night this all happened. It does no good to look into the past. The only thing the two of you need to be focusing on is getting back to where you were before."

I nodded and held onto her tighter.

"Is everything okay?"

The sound of his voice caused a flutter in my stomach. Stepping back away from Debbie, I gave her a reassuring smile. "Yes, your mom and I were just talking."

Holden walked up and cupped my face in his strong hands. They were already callused again like before. The feel of them against my skin sent tingles down my body straight to between my legs.

Tonight was going to be the night. I couldn't wait another minute. We'd been staying in his parents' house since Holden came back from California. Each night he snuck to my room and pleasured me over and over again. Never once letting me return the gesture. In some silly way, I knew he was trying to punish himself for everything.

Each evening, he had taken me out to our pasture and made a bed in the back of his truck so we could look at the stars. We talked for hours in between making out like silly teenagers.

His thumbs gently moved across my wet cheeks. "Why the tears?"

"Just being emotional, that's all. I'm fine, I promise."

The way his eyes filled with concern and he searched my face to see if I was speaking the truth, touched my heart so. I loved this man. Even with everything that had happened, I loved him.

"How about dinner at my place tonight?"

Wiggling his brows, he leaned down and gently brushed his lips over mine before placing a soft kiss on them. "I think that sounds amazing."

"I'm going to try a new dish on you."

Holden laughed. "If my memory serves me right, the last time you did that, we had to go to Whataburger for dinner."

Slapping him on the chest, I shot him a dirty look. "Well, that is not an option since we are not in College Station and pretty much only have peanut butter and jelly."

Holden glanced over my shoulder, pulling me closer, he softly spoke. "She went inside so now I can really tell you what I want for dinner."

My heart rate spiked and I asked, "Wh-what do you really want?"

"My face buried between your legs, tasting that sweeter-than-honey cream of yours."

I swallowed hard then parted my mouth open. "Oh."

With a smile that made my legs weak, his hand moved under my T-shirt and up to my breasts. Pushing my bra up, he pinched a nipple, causing me to gasp. "God, do you have any idea how much you turn me on, Em?"

Gripping onto his arms, I tried to form words but my head was spinning, causing me to sway. "I know what I want for dessert," I finally managed to say.

Now his lips were on my neck, placing one burning kiss after another on my skin. "What's that, baby?"

"You, buried inside of me, Holden. I can't take it anymore. I want you so much."

His head pulled back with a concerned look. "Are you sure?"

Pulling my lip between my teeth, I nodded. "I've never been so sure of anything in my life."

"Fuck if I don't want to take you right here, right now."

My eyes darted to the barn and I was about to make a suggestion. To hell with the dinner and making everything special. I needed him. Now.

"Well, you can't."

Holden and I both froze at the sound of Becca's voice. When he lifted his gaze, Holden frowned. "Hey y'all."

My heart dropped and disappointment rushed over my body when I saw Becca standing there.

Becca lifted her brows as she looked directly at me. "Wow, sounds like things were getting a little hot and heavy out here. I take it you've moved from the slow lane to the fast lane." Making a sexual reference with her hands, she added, "Vroom vroom."

I snarled my lip up at Becca then rolled my eyes. "You always did have terrible timing and a dirty mind."

She laughed and shook her head. "Mason asked me to see if you can go help the boys in the south pasture, Holden. I guess a couple sneaky cows decided to bust out."

Holden grunted. "Why can't he go?"

Leaning back against his chest, he wrapped his arms around me and I settled into his body.

"The security people are here to upgrade the systems on all of the houses on the ranch. They're starting with the main house, and Sam and Debbie said they were heading into town and asked Mason to handle it."

With what sounded like a snort, Holden dropped his arms from around me. "I guess this is the punishment of the prodigal son. My turn to do the grunt work since Mason's been doing it."

I tried hard not to laugh, but it was true. Sam was at times treating Holden like one of the ranch hands he was testing out to see if they could hang. I was impressed Holden was taking it like a champ. Not only was he trying hard with us by taking things slow and showering me with attention, but he was bending over backward to please his father. I'd overheard Sam telling Mason this morning to give Holden two more days of hard work, then bring him up to speed on the upcoming hunting season.

"Do you want to head to your house together, in case those assholes are still hanging around?"

Lifting my hand to his cheek, he leaned gently into it. "No. I'll

253

be fine."

His face constricted and he was about to argue. "Holden. We can't hide forever. The sooner we move on and let Daphne know she hasn't won, the better."

"Yeah. If only it was that easy. I'm so sorry, babe."

"Hey, it's you and me remember? Nothing is going to come between us."

With a smile that reconfirmed my words, he kissed me. Not just any kiss. A kiss that I felt in the tip of my toes.

"I'll be at your place around five."

"Perfect."

An evil grin moved slowly over his face. "I'll bring sandwiches, just in case."

Slapping him on the chest, I gave him a push as he grabbed his hat from the chair and put it back on.

Holden in a cowboy hat. Yummy.

I watched while he made his way to the ranch truck. The way his jeans hugged his firm ass only ignited the desire more. Maybe I'd just make something quick for dinner, like tacos.

Becca walked up and stood next to me and purred, "Gotta love those Wranglers, huh?"

"Oh yeah," I replied with a chuckle.

We both sighed and then laughed. Looping my arm in hers, we headed into the house. "I've got a few things I need to catch up on at my desk then I'm going to venture through the mess at the front entrance."

"Do you want me to go back with you?"

Brushing off the gesture with my hand, I replied, "Nah. Honestly we need to move on. Let them take their pictures and spit out their words. I'll put my headphones in and ignore them."

Becca laughed. "That's my girl." We stopped outside the door to my office. Becca leaned against the door jam and asked, "So dinner tonight at your place, huh? Are y'all going to feed the kitty?"

Narrowing my gaze, I looked at her with a confused expression. "What kitty?"

She rolled her eyes. "Hide the snack in the bush?"

"What in the hell are you talking about?"

She sighed while placing her hands on her hips. "Come on, Em. Are y'all going to churn the butter?"

I stared at her with a blank expression.

"Part the pink sea?" Her brows wiggled and it finally hit me what she was trying to say.

"Ohmygawd. You are … good lord, Becca! No wonder you got pregnant so young!"

"What's going on?" Mason asked walking up.

Shooting Becca a disgusted look, I turned to Mason and pointed to Becca. "Good luck with this one."

I walked into my office and shut the door. The quicker I finished ordering the protein pellets for the feeders and the seeds for the fall food plot, the faster I could get to the store to buy everything I needed for the creamy chicken fajita pasta I was going to make Holden.

With a smile on my face and feeling completely and utterly happy, I got to work. There was no way to explain it, but knowing Holden and I would finally be making love tonight, I knew everything was going to be okay.

Daphne was never going to win.

Ever.

CHAPTER 32

Holden

PULLING UP TO Emylie's small two-bedroom house, I parked in the driveway. Glancing around, I noticed there were no press to be found anywhere.

I got out and shut the door as I took another good look around while I made my way up the porch to her door. Before I had a chance to ring the doorbell, the door opened. My mouth fell open at the sight before me. Emylie was dressed in a light purple sundress. The way it hugged her perfect body made my dick instantly hard. My gaze traveled down her body. I could already picture those legs wrapped around my back as she urged me deeper inside of her.

With a groan, I ran my hand through my hair and looked back up at her. The way her brown eyes caught the light had my stomach jumping and a tightness growing in my chest. I handed her the bouquet of wild flowers. "You look beautiful, Em."

She motioned for me to come in. Burying her nose in the flowers, she inhaled deeply. "You're spoiling me with all these flowers,

Mr. Warner."

With a tender smile, I replied, "I could never spoil you enough, Em."

She motioned for me to come in. "Come on in before the vultures show back up."

Stepping into the house, I asked, "Speaking of, where did they go?"

"I picked my mom up on the way back home after the store. I hid in the back seat and she wore a hat and sunglasses. She pulled into the garage and I got out and unpacked the groceries. Then she pulled back out and they all followed her. They think I'm currently at my poor parents' house."

With a moan, I dropped my head. "Mario is going to kill me."

Chuckling, I reached up on my toes and kissed his lips. "He loves you."

"Ha!" I said as I took off my hat and tossed it onto the table in the foyer. "Tolerates me is more like it."

Taking in a deep breath through my nose, I asked, "What is that heavenly smell?"

Emylie headed into her kitchen as I followed her. "Pasta."

I took everything in as I made my way through her house. "I like what you did to your grandma's house, Em."

She stopped and turned to me. "Want a tour? I forgot you haven't seen it since I moved in."

My stomach growled and she glanced down. "Sounds like you'd rather eat first."

"I'm starving."

She giggled. "Then let's eat!"

I watched her move about the updated kitchen as she stirred something in a stock pot. My dick grew harder the more I watched her. Each time she leaned over or reached for something, her dress lifted a bit more, teasing me until my cock was so hard it ached.

"Will you please get the wine over there on the counter and two glasses?" she asked with the sweetest smile on her face. "If you'll bring it into the dining room, that would be wonderful!"

"Sure," I said as I adjusted my cock and grabbed the bottle of Shiraz along with two wine glasses. Pouring us each a glass, I set it next to each dish. The smell of spices filled the room when Emylie placed the bowl full of pasta onto the table.

"Damn, Em. That looks amazing."

With a huge grin on her face, she softly replied, "Thanks. It's creamy chicken fajita pasta. It's a bit spicy. I hope you still like spicy food."

Her face blushed and I wasn't sure why. Did a memory surface maybe?

"I love spicy food."

Her teeth sunk into her lip and she crossed her legs. Oh hell. She was as turned on as I was. *What in the hell is she thinking about?*

Then it hit me.

The Mexican restaurant in College Station we ate at when I surprised her with a visit our sophomore year. The dish we ordered was so fucking spicy we could hardly eat it. We ended up having to pull over on the side of the road because Emylie had drank so much water trying to cool her mouth down. She had to pee and couldn't wait to get back to her place. Before I knew it, I was fucking her up against my truck on the side of the highway. Impulsive sex is the best.

I watched as Emylie looked my body over. When she took a step closer to me, I knew she wanted me as much as I wanted her. This wasn't how I wanted our first time back together to be. No, I had it all planned out. I was going to give her body the attention it deserved and slowly sink myself into her then make love to her all night.

"Holden," she whispered. "I need you so badly it hurts to breathe."

My heart slammed in my chest. "Jesus, Em. I want to bend you over this table and take you from behind, but that's not how I wanted our first time back together to be, baby."

She nodded, a look of disappointment washed over her face. Walking over, I pulled out her chair as she sat down. My fingers lightly moved up her arm. I watched goosebumps erupt over her delicate skin and it was a glorious sight.

Taking a seat across from her, I lifted my wine glass. "To us."

She grinned and mimicked the motion. "To us."

The taste of the wine seemed to only heighten my desire for Emylie. I wasn't much of a wine drinker, but for some reason that wine on this night with the love of my life sitting in front of me, was the best tasting wine I'd ever had.

"I like the wine," I said while I took another drink.

"It's one of my favorites. My dad picked it up at one of the wineries in Fredericksburg he took mom to for their anniversary. I've been hooked ever since."

For some odd reason, I wanted to ask her if she and Mason had drunk it together, but I pushed the jealous thought from my mind. I took a bite of the chicken and pasta and moaned in heavenly delight. "Holy shit. This is amazing."

Her chest puffed out and she wore a proud expression. "See. I told you I could cook. I learned a thing or two while you were … um … gone."

I forced a smile. What other things had she learned and how much of it was from my best friend?

Fuck. Stop this, Holden. What in the hell is wrong with me?

Emylie started making small talk. Asking me about the fence. Was there a lot of paparazzi at the gate when I left? Did I think my father would work me like a first year ranch hand all summer? Anything to keep the conversation going.

I answered each question with a question of my own. How did she like working for my father? What her last year in college was like? And when Becca finally wised up to her cheating ex. We laughed, drank more wine, ate a second helping of dinner and then cleaned off the table. It was clear the direction of the conversation moved us both away from the hungry desire to rip each other's clothes off.

When I dried the last plate, I turned to see her standing there. She looked so damn innocent, but her eyes were telling another story. Her brown hair was pulled up exposing her neck to me.

Dropping the towel on the counter, I made my way over to her. My lips gently kissed along her neck, pulling out a long soft sigh from her.

"I can't wait any longer, Holden. I'm going to explode."

She turned and pressed her body against mine as our lips locked together. The kiss turned frantic and needy. Our tongues moved against each other so fast and our teeth clashed.

"Take this off," she mumbled against my lips as she tried to untuck my shirt. I reached up and pulled it out as she hurriedly unbuttoned it. The second her hands landed on my bare chest, we both let out a moan. She pushed the shirt off my shoulders and began working on my belt buckle.

"Faster, Holden. I need you now."

Helping her out, I ripped my belt off my jeans. "I'm so fucking hard, Em. I swear if you touched me, I'd come."

She smiled and lifted her dress over her head only to reveal she hadn't had any panties or bra on. "Jesus ... did the whole fucking house just shake?"

Her hands came up to her tits and she cupped each one, causing me take myself in my hand. It was hot as hell watching her play with her nipples.

"My God, I've missed you."

"I've missed you, Holden. So much."

Reaching out, I pushed her hand away and took a nipple into my mouth.

Slow.

Go slow.

Her hand laced into my hair where she grabbed it and pulled me closer to her. Silently begging me for more.

When her other hand made its way between her legs, she let out a low growl from the back of her throat, I lost it.

"Fuck slow," I mumbled as I lifted her up. "Em, I can't do slow or romantic. I need to fuck you like I've never fucked you before."

She wrapped her legs around my body. "I'm yours, Holden. Please. I can't wait another second."

Moving my cock, I felt her warm wet pussy. My eyes about rolled to the back of my head. "Oh, baby," I whispered as I set her down and she sank slowly onto me.

"Oh God," she whimpered.

"You okay?"

She wrapped her arms around my neck. "Don't stop. Please don't stop. It's tight, but it feels so good."

"It feels better than good. It feels fucking amazing."

"More. I want more."

Walking her back against the wall, I pulled out and pushed back into her, causing us both to hiss out a "*Yessss.*"

The way her pussy clenched down on my cock had me fighting like hell to keep from losing it.

Every time with Emylie was fantastic, but this time it was so much more. I wanted to go faster. Harder. Each time I pulled out, I pushed in harder while fighting to hold off until she came.

"Em ... I'm so close."

She dropped her head back against the wall and panted out. "Harder."

I gave her what she wanted. The feel of her pussy starting to bare down on my cock was more than I could take. I fought it off. There was no way I would rob her of an orgasm. Moving my hips slightly, I hit the spot she needed. Calling out my name, she dug her nails into my shoulders.

"Yes! I'm going to come. Oh God!"

One more hard push in and I was coming along with her. My face buried in her neck and her name being called out. I was almost positive she was still coming as I felt her pulling every drop out of me.

Everything went dark as I held her trembling body. Forcing my own body to stay upright.

I didn't want to move. I wanted to stay inside her forever. Like this, we were perfect. Everything was perfect. The outside world didn't exist.

"Holden?" she spoke my name so quietly I barely heard it.

"Yeah, babe?"

"I love you."

I tilted my head back so I could look into her eyes, and my breath caught when I saw her tears. "Baby, I love you too. Please tell me those are happy tears."

She nodded while pressing her lips together tighter. "Tell me why you're crying."

With a trembling chin, she answered me. "I've been dreaming of this moment for so long. My head told me I needed to move on and forget you, but my heart never gave up hope."

"I don't deserve your love, Em. But I promise I'll show you every day how much I treasure it. You're my air. The reason I breathe. I was made for you. Only you."

Her smile seemed to lit up the entire room. For the first time in a long time, I finally felt whole.

Kissing the tip of her nose, I said, "Let's take a shower, then I want to make love to you."

With a giggle, she replied, "I like that plan!"

The moment I pulled out of her, we both knew. Placing her on the floor, our gaze drifted down.

"Shit. Oh God, Em. I'm so sorry."

I looked back up at her. She was still staring as she whispered,

"Oh no."

As if my heart wasn't still beating fast from what just happened to us, add in the fact that I realized I forgot to wear a condom and then add the panic in of Emylie's voice.

"Please tell me you're on the pill."

She glanced up and the fear in her eyes made me take a few steps back. "I ... I am ... I was."

"Was?"

Her fingers went to her temples and she rubbed them quickly. "Oh God."

Spinning on her heels, she dashed through the house and to her bathroom.

My heart felt like it was going to beat right the fuck out of my chest. Holy shit. How could I be so fucking stupid? Another costly mistake. Emylie was never going to forgive me.

Reaching down, I grabbed our clothes and followed her. When I walked into the bathroom, she was sitting on the edge of the tub. "I'm so sorry I let you down."

Her head lifted. "What? You didn't let me down. Holden, we both forgot. This is no more your fault than it is mine."

"It was my responsibility, and I fucked up. Again."

She shook her head. "No. It was both of ours and we were totally caught up in the moment."

Sitting down next to her, I took her hand in mine. "So, what about the pill?"

"I've been taking them, but the last few days, I haven't taken any. With everything going on and staying at your parents' last minute, it totally slipped my mind."

Lifting her hand to my lips, I kissed the back of it. "Are you angry?"

Her beautiful brown eyes looked into my green. "No. Are you?"

"Hell no. That felt amazing, and I loved not having anything between us."

She grinned. "Me too."

"But, we have so much to work out together, that I don't think it would be wise for use to keep having sex without some kind of birth control. Don't get me wrong, I want to have kids with you some day, Em. But I really want to be with you right now."

"I feel the same way. Let's not think about it, until we need to think about it. Worrying isn't going to do any good."

"Agreed."

We both put on fake ass smiles, but I knew we were both freaking the hell out on the inside.

As much as I was dying to make Emylie my wife and plan our future, we needed to focus on us. I said a silent prayer as I turned on the shower and pulled her in. I also made a mental note to grab the condoms out of my wallet and put them next to her bed.

CHAPTER 33

Emylie

THE SICK FEELING in my stomach hadn't settled any as Holden and I snuggled up on my sofa. After the hot shower, Holden laid me on the bed and gave every single inch of my body attention. From soft kisses to massages with his magical hand. He slipped a condom on and slowly made love to me. I didn't want to tell him how much better it felt with no barrier, but there was no way we could risk having sex with no condom. I was going to be in full-on freak out mode until I was able to take a test.

I was about to say something when someone started pounding on the door.

"Fucking reporters," Holden mumbled as he got up from the sofa.

"Don't even go to the door," I cried out.

"Em? Holden? It's Becca!"

Jumping off the couch, I raced over to the door just as Holden opened it. Only a few paparazzi stood out by the street, snapping a picture as soon as they saw us.

"What's wrong?" I asked as Becca pushed her way into the house. Mason followed behind closely.

"Nothing. As a matter of fact, everything is amazing! Well, wait, tell me your kitty got fed first, then I can say everything is amazing." Glancing over to Holden she asked, "Sex. Did y'all finally have sex?"

With a roll of my eyes, I groaned.

"What in the hell?" Holden asked as he gave Becca a shocked look before asking Mason, "What do you see in her?"

Mason laughed and slapped Holden on the back. "Love is blind."

Everyone stopped moving as Becca sucked in a breath.

"What did you say?" I asked.

Mason glanced between all three of us. "Um. I don't know. Why are you all looking at me like that?"

I clapped my hands together and did a little jump. "Mason! You said love is blind."

Becca stood there speechless. Her eyes were beginning build with tears as she waited for Mason to say something.

"Oh. Well, um, shit. I didn't want the first time I said that to you to be a slip up, Becca."

I was positive Becca didn't care how Mason told her he loved her. She threw herself into his arms and kissed the hell out of him. Holden and I exchanged smiles and he mouthed that he loved me.

Before I had a chance to do the same, Becca pulled back and gasped, "Oh my God. As amazing as that was, we have something even more amazing! Well, no, it's not more amazing. It's right up there, but Mason saying he loved me is the ultimate amazing."

"Becca!" I shouted.

Holden chuckled and headed toward the kitchen. "Nothing could make this night anymore amazing, Becca. Sorry." Glancing back at us over his shoulder, he asked, "Beer anyone?"

"I'll take one," Mason said as he plopped down onto my sofa. I moaned internally. As much as I loved Mason and Becca, I really wanted to spend some alone time with Holden.

"Are you going to tell me why you're here and what is *so* amazing that you had to interrupt our evening?" I asked.

With a huge grin on her face, Becca sat down next to Mason. "Yes! Okay so you know how the security company came today to upgrade the main house?"

I nodded as I took the bottle of beer Holden had offered me. "Yeah. What about it?"

Becca took a bottle from Holden as well. Except she placed hers on my coffee table.

"Well, when we were in Mason's office, they had the tapes pulled up from one of the cameras. I, of course, thought about the naughty moment you and Holden had shared earlier on the back porch and I wanted to find it to see exactly what you two were up to."

Scrunching my nose, I shrieked, "What? Becca, that is so wrong!"

She made a sound with her mouth and waved me off with her hand. "Please. Don't act like my nosey, butting-in self has not saved you a time or two. Even you have to admit, Holden, I've saved your ass a time or two."

Holden nodded and chuckled. "Yes, you have."

"Thank you for that," Becca said beaming with a weird sense of pride.

"Becca, please get to the point," I pleaded, falling back against Holden's body.

"Right. Anyway, the tapes where all the way at the beginning for some reason. As I was fast forwarding them, I saw something interesting."

I leaned forward. "What was it?"

Her face lit up like the fourth of July. "It was Daphne on the back porch. I was curious if maybe she might have said something that hinted to her deceit. I hit play and you will *never* believe what Ms. Weston was talking about."

Now it was Holden who leaned forward. "What?" we both spoke at once.

Leaning closer to us, she started telling us what she had heard. "She was on the phone with her daddy, telling him she still hadn't been able to get pregnant and if it didn't happen soon, she was going to have to pretend to have a miscarriage."

I gasped and covered my mouth. I still couldn't believe her father was going along with her crazy plan. "What kind of a man agrees with something like that?"

Holden stood up and began pacing. "The same kind of man who would pay off a doctor to say Daphne wasn't as far along as she really was. The same kind of man who pretty much forced me to marry his daughter out of guilt and helped her with that damn news conference."

Becca injected, "You know the saying, bad press is better than no press. Maybe in some sick twisted way, he thought this would give attention to his movie."

"Or maybe he doesn't know that Holden knows the truth. Daphne could have hidden it that from her father," I stated as I looked around at everyone.

"That's possible," Holden replied.

"It gets better," Mason said with a big Cheshire cat grin. "Tell them, Becca."

Becca snapped her head back to us and went on. "Right. So she goes on to talk about how much she hates Texas, your family, and most of all, your ex-girlfriend. She even makes a reference to Emylie being part-Hispanic."

My mouth fell. "Oh no, she didn't!"

Becca nodded. "Oh yes, she did! Then, she said she wished she could go back to the night she *drugged* Holden. If she could, she'd had chosen someone who wasn't madly in love with his girlfriend or didn't have a girlfriend at all."

All the air left my lungs. "Ohmygod. She admitted to everything! And we have it on tape?"

Holden stood next to me with a stunned look on his face.

Mason and Becca smiled as they looked at us. "Yep. I already duplicated it and saved that part of the surveillance video to my computer. I emailed it to Sam, Debbie, Emylie, and you, Holden."

I stood and walked up to Holden. "What are you going to do? Release it to the press?"

Holden's face looked pained. As much as we all hated Daphne, I knew the right thing to do would be to show the actual proof we had to her and get her to retract her statements. I could see Holden thought the same.

After taking a few moments to think, Holden answered. "No. There's no way I'll stoop to her level. But what I will do is send it to her dad, along with the fact that I know he helped in the manipulation of her due date to make me think the baby she lost was mine. If we have this that shows he knew she did all of this, including drug me, then I'm positive he will make it all go away. He cares about his daughter, but he loves his movies more and wouldn't want to taint his own reputation."

"Damn. I was really wanting to see that little bitch's face when she was outed for being a crazy lying no good for nothing bitch."

We all put our gaze onto Becca. She lifted her shoulders and asked, "What? Don't try and say you don't agree with me."

Mason stood and reached for Becca's hand. "Come on, let's leave and let them celebrate the good news. Hopefully, life will go back to normal around here soon. Shit, Warner. You blow into town and all hell breaks loose."

We all let out a laugh as Holden and I walked Mason and Becca to the door.

"I believe y'all have some celebrating to do also with Mason dropping the L word!" I said as I winked at Mason.

Becca's face lit up again. I was so happy for them both. It seemed like things were finally how they should be. At least, I sure as hell hoped so.

Three days later

Holden held my hand while we sat in the waiting room of Mr. Weston's office. My heart was racing. Holden leaned over and whispered, "It's almost over, baby."

I responded with a frustrated sigh. "I hope so."

"Mr. Warner, Ms. Sanchez, they're ready."

Holden glanced over to his lawyer Troy. I'd finally asked Holden why he had hired Troy and he said it was after Daphne's father pressured him into asking for Daphne's hand. He was having Troy draw up a prenup. Since Holden was set to inherit everything from his parents, he didn't want Daphne to get her hands on anything.

"Let's do this," Troy stated with a grin.

When we walked in, Daphne and her father shot me a dirty look. I kept my chin up and didn't let them see that they affected me in any way.

Mr. Weston's nostrils flared the moment he saw me next to Holden. His voice was laced with anger as he spat out, "I hope you have a damn good reason why you're here in my office."

With a smile, Holden opened his laptop, set it on Mr. Weston's desk and hit play.

The video of Daphne on the back porch started. I'd never seen two people turn white as ghosts before.

Daphne's father glared at Holden while his daughter sat next to him wringing her hands together. "Are you going to release this to the press?" he asked, attempting to keep his voice calm.

Holden reached for my hand. "No. But I want Daphne to retract her statement."

Daphne laughed, but then quickly stopped when her father turned and shot her a look that clearly told her they had lost.

"She'll do it today," Weston replied with a look of defeat.

Daphne's head snapped as she turned to her father then back to Holden. "What in the hell am I supposed to say?"

Holden wore a glowered expression. His nostrils flared slightly and his expression was cold and distant. It was clear he was still very angry for all of the shit this crazy woman put us all through.

"I don't give a shit what you say, Daphne. That's not my problem. You're damn lucky I'm not releasing it to the press after the shit you pulled with me. The years I lost and the hurt that was caused because your twisted, fucked-up mind thought you could get away with this."

Holden turned to Mr. Weston. "And I'm sorry sir, but knowing you played a part in this too, well I think I'm being more than fair, don't you?"

Daphne's father leaned back in his chair. I'm sure he thought his money would be able to get him out of anything, and it probably would. Even this. But he wasn't going to risk it. That was clear.

"Daphne will make a statement saying that things between the two of you have been declining for some time. You both thought that marriage was the key, but quickly realized that was not the way to go. She suffered a small breakdown after you both agreed to split amicable, and that she apologies to Ms. Sanchez for the undue stress she has caused."

"The miscarriage?" Holden asked.

Weston cleared his throat. "She'll say she suffered a small breakdown when she realized that relationship was not going to mend itself and she found out she was indeed never pregnant."

Daphne jumped up. "Like hell I'm going to say I suffered a

breakdown!"

Mr. Weston slowly turned his chair and practically shot daggers through his daughter. "Would you rather that or be labeled as a jealous crazy person who drugged a man, lied about him being the father, then turned around and faked a goddamn pregnancy? I'm through with your bullshit, Daphne. This time you're not getting your way. You'll make the statement, and then you're going to forget Holden Warner ever existed."

Four months later

The knock on my office door had me drawing my head up. "Come in."

"Hey."

Smiling, I leaned back in my chair and replied, "Hey. How's everything going?"

Holden walked up to the chair in front of my desk and sat. "Going good. Mason got the hunters all settled into the cabins and looks like they're planning on an evening hunt."

"That's good. I saw a really nice, large, non-typical with at least fourteen points and a drop tine over on the bluff near three points."

He smiled and replied, "Damn. Someone should really pat the wildlife manager on the back."

My cheeks heated. "We've got some nice looking bucks this season."

"We'll take them over there. I'm thinking I want to do things a bit differently. Since Mason and I can split up and take the hunters to different locations on the ranch, I think it's going to work out even better. Dad seems to really be on board with it. Split them up so they aren't all fighting for the same damn buck."

I nodded. "Well since we cut back the number of hunters this year, I think we have a really good chance of having even better bucks next year, especially with the feeding plan I've implemented."

"I love it when you talk like that."

With a chuckle, I rolled my eyes.

I loved how life had settled into place for all of us. With all of the drama with Daphne finally over, we were able to start our lives. After Daphne made her statement, the press quickly forgot about us and focused on Daphne and her mental breakdown. Last I heard, she had pulled out of her father's movie and checked herself into some mental health resort in Europe somewhere.

"I'm glad that your dad agrees with the new plans."

"Yeah, me too. I've missed this. All of it."

The way Holden was staring at me told me there was something on his mind other than hunting season. Tilting my head, I gave him a pondering look. "What's on your mind?"

"You. Always you."

My stomach fluttered. "I was hoping you were going to say the house."

A small chuckle passed through his lips. "That too. The builder said he's almost positive we'll be in by Christmas, if not sooner."

A bubble of excitement built in my stomach. Holden had worked hard with talking me into moving in with him when he said he was building a house on the ranch. It wasn't anywhere near the main house that was his parents', but closer to the south side of the ranch. It had been a part of our original plan back when we made one. I couldn't help but think about how far we had come in the last few months. One of my best memories was of Holden whisking me away to Fredericksburg for the weekend. We spent one day wandering the shops and picking out things for the house. That night and leading into the next day, we spent in our room. Making love and talking. It was amazing.

"That will be fun! Decorating our very own home for Christmas!" I said with a big grin.

His eyes turned dark. "I was thinking it would be more fun breaking in each room with hot sweaty sex."

Heat pooled between my legs causing me to press them together. Things between Holden and I had been steadily heating up and definitely not slowing down.

My tongue instinctively ran over my lips. Holden stood, placed his hands on my desk, and leaned closer to me. The smell of his woodsy cologne fueled my libido even more. "You know. Come to think of it, we've never had sex in your office or mine."

The beating of my heart was so strong I felt it through my entire body. Trying to keep my cool, I replied, "That would be rather tricky since your father is sandwiched between both of our offices."

"We can be quiet."

Lifting a brow, I entertained the idea for a few brief moments. When his green eyes met my brown, something ignited between us. It didn't take much to heat things up with us. We never seemed to be able to get enough of each other. I had thought it was only because we were making up for lost time, but things seemed to be growing even more intense as the weeks passed. Each time we were together was more incredible than the time before.

"I don't know. You tend to bring out another side of me when we're together."

Holden's gaze turned dark, and I knew that look. He was turned on and the chances of us having sex were increasing by the second.

He walked around the desk and reached for my hands, pulling me up. "I bet if you try really hard, you can be quiet."

My gaze drifted over to my office door.

"I already locked it."

Focusing back on Holden, he wore a devilish grin. "So you had this all planned out?"

"It's called positive thinking, baby."

I lifted the left corner of my mouth in smirk. "Is that so?"

"Yep. Just like I'm positive if I slip my hand down those panties, you're going to be ready for me."

My body trembled and a rush of wetness hit my panties. Holden took a deep breath in. "Fuck you smell so damn good."

I pressed my lips together, silently wishing he would do what he said and give me the orgasm I so desperately wanted.

His hand came up and caressed the side of my face so gently. "You're so beautiful. You make it hard to breathe when I'm around you."

My own breathing became shallow as I looked into his eyes. "If I bend you over this desk and fuck you, can you be quiet?"

All I could do was nod in response to the sweet action mixed with his dirty talk.

"Is that a yes, Em? Because right now all I want to do is sink my—"

The knock on my office door caused me to gasp and Holden to curse under his breath.

"Just when it was getting good," I whispered.

"Emylie?"

It was Holden's dad. I went to walk over to the door, but Holden grabbed my arm and shook his head.

"What?" I mouthed. There was no way I was going to get it on knowing Sam was standing on the other side of my door.

"He'll go away," Holden whispered.

I covered my mouth to hide my smile. "You're crazy!"

His mouth pressed to mine, kissing me like he hadn't seen me in days. His tongue explored my mouth with pure desire. When his hand slipped up under my dress, I opened my legs wider for him.

One sweep of my panties to the side and his finger was massaging my pulsing walls.

"Jesus, you're fucking wet," Holden whispered.

Dropping my head to his chest, I relished in the feel of his touch.

Pressing his thumb against my swollen clit, I gasped.

"Are you close?" he asked, slipping another finger in.

"So. Close."

Just as my body was winding up with my orgasm, he pulled his finger out and unbuckled his belt. He wasn't trying to be quiet at all. When I saw his hard dick slip from his pants, I let out a moan.

"Commando," I whispered. My teeth sunk into my lip and my body shook knowing he would be buried inside me soon. "That's so damn hot."

I wanted to drop to my knees and take him in my mouth. Run my tongue along the pulsing vein that ran the length of his dick.

"Put your hands on your desk."

Doing what he asked, I held my breath.

"Are you ready, baby?"

My breaths were labored and the need to have him inside of me was almost too much to take. If I slipped my fingers down to my clit and pressed, I'd come on the spot.

He pressed his dick against me, slowly inching in as he ran his hands over my ass cheeks. "Damn, you look hot like this. There are so many things I want to do to you, Em."

"What kind of things?" I asked while glancing over my shoulder.

We were still whispering but I gasped when he pushed into me hard and fast. Leaning over my back, he bit my earlobe and said, "Lots of dirty things."

"Oh God, Holden," I whispered while I gripped the desk harder.

That's when we both heard the door unlock.

Pulling out of me, he grabbed me and pulled me down to the floor.

"Emylie?"

The sound of Sam's voice caused my eyes to widen. Holden covered my mouth.

"Why would she lock her office door?" Sam asked.

"Not sure," Debbie replied.

I prayed they wouldn't walk into the room any farther. If they did, they would surely see us.

Then it happened.

My entire world came to a stop and I was positive Holden was about to pass out.

My father spoke.

"Maybe she went out on the ranch with Holden?"

Pure panic filled me as I looked at Holden. He acted calm, but I knew deep down inside he was seeing his life flash before him.

"You know what, I'm pretty sure she told me she had a few errands to run. I bet that's where she is."

"Huh. I swore I heard her and Holden in here talking," Sam said.

Holden closed his eyes.

This is not happening. My father is not standing in my office next to Holden's parents with the two of us down on the floor with Holden's dick hanging out of his pants.

Maybe if I squeeze my eyes closed tight enough, I can make this a dream.

"How about a piece of pecan pie, gentlemen?"

"That sounds heavenly. Just don't tell Kim I said that," my father stated with a chuckle.

The door shut and the sound of muffled voices disappeared. I quickly pushed Holden's hand off my mouth and jumped up. Attempting to straighten myself out, I looked directly at Holden. "Your mother knew! Oh my God ... she must have seen us?"

His face turned white. "No," he whispered. "There was no way she saw us."

"Oh, she knew! I didn't tell her I had errands to run! Oh my God. Your mom knows we had sex in here. I'll never be able to look at her again."

After tucking his dick back into his pants, Holden laughed.

"Nonsense. She doesn't know."

The door opened and we both froze.

Debbie cleared her throat and we both slowly turned to face her. Her furrowed brows were lifted and her hands laid on her hips.

"Oh, hey, Mom," Holden said with a nervous chuckle.

My mouth opened to say something, but nothing but an awkward sound came forth.

Debbie glanced between us then focused back in on Holden. "You're both grown adults who are building a future together. Now I know what it's like, believe me. Sam and I had some fun times in his office, and the barn, and on the tractor."

Holden's hands flew up to his ears. "Mom! Oh God, why?"

She walked in and pointed to Holden. "If my mind had to go there, then so did yours."

Glancing my way, I felt my cheeks burn with embarrassment. "Chuck, the contractor, is looking for you both. They have some questions about the kitchen cabinets."

I nodded. "Yes ma'am."

Debbie winked and gave me a smile. "Now get back to work, both of you."

Holden's mom turned and headed out of my office, leaving the door wide open. I let out a sigh of relief and plopped on my chair.

"How did she know?" Holden asked.

My head shook. "I don't know." My heart was hammering in my chest. I was never having sex in my office or this house or anywhere other than my bed ever again.

"That was kind of exciting!" Holden stated with a laugh. My head snapped over to him.

"What? That was sheer horror. How can you say that was exciting?" I questioned.

He wiggled his brows then leaned down and pressed a kiss to my lips. "The thrill of being caught." His face lit up with amusement and I couldn't help but giggle. "Listen, I've got to go, but I'll call

Chuck and set up a time to meet with him at the house."

"Okay, sounds good."

Leaning in closer, he kissed the spot on the side of my neck that caused my heart to accelerate. "I promise to pick up where we left off tonight."

My stomach dipped and a wave of heat washed across my body. This man could melt me into a puddle of mess with a few simple words and one touch.

"I can't wait," I said with a breathy voice.

Holden stood back and flashed me that smile I loved so much. "Bye, babe. Love you."

"Be careful, and I love you too."

Watching him walk away, I couldn't help but let the feeling of utter happiness settle over my body.

Life was moving on and we were together. That day in the barn when we held each other close and talked of a future together no longer seemed like a lost dream.

CHAPTER 34

Holden

MY GAZE DRIFTED up again to my rearview mirror. The sheriff had been following me for about a mile now.

Glancing over to Emylie, she had her face buried in her phone, looking at backsplash samples.

"I guess we need to figure out which one so we can get this over to Chuck."

"You pick, babe. I'm good with anything you want."

With a sigh, she looked my way. "No. This is our house, Holden. Really it's your house, and you talked me into moving in with you."

"Baby, it's our house. We're doing this together. Remember you forced me to let you pay half on the loan?"

She chortled. "Okay, then you have to be part of the decision."

I glanced in the mirror again.

"Did you call Mason and Becca to tell them we're on the way?"

"Yep," she said absentmindedly. "Becca sure seemed excited

about something."

I rolled my eyes. "When is she not excited about something."

"Stop it. She's happy and that makes me happy. Sage is over the moon in love with Mason. Did Mason tell you she called him Daddy the other day?"

Warmth spread through my chest when I thought back to Mason standing there with tears in his eyes. I knew then I didn't want to wait. Life was short and I was ready to start my life with Emylie. That's when we decided to come up with the plan.

My hands started sweating as the sheriff got closer to me.

"Uh … yeah. He told me. He was pretty um, emotional about it."

"I bet!" Emylie said with a soft chuckle.

"What's wrong? You seem so nervous."

"Cop. He's been following me since I pulled out of the drive-way."

Emylie turned around and looked out the back window. "It's probably nothing. You're not speeding are you?"

"No."

"Do you have a taillight out?" Emylie asked.

"Not that I know of."

"Lights working on the license plate?" she asked, attempting to hold back a giggle.

Rolling my eyes, I replied, "Ha ha."

She reached for my hand. "You're being silly, Holden. It's fine."

"Right. I'm just a little on edge tonight and you know my track record with cops."

"I noticed and yes, I know."

I glanced up again before swallowing hard. His lights turned on and I let out a curse.

"He's pulling me over."

Emylie looked over her shoulder again. "Damn. We're going to be late. You have the worst luck with cops."

I pulled over into the parking lot of the gas station and took in a deep breath. Glancing over to Emylie, she shrugged. "Maybe you were speeding and didn't realize it."

The sheriff walked up as I let the window down.

"Holden Warner?"

"Uh, yes, sir that's me."

He opened the truck door and said, "I'm going to need you to keep your hands where I can see them and step out of the truck."

Emylie's looked at me with a terrified expression. "I don't think it was a light out."

Another sheriff appeared on Emylie's side of the truck. "Ms. Sanchez?"

"Y-yes?" Emylie stuttered.

"Please step on out of the truck ma'am and stand on over here."

Emylie did as she was told, but true to her personality, she started with the questions. "Are you going to tell us why you pulled us over? Is it because he's been pulled over so many times?"

"Hey!" I looked at her. "Seriously, Em?"

She shrugged and made a face. "Sorry!"

The sheriff replied with only a "No."

"Oh. Well, do we get a hint?"

I tried like hell not to laugh. The sheriff walked me behind the truck while the other sheriff did the same thing with Emylie.

"Sir, we need you to stand here while we call for backup."

"What in the hell did you do, Holden?" she gasped.

"Me? How do you know it's me?"

Her mouth dropped. "They said your name!"

I motioned to the sheriff standing next to her. "He said your name."

She went to say something and stopped.

Then dispatch came over his radio.

"Contain the suspects until backup arrives."

Emylie looked between both cops and then back to me. "This is not looking good!"

"Sir, I need you to put your hands behind your back and get down on the ground."

Emylie's gaze widened. "Holden," she whispered then peeked at the sheriff standing next to her. She pulled her head back in shock. "Why are you recording this on Holden's phone? What in the hell is going on here?"

The sheriff placed the box in my hand as I dropped to one knee. Behind Emylie, I saw everyone approaching. I drew in a deep breath and started talking.

"Em?"

She focused back on me. Her chin quivered as she looked at me. "It's always been said since I can remember that you and I were meant to be together. I knew the first moment you smiled at me you would always be a part of my life. Then one day, something inside me changed and you were no longer my best friend, but the woman I loved. Over the years, I dreamed at night about how I wanted to make you my wife. How would I ask you? Would I be able to make it special enough? Could I make it something we would never forget?"

I pulled my hands out from behind my back and opened the small red velvet box that held her engagement ring I bought back when we were in college. I'd had the ring stored in a safety deposit box in California and was the only real reason I had flown back when everything went down with Daphne. Her hands went over her mouth as she let out a sob.

"It's been one hell of a bumpy road for us. If I could go back and change one thing, you know I would, but I can't. So all I can do is promise you from this day forward that I will love you and take care of you. I vow to never in this lifetime hurt you again. You were made for me and I was made for you. Will you marry me, Emylie Sanchez?"

Tears flowed down her face as she nodded her head and rushed over to me. I got up just in time to catch her in my arms.

Our family and friends quickly began cheering as Emylie and I kissed. Laughing against my lips, she pulled away and looked back at everyone and then at me.

"How did you do this?"

Setting her down on the ground, I placed the diamond ring on her hand and kissed her. "I called in a favor from a friend."

She glanced up and looked at Dave. "Oh my God, Dave Jones! I didn't even know that was you!" Emylie rushed over and hugged him. "You scared the shit out of me!"

Dave threw his head back and laughed. "Was it a moment you'll never forget?"

Emylie chuckled. "Yes! I will for sure never forget it!"

"Good. Then we did our job."

Walking back over to me, Emylie buried her face into my chest while I wrapped my arms around her. Becca and Kim were the first ones over to us, pulling Emylie from my arms and demanding to see the ring. Mario and I shook hands as he gave me a pat on the back.

"Good job, son."

After thanking him, it was my father's turn. We shook hands then he pulled me in for a quick hug. I hugged my mother who promptly turned to Kim and started talking about wedding plans. I walked over to Dave and his partner Jim and thanked them again for helping me out.

"Any time," Dave stated with a quick handshake. Jim handed me the camera he used to record the proposal and congratulated us again.

After all the hugging and congratulating, Mario whistled and got everyone's attention.

"Now that Holden has made it official, it's time to throw a party for these two! Finally!"

The cheers erupted again as Emylie walked up to me and I

wrapped her in my arms. Kissing the top of her head, I held her close.

"Are you happy?" I asked with my mouth pressed next to her ear.

"I've never been so happy in my entire life. But we need to talk alone."

My heart dropped. Shit. Maybe I asked her to soon? I originally was going to ask her the day we moved into the house, but I couldn't wait any longer.

Forcing a smile, I managed to speak. "Sure, okay, well let's head on over to your folks' place, I'll take the long way."

She reached up with her hand and gently placed it on my cheek. "It's nothing bad so get that look out of your eyes."

Leaning into her touch, I tried to ease the fear in my chest. Everyone scattered off into different directions as I held the truck door open for her. Once she was in, I slowly walked around the front of the truck while I attempted to settle my racing pulse.

I climbed into the cab of the truck and started it. Emylie instantly blurted out, "I want to elope."

My head jerked back as I turned to face her. "What?"

"Run off and get married."

"Um, now?"

She smiled as she chuckled. "No, not right now. Maybe after hunting season or even around Christmas. I've always wanted to get married at Christmas time."

Holy shit. I could hear my heart beating in my ears. When I didn't say anything, her face fell. "If you're not ready to…"

"Yes! Yes, I want to get married. Shit, I would do it today if you wanted to. But, what about a wedding? You don't want a big wedding with our family and friends?"

Taking my hand in hers, she stared into my eyes. "I know this is going to sound insane, but with everything we've been through, I really want it to only be us. Somewhere amazing and romantic, with only me and you. Something we can share together. We can have a huge reception when we get back. But when your mom and my mom started talking wedding plans, I knew right then and there what I truly wanted."

"Baby, if that is what you really want then that is what I want. Whatever makes you happy."

She grinned wide and before I knew it, she was on my lap with her lips pressed to mine. It didn't take my hands long to find her soft skin under her shirt. When she pressed her warmth into my hard dick, we both moaned.

"Sex in the truck … I like it," I spoke against her lips.

We both yelled out when someone tapped on the window. Turning, we saw Dave.

"Oh. My. God. Two times in one day!" Emylie gasped as she quickly retreated and sat in the passenger seat.

I rolled the window down and Dave shook his head. "Dude, seriously?"

With a deep roar of laughter, I held up my hand. "Sorry! We got caught up in the moment. Leaving right now."

He nodded. "Good." Leaning in and looking directly at Emylie he said, "And stay buckled up. We don't need him distracted while he's driving."

Her face turned fifty shades of red. "Right. Got it. Staying in my seat."

"Talk to you soon, Warner."

With a nod, I started up the truck and we headed to her folks' place.

"I have one more surprise for you."

There was no doubt I could feel the happiness pouring off of her and I knew this would be the cherry on top.

"Oh yeah? When do I get it?"

"Soon."

Ten minutes later we pulled up to Mario and Kim's house and

parked on the street behind Mason's truck.

"Wow how did everyone get here so quick?" Emylie asked.

"Well we did have that moment in the parking lot of the gas station."

She giggled. "You mean the one where the cop told us to knock it off and get a move on?"

"At least we'll have something to tell our kids when we're older."

Her smile grew bigger. "You think about kids?"

Lifting her hand to my lips, I turned it over and kissed her wrist, but not before running my tongue lightly over her skin. She inhaled a deep breath. "Yes. All the time. I picture you pregnant and standing on our back porch with my hands wrapped around you and resting on our child while we watch the sun set."

Tears filled her eyes. "That sounds amazing."

I placed my hand behind her neck and pulled her closer to me. The kiss was soft and tender, yet filled with so much love you could feel it pouring between the two of us.

"Ready for your surprise?"

She nodded her head. "I am!"

Pulling away from her, I opened my door and called out over my shoulder, "Then let's get inside!"

I rushed around the front of the truck and took her hand in mine as she got out. We headed up the stairs of her parents' house. The door opened and Carter stood there with a huge smile on his face.

"Carter?" Emylie gasped. "Oh my gosh! What are you doing here?"

She threw herself into his arms as he gave her a hug. Tori appeared next to him with a glow that practically lit up the entire room.

"Tori! Oh my gosh!" Emylie squealed with delight as the two women embraced each other.

Tori pulled back. "Let me see the ring!"

Carter reached out and shook my head. "Congrats, dude. I'm

happy for you."

"Thanks, Carter. The same to you."

"Let me see your ring!" Emylie exclaimed. Both girls took off for the living room to join Becca and a few other friends.

Carter and I hung back a little way. "So? I asked as I looked at him.

He pushed his hand through his hair and my heart dropped a little. Then he smiled the biggest megawatt smile I'd ever seen.

"Holy shit, dude. Are y'all?"

He nodded. "Yep. She's barely five weeks so we don't really want to say anything yet, but, Tori really wants to be the one to tell Emylie."

"I understand, and I get not wanting to tell folks yet. Do your parents know?"

He shook his head. "No. Dad's officially cancer free, so we've been riding that high for a few days. We decided to wait until we're nine weeks, then tell everyone."

I grabbed his shoulder and gave it a slight squeeze. "I'm so happy for you both."

His eyes watered up and he glanced over to Emylie. "I don't know what would have happened if I hadn't met Emylie up at Jamie and Jax's place. I truly believe she was placed there at the right time and for the right reason. If it hadn't been for her, I'm not sure if Tori and I would have found our way back to each other."

My gaze was locked on my beautiful girl. Her long dark hair was pulled up and a few strands of hair framed her beautiful face. You could see the excitement of today shining off of her. From her rose-colored cheeks to the way her smile lit up the room.

She must have felt my stare. When she looked over at me, our gaze locked and I was overcome with the way she held my attention like we were the only two people in the room. This amazing woman loved me even after all the shit I had put her through. She was my rock. The only thing that I would ever need in this world to make me happy.

With a huge smile, I kept my focus on her. "Y'all would have found your way back to each other trust me. That's the great thing about love … when it's real and it's meant to be … there is *nothing* that will stand in its way."

"Isn't that the truth," Carter added with a slight chuckle. "At times, it was an uphill battle that I thought I wasn't going to win."

I nodded in agreement. "We both walked along a broken road to get back to the women we loved. But every mistake, lost dream, and broken heart led us to right now."

Emylie's gaze never left mine as I spoke.

My chest tightened and I slowly lost awareness of my surroundings. I felt completely whole as we got lost in one another. "I'll treasure this day for the rest of my life."

For one moment in time it was only the two us in that room. No words needed to be said. We felt it. An emotion so strong it about brought me to my knees at least once a day.

Love.

Our love.

CHAPTER 35

Emylie

Thirteen months later

TRYING TO CATCH my breath, I leaned against the wall
and watched everyone dancing.

"Don't tell me the dancing queen is tired."

Turning to face Carter, I rolled my eyes. "Hardly. But consider-
ing I've been dancing circles around you for the last few hours, I feel
as if I deserve a break."

He grinned and looked out at the dance floor. It was three days
before Christmas and two days before my one-year wedding anniversary. Holden had decided to throw a huge hoedown, and of
course, Carter and Tori had to be here. Their little girl Carrie was
almost five-months-old and the apple of Carter's eye.

My gaze drifted across the dance floor and landed on Holden.
"Seems like someone is stealing your girl."

Carter let out a gruff laugh. "Please. She knows who the true
man in her life is. Her daddy."

I could hardly breathe watching Holden dancing with little Carrie. It was the sweetest thing I'd ever seen. No, that wasn't true. The sweetest thing I'd ever seen was the first time he held her. We had flown up after the birth and when Carter placed his daughter in Holden's arms and he teared up, I wondered how I could possibly fall more in love with him.

"You excited?" Carter asked.

"Yes."

"Getting closer," Carter whispered as he nudged my arm with his.

With a light-hearted laugh, I nodded. "I know."

"Don't worry. Everything is going to be perfect."

I chewed on my lip. "I hope so."

Carter grabbed my arms and turned me to face him. "Talk to me, Emylie. I see it in your eyes."

The sting of the threat of tears, forced me to close my eyes tightly then re-open them. "I'm worried that she's going to show up again."

His expression softened. "She won't. You haven't heard from her since that day you left California right?"

I nodded.

"Then stop worrying. Even if she did try something, you know Holden would stop it before it started."

Sighing, I blew out a breath. "I know I'm being silly."

Carter kissed the top of my forehead. "Yes, you are. Now come on, I think you have one more dance left in you."

As we headed to the dance floor, "That's My Girl" by Russell Dickerson started. Carter and I danced to the first verse before Holden cut in.

Motioning over to Carter's daughter, Holden gushed, "I believe you have a blue-eyed beauty wanting you."

A wide grin spread over Carter's face. "You don't have to tell me twice."

Holden wrapped me up in his embrace. "How's it going?"

"It's going."

"You having fun?"

With a smile, I nodded. "But you know what I really want?"

His mouth trailed kisses across my neck until his hot breath hit my ear, causing my body to tremble.

"Tell me, baby."

"I want to be wrapped in your arms in the back of your truck looking up at the night sky."

"Hmm, that sounds like heaven. Me and you and no one else. The crickets playing our song while the moon shines down on us." Pulling back, he observed my face. "You sure you feel up to it?"

With a nod, I smiled. "Positive."

Holden soon had my hand in his as we bid everyone a good night and informed Carter of our plans. Tori leaned over and placed a soft kiss on my cheek. "Don't get caught by anyone if y'all do the deed."

My cheeks burned as I let out a chuckle. "Don't stay up and wait for us."

"Oh, trust me, we won't. I'm going to crash when we get back to your place, and I know Carrie will be out like a light the moment she hits the car seat."

Carter, Tori, and Carrie were staying with us while they were in town visiting. I loved having them stay with us. It brought such a new life to the house.

I laughed and gave Carrie a quick kiss on the cheek. "I'll see you later, if not in the morning."

Tori wagged her brows and teased, "Have fun!"

Holden practically dragged me away and out to his truck. It didn't take us long to drive out to the south pasture and park in our favorite spot. Sitting in the back of his truck and looking at the stars wasn't something new. We'd been doing it since high school. Holden always carried a blanket and two pillows in his truck, just in case we found ourselves in the mood.

After getting it all set up, he helped me up on the step that led to the bed of his truck. I couldn't help but chuckle. "I figured you would be more comfortable if we sat up."

"Probably," I agreed. I stood in the bed of his truck and looked up at the night sky.

His hands landed on my nine-month swollen belly. "How are you feeling tonight, Mrs. Warner?"

"Very pregnant."

The moon shone perfectly on his face and I could see his wide smile. "You look beautiful."

With a frown, I shook my head. "I don't feel like it."

He carefully led me over to the area he had set up for us. Holden sat first then guided me down. I let out a contented sigh and molded right into his warm body.

I felt Holden's chest vibrate as he let out a chuckle. "You know, I really do think we conceived this baby in this exact spot."

Warmth spread over my body. "I think so too."

"Are you happy, Em?"

Dropping my head back against his chest, I looked up at the stars. "I've never been happier."

His hands rubbed lightly over my stomach. "Oh, I think something will make you a bit happier if she would ever make her appearance."

With a grin, I let out a soft sigh. "Are you nervous?"

"Yep. You?"

"Scared to death."

His lips found that area beneath my ear that always made my panties wet. "Do you need a bit of stress relief?"

I let out a moan and whispered, "Yes."

His hands expertly found their way to my clit as he softly built up my orgasm. The things he whispered in my ear that he wanted to do to me had me squeezing onto his legs as he slipped his fingers inside of me. I must have been desperate for the release because it hit me hard and fast. My eyes closed as bursts of lights danced behind my lids. With my body trembling, I called out Holden's name into the night sky.

"Oh, baby, I love hearing you cry out my name when you come."

My breathing was labored and my heart raced. When his hands touched my stomach again, I froze.

"Damn, why is your stomach so tight?"

I gripped his legs again. "Oh God. Contraction."

"What!" Holden said as he somehow managed to get out from behind me without me falling back.

"Did you say … contraction?"

With a slight giggle, I looked up at him. I wasn't sure if that was fear or excitement I was seeing on his face as the moonlight hit him.

"Looks like that orgasm gave her a little wake-up call."

He reached and helped me stand. "Come on, let's get back to the house. I'll start timing them," Holden said as he jumped off the bed of the truck and then helped me down but kept me in his arms.

"I can walk, you know."

He laughed and then stopped walking. "Did you just pee on me?"

My smile fell.

Biting into my lip, I drew in a deep breath before exhaling it. "My water broke."

He slowly set my feet on the ground and cupped my face within his hands.

"Holy shit!"

I reached up and took a hold of his arms. "I know! This is it."

He shook his head. "No! That was so close. Thank God you weren't in my truck when your water broke."

And just like that, my fear slipped away and I started laughing.

Life from this point on would never be the same.
It would be better.
So. Much. Better.

Emylie

Two years later

"ARE WE READY?" I called out while lighting the candles on Alana's birthday cake.

I heard a loud crash and cringed. I didn't dare ask what happened. "Almost!" Holden called out.

Sage came running into the kitchen. "Um, Aunt Emylie?"

"Yeah?" I asked as I lit the last candle. Our folks were running behind and told us to start since Alana was past her naptime and on the verge of a breakdown.

"Daddy and Uncle Holden broke Alana's new swing set."

My mouth dropped. "What do you mean, broke it?"

She placed her hands on her hips and I was instantly taken back to a time on a playground when her mother did the same thing at almost the same age. "I told them not to get on it, but they insisted it would be okay. The seesaw broke, but Daddy promised Mommy he could fix it."

With a frustrated moan, I walked over and looked out the window to the backyard. I covered my mouth as I watched a very pregnant Becca yelling at Mason and Holden. Alana was standing next to her looking up taking it all in. Every now and then she would jump up and down laughing.

"Oh geesh. We better go save your dad and Holden."

Sage's gaze lit up. "Alana's birthday cake is so pretty!"

I glanced down at the Winnie the Pooh themed cake. Winnie the Pooh was Alana's favorite. Everything in our life was that stupid bear right now.

"Thanks! Okay, let's get it out there and get this birthday party started. Will you grab the plates, Sage?"

"Sure!" She quickly grabbed them and was smart enough to grab the bucket full of plastic forks and napkins.

When I stepped out onto the back porch, I looked at Sage and nodded. We both started singing happy birthday. Alana shrieked with happiness as we made our way over to the table. Holden scooped her up and placed her on his shoulders as we sang to our two-year-old daughter. She clapped and laughed and screamed out "Pooh" when she saw the cake up close.

Leaning her over the cake, we all counted to three and blew the candles out with her then clapped. Holden set her on the table and before any of us could do a thing, her entire face landed on the top of the cake and she went to town eating it.

All we could do was stand there stunned as she lifted up her head and flashed a huge grin. "Yummy cake!"

I covered my mouth and tried not to laugh. Becca, on the other hand, lost it laughing, as did Sage.

Holden and Mason looked devastated. All they had been talking about for the last four hours was wanting a piece of cake.

Dropping my hands, I glanced around at everyone. Holden actually looked like he had tears in his eyes. "I had cupcakes made as well. They're in the dining room."

It was like watching a race with the way Mason, Sage, and Holden ran into the house.

Becca rolled her eyes as I attempted to get Alana away from the cake.

"Yummy cake, Mommy!"

Wiping her face off, I replied, "I wouldn't know, princess. You face-planted in it."

She laughed like I had told her the funniest thing in the world.

"Oh, man. I can't wait to do all of this again," Becca confessed while rubbing her stomach.

With a sigh, I shook my head. "I'm beginning to think I should have my head examined thinking I wanted another this soon."

I picked up my little messy girl and nestled her above my swollen belly.

"I think doing them close together is smart. I loved that Mason wanted to focus on us and Sage for a bit though. It really made it special that Sage and Mason got to bond like they have."

A warm feeling spread across my chest. Mason had asked Becca to marry him a week after Holden had asked me. They choose a simple wedding on Sam and Debbie's ranch a few months after Holden and I eloped and got married in Belize. It was perfect, and I'd never seen my two best friends so happy before.

"He really is a great guy. I'm so happy for you two."

Becca reached for my hand and squeezed it. "I'm happy for both of us."

"More cake!" Alana cried out.

"Oh no! You ate almost half of it in three bites, you little stinker."

Holden came walking out and down the back porch. He took Alana out of my arms and kissed her on the tip of her nose. "You look so cute sitting on top of Mommy's pregnant belly with cake all over your face."

Alana looked down at my stomach. "Little bweother."

"That's right, baby girl. In three months, your little brother, Carter, will be here."

"Hey, how are Carter and Tori?" Becca asked as she attempted to lower herself into a chair.

With a wide smile, I answered her. "They're doing great! The youngest, Emma, will be six weeks old tomorrow."

"Oh wow. I still can't believe they have three kids."

I shuttered. "I know. I can't even handle one."

Holden and Alana were now chasing each other and I was waiting for it to hit them both.

Almost like clockwork, they both stopped running around.

"And here we go."

"Mommy!" Alana cried out as she made her way over to me.

"Upset tummy?"

She nodded.

"Oh hell. I'm about to throw up," Holden stated as he walked up to me with his hand on his stomach.

"How many cupcakes did you eat?"

"Four."

My brows lifted and I gave him a questioning look. "All right, I slammed six of them."

"Six?" Becca and I both said.

Right about then Sam and Debbie walked out. "Are we too late?"

"Grammy! Pampa!" Alana shouted as she took off running. I wasn't sure where she got her second wind. Probably the sugar high from the cake.

"Well, if you wanted cake or cupcakes you're out of luck."

Debbie laughed as she gave me a hug. "What happened?"

I glanced over to Holden. "Well, Alana face-planted in the cake and went to town. Then your son, Mason, and Sage fought like wild animals to get to the cupcakes."

Sam laughed. "Wait until Mario finds out he isn't getting any cake."

Becca walked up next to me and poked me in the stomach. I ignored her. "Well he can have it if he wants to cut off what Alana ate."

Sam took a peek over at the table. "I see a perfectly good cake that can still be saved."

"Really?" Holden asked with excitement in his voice.

Becca pulled on my shirt. "Um, Em?"

Turning to her, I frowned. Her face was white as a ghost. She took in a deep breath and slowly let it out.

"We probably need to let Mason know his son is on the way."

My hands flew up to my mouth as I gasped. "What? You're not due for another week."

She gave a light hearted laugh. "Well, tell the baby that, because I've been timing my contractions and they're getting closer."

"What?" Debbie and I both yelled out.

"You're never this quiet about things! Why in the world would you pick now?" I asked.

She shrugged. "It's Alana's party. I didn't want to ruin it."

I jumped like a crazy person. "What if you have him on Alana's birthday. Oh my gosh, we can do double birthday parties. How fun would that be?"

Debbie nodded. "Oh that would be fun."

Becca forced a smile. "Uh-huh. Yeah. Super fun. Right now I'd really like to get to a hospital to get this kid out of me."

"What? It's time?" Mason asked as he came running up.

Becca smiled so lovingly at him, that I practically melted on the spot. "It is. You ready?"

Mason cupped Becca's face and gave her a tender kiss. "Never been more ready. Let's do this."

And just like that he calmly guided her around the side of the house and to his truck. After Holden and I got Alana settled with his parents, I called mine to let them know we were heading to the hospital with Becca, Sage, and Mason.

As we followed Mason's truck, Holden reached for my hand and pulled it to his lips. Turning my wrist up, he gently kissed it. It was a simple gesture he had done for as long as I could remember. Yet it was one that spoke more than words could.

My stomach flipped and I had to push my legs together. Holden saw my expression and smiled.

"Oh no. I know that smile," I said, trying to pull my wrist away.

He let go of it and let off the gas at the same time.

"Holden Warner. Don't you even think of it."

"We are alone. Alone, Em."

My tongue ran over my lips. "That doesn't happen often."

"Never. It happens never."

Looking back at Mason's truck, it was pulling away. "Can you be quick?"

Holden made a pft sound then said, "Please. Baby, I can go slow or I can go fast. You just tell me what you want."

"Fast. It has to be fast. If I miss the birth of this baby because of sex, I'll never forgive you."

Holden put on the turn signal and pulled down a driveway. It was an old abandoned house so there was no way anyone would be driving down it.

Ten minutes later, I was on top of him in the back seat riding my way to one hell of an orgasm. Holden gripped my hips and lifted up as he grunted and called out my name.

Dropping my head against his chest, we both fought to get our breathing in check.

"Damn. Every single time it gets better with you, Em."

Lifting my head, I smiled. "Same goes for you. That was incredible and probably the last time we'll be able to do that with the rate this little boy of yours is growing."

Holden's face beamed with pride.

"Think we have time for one more round?"

I rocked my hips and laughed. "You ready to go that soon?"

The tap on the window had us both freezing.

Slowly turning, we saw blue and red lights.

"You've got to be kidding me," Holden said with a frustrated moan as he dropped his head back on the seat.

Letting out a chortle, I replied, "At least we got to finish this time."

The End

Selena Gomez – "Nobody" – Prologue

Vince Gill – "Down to My Last Habit" – Emylie and Mason at the dance hall

Jennifer Nettles – "Unlove You" – Emylie seeing Holden after he comes back

Jena Kramer – "Circles" – Emylie talking to Holden in the pasture

Tove Lo – "Talking Body" – Emylie and Mason dancing at Twin Oaks as Holden watches

Kelsea Ballerini – "First Time" – Emylie waiting on Holden to meet her for lunch

Rascall Flatts – "Come Wake Me Up" – Emylie leaving for Utah

Christina Perri – "The Words" – Emylie in Utah

LoCash – "God Loves Me More" – Holden going after Emylie in Utah

Lo Cash – "Drunk Drunk" – Carter and Emylie dancing at the bar in Colorado

Vince Gill – "Make You Feel Real Good" – Holden and Emylie dancing at bar in Colorado

Russell Dickerson – "Yours" – Holden and Emylie dancing at bar in Colorado

Maroon 5 – "Wipe Your Eyes" – Holden and Emylie when he comes back from California

Dierks Bentley – "Black" – Holden and Emylie making love at her house

Kenny Chesney – "Me and You" – Holden asking Emylie to marry him

Dan + Shay – "From the Ground Up" – Epilogue

Full playlist is listed on Spotify

Erin Noelle – Thank you for taking care of yet another one of my books! You're the best! **wink**

Holly Malgieri – Thank you for squeezing in a proofing and putting your touch on the process as well.

Ari Niknejadi – Thank you for being such an amazing friend and for designing the best website ever. I love you!

Danielle Sanchez – Thank you for all you do for me! Don't know how you keep up with everything, but I'm sure glad you do.

Kristin Mayer – Thank you for always reading my stuff before anyone else and helping to make it a stronger story! I love you, Special K!

Laura Hansen – Thank you so much reading these crazy stories when half the time they don't make any sense! Your input means the world to me! Love you girl!

Stacy Solis and Ana Winegar– Thank you so much for giving the manuscript one last read through!! I truly appreciate you help!

Nikki Sievert – As always thank you for be one of the last set of eyes on the manuscript!

Julie Titus – You never cease to amaze me with your formatting skills. You bring the books to life with your vision and make formatting one of my favorite processes!

Shannon Cain – Thank you for working so hard to capture the perfect picture when we shoot for these books. You're crazy talented and I hope you know that! Thank you also for the beautiful cover!

Emylie and Holden – You two were so much fun to work with! Thank you for letting me use your names as well. I hope we can do it again for another book!

Sugar Berry Inn and Breakfast – Thank you for letting us take over one of your cottages for not one, but two photo shoots. I loved staying there and look forward to returning!

My readers – Without you, none of this would be! Thank you for taking a chance on me and for reading my books and sharing them with your family and friends! Your support means the world to me and I hope you realize how much I love y'all. I hope you enjoy this one!

Darrin and Lauren – As I sit and type this, I can't help but think of how lucky and blessed I am to have you both in my life. I love you both more than anything. Thank you for putting up with my crazy world.

And last but not least, thank you, Heavenly Father, for blessing me with the gift of story-telling and this amazing life you've given me.

ABOUT THE Author

K elly Elliott is a New York Times and USA Today bestselling contemporary romance author. Since finishing her
bestselling Wanted series, Kelly continues to spread her
wings while remaining true to her roots and giving readers stories
rich with hot protective men, strong women and beautiful surroundings.

Kelly lives in central Texas with her husband, daughter, and two
pups. When she's not writing, Kelly enjoys reading and spending
time with her family.

To find out more about Kelly and her books, you can find her
through her website. www.kellyelliottauthor.com

Stand Alones

The Journey Home
Finding Forever (Co-written with Kristin Mayer,
previously titled *Predestined Hearts*.)
Who We Were (Available on audio book)
Stay With Me
Searching For Harmony
The Playbook
Made For You

Wanted Series

Book 1– *Wanted*
Book 2 – *Saved*
Book 3 – *Faithful*
Book 3.5 – *Believe*
Book 4 – *Cherished*
Book 5 Prequel – *A Forever Love*
Entire series available on audio book

The Wanted Short Stories

Love Wanted in Texas Series
Spin off series to the WANTED Series

Book 1 – *Without You*
Book 2 – *Saving You*
Book 3 – *Holding You*
Book 4 – *Finding You*
Book 5 – *Chasing You*
Book 6 – *Loving You*
Entire series available on audio book
Please note *Loving You* combines the last book of the **Broken** and
Love Wanted in Texas series.

Broken Series

Book 1 – *Broken*
Book 2 – *Broken Dreams*
Book 3 – *Broken Promises*
Book 3 – *Broken Love*
Book 1-3 available on audio book

The Journey of Love Series

Book 1 – *Unconditional Love*
Book 2 – *Undeniable Love*
Book 3 – *Unforgettable Love*
Entire series available on audio book

Speed Series

Book 1 – *Ignite*
Book 2 – *Adrenaline*

YA Novels written under the pen name Ella Bordeaux

Beautiful
Forever Beautiful (Releasing October 2016)
First Kiss (Releasing early 2017)